The man who walked out from behind the bushes was tall.

That was the first thing Alexia noticed as she drew a bead on his chest directly over his heart. Then she looked up into his face. He was one of the most beautiful things she'd ever seen. Not beautiful like a woman, but in the perfect harmony of his features: the strong chin, straight nose, high cheekbones, expressive lips.

And his eyes. They were dark…not maroon like those of a Nightsider, but the deepest sapphire imaginable. His short hair was not white, like most vampires, but a hue somewhere between brown and gold, and his skin was deeply tanned.

Alexia swallowed. She had met her first Daysider at last, and he was so much…more than she had expected.

DAYSIDER

SUSAN KRINARD

MILLS & BOON

First published in Great Britain 2013
by Mills & Boon, an imprint of Harlequin (UK) Limited,
Eton House, 18-24 Paradise Road, Richmond, Surrey TW9 1SR

© Susan Krinard 2013

ISBN: 978 0 263 90410 9
ebook ISBN: 978 1 472 00674 5

089-0813

Harlequin (UK) policy is to use papers that are natural, renewable and recyclable products and made from wood grown in sustainable forests. The logging and manufacturing processes conform to the legal environmental regulations of the country of origin.

Printed and bound in Spain
by Blackprint CPI, Barcelona

Susan Krinard has been writing paranormal romance for nearly twenty years. Her books include a number of novels for Mills & Boon. With *Daysider* she begins a series of vampire paranormal romances, the NIGHTSIDERS series, for Mills & Boon® Nocturne™.

Sue lives in Albuquerque, New Mexico, with her husband, Serge, her dogs, Freya, Nahla and Cagney, and her cats, Agatha and Rocky. She loves her garden, nature, painting and chocolate...not necessarily in that order.

With thanks to both "L's" for their
patience and support.

The first known offspring of a voluntary union between a human female and a male Opir, aka "Nightsider," was born in the San Francisco Enclave during the seventh year of the Opir-Human War, conceived during the brief period of the first Truce. The child, Jenna Donnelly, daughter of Special Forces Captain Fiona Donnelly and Opir refugee Kane, remained the only documented example of such a union until the last year of the War, when other hybrid children—christened "dhampires"—and their mothers, who were accused of willingly "consorting with the enemy," were brought into the capital city of San Francisco.

In the final year of the War and immediately afterward, human soldiers sweeping the newly created Zone—otherwise known as "No-man's land"—between Enclave and Opir territories discovered lost, abandoned dhampir children, as well as those in hiding with their mothers. Unlike the women of the first "wave," these mothers had been impregnated by male Opir soldiers without their consent, and they were often unaware that they had conceived until weeks after the encounter.

Such women and their children were given full refugee status in the Enclave, though their acceptance among Enclave citizens was slow in coming. This acceptance was impossible in Opir society, where hybrid children were considered undesirable half-castes and even abominations. It was a common belief in the Enclave that any children born to human serfs in Opir territory, particularly the city of Erebus, were destroyed before birth—a credence that was largely refuted in subsequent years, though the practice was not unknown.

In spite of their awkward status within the Enclave, dhampires soon proved to be invaluable assets. With the ability to see clearly in the dark, along with keener senses, strength and speed than *homo sapiens,* these children were soon recruited by Aegis, the Enclave Intelligence agency responsible for Opir-Human relations.

On its face, Aegis studied Opir society and arranged ambassadorial visits between Erebus and the Enclave, but in practice it also ran covert infiltration, intelligence operations, espionage and counterespionage within the Zone, occasionally inserting specially trained moles, posing as serfs, into Erebus itself.

Though not required to undergo Aegis training, most dhampir youths eventually sought affirmation by serving the Enclave as covert operatives. The only complication in utilizing such resources lay in some dhampires' need for blood, another trait they held in common with their Opir Sires.

With few exceptions, dhampires rejected the taking of blood from humans. While fully sixty percent of dhampires could survive on human food alone, the remaining forty percent, in addition to being immune to the bite of a full Opir, required a special drug to allow them to digest human fare.

In time, scientists developed a means of delivering the drug into the body through a subdermal patch. This allowed the "immune" dhampires to work in the field for extended periods without requiring blood.

But dhampir operatives faced yet another challenge: Opir scouts who, while dependent on blood for survival, were capable of sustained exposure to sunlight. These "Daysiders," outcasts within their own rigid society, nevertheless served as counterparts to Aegis agents and hindered the gathering of intelligence and other clandestine operations within the Zone.

—from the Introduction to *A Brief History of the Nightsider War, San Francisco Enclave*

Prologue

Mommy was crying. Alexia knew it had something to with do the lady on the TV, talking in soft words that didn't match the angry expression on her face.

Behind the lady was a picture of a city, a black, upside-down bowl that gleamed like a beetle's shell in bright sunlight. "Erebus," the lady on the TV said. Alexia didn't know what that meant, but it sounded like a very bad word. And somehow, it was making Mommy sad.

Alexia got up from her seat on the thin carpet and went to Mommy, searching her face anxiously. There were dark blotches under Mommy's eyes, and her nose was red.

"What is it, Mommy?" Alexia asked, reaching up to be taken into her mother's arms.

Mommy picked her up and sat her on the couch beside her. "Nothing's wrong, Lexie," she said, trying to smile.

Alexia always knew when Mommy was fooling. It wasn't

just that she smelled different, or the way her voice got very tight, even though she was smiling. There *was* something wrong, and it made Alexia upset that Mommy was unhappy. Upset and angry.

"What are they talking about?" Alexia asked, pointing at the TV.

Mommy pulled Alexia close and stroked her hair. "It's a city," she said.

"Like San Francisco?"

"Not the same," Mommy replied. She breathed in and out in a funny way that made Alexia's heart hurt. "You remember when we talked about the Nightsiders?"

Alexia made a face. "They're nasty. We had a big fight with them."

"That's right." Mommy bent her head so her nose pressed against Alexia's hair. "That is the city they built in what we used to call the Sonoma Valley. They made it all for themselves, where they don't have to be in the sun."

"Sun kills them," Alexia said solemnly.

"That's right."

"And they used to kill people all the time, didn't they? During the big fight?"

Mommy covered Alexia's eyes as if she didn't want her to see the TV anymore. "You shouldn't know about that," she said, a funny warble in her voice. "No child should know."

"Don't worry, Mommy." Alexia pulled her mother's hand away from her eyes. "The kids at school talk about the bloodsuckers all the time. I'm not scared."

"Oh, God," Mommy whispered. "Do they… Are the other kids…nice to you, at school?"

"Oh, they're okay. Some of the girls are mean sometimes. They give me funny looks. The boys just stare at me a lot."

Mommy cupped both her hands around Alexia's face. "What do they say?"

Alexia shrugged the way she had seen grown-ups do when

they were pretending something didn't matter. "Silly things, about my eyes." She touched her own eyelids. "They say I'm like a cat because I can see in the dark."

"That's right," Mommy said in a completely different voice than before. "Like a cat. And cats are beautiful, aren't they? So graceful and brave." She smiled, moving Alexia to sit in her lap. "But you know what? I think you look even more like a fox. Remember the pictures I showed you?"

Alexia nodded. "It was red, like my hair."

"And quick and clever. Like you."

They were very nice words, but Alexia couldn't help looking at the TV again, and at the ugly city with the scary name.

"The bloodsuckers aren't ever going to come *here,* are they?" she asked, just a little bit scared after all.

"Lexie, that word—"

"Isn't that what they are, Mommy?"

Mommy made a sound a little like a laugh, but it wasn't a happy one. "Yes," she said. "But you don't have to worry about that."

"I'm not worried." Alexia bit her lip. "We aren't ever going to get in a big fight with them again, are we?"

"No." She took a big, long breath. "I wish—"

Alexia wriggled free and looked up into Mommy's eyes. "What do you wish, Mommy?"

"I wish things could be the way they were before…before the big fight."

"When my daddy was alive?"

Mommy's face seemed to crumple all at once. She sobbed, and Alexia knew it was because of what she had said. It was all *her* fault.

"It's okay, Mommy," she said, stroking her mother's trembling hand and soft, wet cheeks. "I won't ever talk about Daddy again."

"Oh, my baby," Mommy said, gathering Alexia up again so tightly that she could barely breathe. "I will never, ever let anyone hurt you. Not anyone. I'm going to keep you with me forever and ever."

Alexia pressed her face to the pulse in Mommy's neck. It was so warm and sweet. It made her feel safe.

But she didn't want to just be safe. She wanted to find a way to make Mommy happy.

And keep those nasty bloodsuckers in their ugly black city from making anyone afraid, ever again.

Chapter 1

"It may be fatal," the Director said.

Alexia laughed. "Since when hasn't that been true of every mission?"

Aegis Director of Field Operations Wilson McAllister regarded her without a trace of amusement. "This isn't funny, Alex," he said. "We're talking about violating our side of the Treaty and striking deep into the Zone. Even the Mayor doesn't know about it."

"At least not officially," Alexia said.

"Not officially enough to send someone to pull your ass out of the fire if you get caught." The steel rims of McAllister's glasses flashed as they caught the cold and sterile light from the overhead fixtures. "Your mission will be to learn everything you can about the Nightsiders' illegal colony without doing anything to attract the Citadel's attention. If you fail or are captured—"

"—Aegis will disavow any knowledge of our actions. I know the drill." Alexia wandered to the window overlooking the glimmering waters of San Francisco Bay. From Aegis headquarters in the old Financial District, she could see a heavily guarded convoy of trucks carrying agricultural products from the Central Valley into the city. The Treaty meant that the Nightsiders were supposed to leave such convoys alone.

Usually they did. But there were always the terrorists, the ones who wanted to ignite a new War. On both sides. And that was what her team would be sent in to try to prevent.

Alexia drifted back into memory, of the year the Nightsiders had first appeared. Not that they'd been *her* memories, not exactly. But she'd seen the archived news vids, the looks of bewilderment and fear on the newscasters' faces when the first reports came in: horror stories of vampires arising seemingly out of nowhere, some emerging from decades or centuries or even millennia of sleep in sanctuaries built far beneath the earth. No one knew—or at least the leeches weren't telling—what had roused them, or why they had chosen that time to rise and claim the earth.

Ten years later—ten years of chaos and plague and terrible war, the time when Alexia's mother gave birth to a half-vampire child—had led to the Treaty, and now most parts of the world were carefully divided into territories: vampire Citadels and human Enclaves, separated by the unclaimed regions known as the Zones.

Just outside the Enclave that embraced San Francisco and the area formerly known as the East Bay, the Zone comprised an immense semicircular region that had once held thriving suburbs, now abandoned and slowly crumbling back to the earth as new forests and fields absorbed stone and concrete, and animals—once driven away by human incursions—reclaimed their original habitats. Beyond the Zone, to the south and east in the regions of the Central Valley, lay the farmlands that produced sustenance for the Enclaves, each surrounded by its own Zone and patrolled by special military forces whose job it was to keep Nightsiders out and human workers safe from them. In theory, as per the Treaty, the workers were protected, and so were the routes to the Enclaves.

To the north, in the area once distinguished by its scenic fields of grapevines and boutique wineries, its rolling hills and towering redwoods, stood Erebus. The Citadel of Night.

Alexia remembered the images on the TV when the construction began. Very little had been known then, because the Zone had just been established, and rumor was more plentiful than fact. Human laborers…prisoners of war…had built the city by day, vampires by night. In a year the Citadel—all black, gleaming, windowless towers and paradoxically Gothic ornamentation—was large enough to hold a population of ten thousand, and that was only on the surface. It was speculated that the underground portion of the city could house five thousand more. Today, the Citadel was twice as big, with its own farms and fields to support its human inhabitants.

Slaves, Alexia thought with that burning anger that never diminished. Blood-serfs. The prisoners, the castoffs from the human Enclaves. The damned.

Like Garret.

"Ms. Fox?"

She turned back to McAllister, who was leaning over his desk with an ominous frown on his lean brown face. His sudden formality wasn't a good sign.

"You aren't listening to me," he said. "Are you sure you're up to this?"

Alexia returned to stand before the desk, taking a formal stance that betrayed none of her emotions. "Yes, sir. More than up to it."

"It's only been a year since your brother was—"

"I haven't forgotten, sir."

He cleared his throat. "The Examiners say you may still

harbor resentment against the Court for sentencing him to Deportation."

Deportation. Such a *nice* way of putting it. "I know the Court weighed the evidence thoroughly, sir. It was a fair trial."

The Director sighed and sank back into his chair. "Was it?"

Alexia knew it was another test, and one she had to pass. "The evidence was conclusive, sir."

"Then you no longer believe it was self-defense?"

The same questions the shrinks had asked her, over and over again, ever since Garret had been sent to Erebus.

"Without the laws there would be chaos, and the Enclaves would die," she said with perfect sincerity. "I blame the leeches, sir. Only them."

"But do you blame them enough to lose your objectivity in an operation of such extreme delicacy? That is the question."

"Have the Examiners suggested that's the case, sir?"

McAllister smiled without pleasure. "If they had, we wouldn't be having this conversation. But the final decision rests with me. If I'm making a mistake—"

Alexia straightened, staring hard at the framed mission statement hung on the wall behind the Director's chair. "You aren't, sir. When do we go?"

McAllister made a show of shuffling a few folders on his desk and slid one of them across the desk. "Tomorrow. You and Michael will be the only team for the time being, and your mission will be to observe, and observe *only*."

"Understood, sir."

"Call Carter and study the report. There'll be a briefing at 1100 hours."

Before Alexia could salute, McAllister was back to his computer, typing away as if she had already left the room. She knew he preferred it that way. And so did she.

She returned to barracks and the small apartment that she, as a highly valuable Aegis asset, was permitted to occupy alone. Alexia unlaced her boots and allowed herself a small glass of the rare and expensive Riesling she had bought with the better part of last month's pay. After a short breather she buzzed Michael, and they synced their computers to study the report.

"Looks easy," her partner said when they had gone over it a second time. "In and out."

Alexia glimpsed her reflection in the computer screen, briefly blotting out the image of Michael's habitual smirk: straight auburn hair cut at an efficient and regulation chin length, tilted green eyes, slightly pointed chin. New recruits sometimes thought themselves clever by suggesting how much her appearance matched her surname.

But even a fox might not sneak out of this one. Not even a highly trained dhampir agent like her. If she'd thought Mike was taking this as lightly as his words suggested, she might have been genuinely worried.

She knew better. Her partner was one of the survivors, an agent who had made it through ten missions with only minor wounds and the same partner until Jill had been killed a year ago. Since then, he and Alexia had been on three assignments together, and they'd worked as a perfect team. She trusted him more than anyone else in Aegis, even the boss.

Michael had been deep into the Zone several times, while she'd never gone much beyond the Border. She would be relying on his greater experience, but she intended to pull her full weight. This was her chance to prove just how good she was.

She glanced at her watch. "Briefing in fifteen minutes. See you there."

Michael gave her a mock salute. "Don't even think about finishing that wine. I plan to drink at least half of it when we get back."

"It's a deal." Alexia signed off, laced up her boots and sipped the last few drops of the wine in her glass, wonder-

ing who would be drinking the rest if she and Mike didn't
make it back.

Craving some fresh air, Alexia took the elevator to the
lobby and walked out into the busy morning street. Twenty-
six years ago, on the day she was born, no one would have
believed that San Francisco could ever return to what it had
been in the years before the Awakening.

It hadn't, of course. Not completely. But the rhythms of
human life had resumed after the Treaty had permitted regular farming, manufacturing and inter-Enclave commerce.
There were bankers and office workers, reporters and shop-
keepers, cops and financiers all going about their business
much the same way they had in the twentieth century.

But Alexia could never venture out among the general
public without knowing what *had* changed. Because when
her eyes met those of an ordinary human on the street, she
saw the suspicion. Suspicion, or fear, or hostility—all the
same emotions most humans felt for Nightsiders, only a little
less severe because they knew she wasn't one of the enemy.

The existence of dhampir agents couldn't be kept from
Nightsiders or Enclave citizens. But neither she nor any of
her fellow Half-bloods could pass for human. Not with eyes
like those of a cat and teeth a little too reminiscent of a wolf's.

Or a Nightsider's.

As Alexia paused at a fruit stand to examine a fresh or-
ange, just shipped in from the Los Angeles Enclave, she heard
a child's voice on the other side of the stacked crates.

"Look, Mommy," the little girl said. "Is that a bloodsucker?"

Alexia tried to smile at the mother, hoping to express her
understanding for the child's mistake. The woman looked
mortified, but she couldn't hide her distaste.

"You mustn't say such things, Jenny," she said, jerking
at the little girl's hand. "It isn't polite, and anyway, she's on
our side."

Our side, Alexia thought as she returned to headquarters. Yes, her loyalties could never be in question. It was her late human mother who had raised her, not her unknown and reviled Nightsider father.

But for the dhampires, there would never truly be an "our."

The ferry slid quietly away into the fog, its wake swallowed up in the choppy waves stirred by a brisk late-summer wind off the Pacific. Unless an observer were standing nearly on top of Alexia and Michael at the old Larkspur Ferry Terminal, he or she would hardly know a boat had ever been at the dock.

But then again, Alexia thought, this was still technically part of the San Francisco Enclave, and there shouldn't be any leeches here. Which didn't mean a damned thing. They were standing almost at the border of the Zone, where the Redwood Highway crossed over Mission Avenue in the crumbling city of San Rafael. It was an arbitrary border, like so many of them, but it was quite real. Broad daylight, more than any mere treaty, was what protected them now.

The abandoned stronghold of the former San Quentin Correctional Facility stood within view across the inlet to the southeast, and beyond it the twisted halves of the Richmond Bridge, separated by a kilometer of empty water, reached out from each side of San Rafael Bay like hands desperate to touch one last time before an eternal parting.

Alexia tightened the straps of her pack and nodded to Michael, who was already scanning the disintegrating ferry buildings for any sign of movement. She watched him for a moment, grateful that she'd never felt the slightest romantic interest in him in spite of their close partnership. It would have made things very complicated, and fraternization was against Aegis policy in any case. But with his rugged good looks, heavily muscular build and sun-streaked blond hair, he had plenty of female admirers.

"All clear," Mike said, oblivious to her inspection. He checked his weapons, traditional XM30 assault rifle and VS120 "Vampire Slayer" pistol and combat knife. The XM30 was powerful enough to slow a vampire down, even stop one for some time when used by an expert marksman, but the Vampire Slayer was the only weapon that could kill a leech. And it was to be used as a very last resort, because the damage it inflicted on a vampire, as well as any other creature unfortunate enough to be on the receiving end, couldn't be mistaken for anything but what it was. It almost literally blew its target apart.

After checking her own weapons, Alexia instinctively touched the underside of her arm, tracing the raised shape through the heavy fabric of her uniform jacket and the shirt beneath. The patch was exactly where it should be, attached to her skin by a thin graft of synskin that held it in place and continuously fed the necessary drugs into her bloodstream. It was new, replaced only yesterday, and would remain effective for up to a month.

Without the drugs, she—like approximately forty percent of dhampir agents—would be unable to take nourishment from human food, and since Half-bloods never fed on blood, death was the inevitable result. At least she, unlike the other sixty percent, was immune to any risk of conversion by a vampire's bite.

And that was a horror far worse than death. Michael noticed her gesture and touched her shoulder. "Don't worry," he said. "We'll have this over and done within a week."

Alexia quickly dropped her hand. There were eleven hours of daylight left, but it was a good thirty miles northeast across the Zone. If the garbled reports were correct, the illegal colony was just west of the old city of Santa Rosa, on the other side of the Sonoma range and at least three miles from the eastern border of the territory claimed by Erebus.

And the closer they got to Erebus, the more likely they

were to run into the Citadel's own agents, both Nightsiders and the elusive Daysiders.... That is, *if* they managed to make it past the mutant creatures even the Nightsiders wouldn't allow near their city.

Without exchanging another word, Alexia and Michael set off toward Highway 101.

Damon crouched at the crest of the hill, looking down into the valley below. From this elevation, the abandoned city was a maze of streets and decaying buildings, empty of human life. Rusting automobiles caught the sun's light—brief, glaring beacons that appeared and vanished in a matter of seconds like the signals of an unknown code.

But he knew the emptiness was only an illusion. Somewhere, nestled at the foot of these hills, was a society that shouldn't exist.

He smiled, though there was no one to see. It wasn't as if the Council hadn't known about the colony. They hadn't shared that fact with their field agents, but those the humans called Daysiders, despised minority that they were, had their own secret channels of communication within Erebus. Certain powerful Bloodmasters had simply failed to acknowledge the "problem"...as long as the humans, other than the serfs in the colony itself, didn't know about it. After all, it was to Erebus's benefit if the Opiri gained a strong foothold in the Zone. One step here, another there, testing the waters, seeing just how far they could push.

But the colony wasn't a secret any longer. Word had come that the Enclave knew something was up, and at this very moment Aegis operatives were on their way to investigate.

And that could mean war. A new war the Expansionists would be eager enough to encourage, if the humans would be cooperative enough to instigate it. Some believed the Expansionists had established the colony themselves for that very purpose.

Even if they hadn't, Damon had no doubt that the conservatives were secretly giving the settlement their full support, perhaps even providing serfs for the colonists. Not so the ruling Independent. They still controlled the Council, and they had no intention of letting the fragile Armistice be destroyed.

But they faced a problem that wasn't likely to be solved without significant conflict. Damon knew the establishment of the illegal colony had been motivated by a very simple instinct shared by both Opiri and humans: the need to survive.

For Opiri, survival meant not only blood but room to live as their very biology demanded. Erebus was beginning to outgrow itself. Opiri were not meant to dwell in close proximity to each other like humans or rabbits, squeezed into apartments stacked like blocks under a single roof. Though Bloodmasters and many Bloodlords were accorded their own towers to accommodate their many serfs and vassals, there was little room in the Citadel for upward mobility. And Freebloods needed blood as much as any other Opir.

Sooner or later, the pressure to increase their territory would incite certain Opiri to violence. The only thing to be done was to delay the inevitable until some new bargain could be reached with the human government…or the Expansionists found a way to break the power of the Enclaves forever.

Damon had no personal stake in the colony's fate one way or another, and his opinions were of no consequence except where they related directly to his work. He belonged to no Bloodmaster. He served only the Council, and Erebus. Because that was his nature, and his destiny.

To be forever alone. Neither human nor Opir, too valuable to be discarded like the Lamiae, too different to ever fully integrate into Erebusian society. But vital to the Citadel nevertheless, and free in a way no vassal could ever be.

Squinting against the lowering sun, Damon started down the slope, his feet deftly finding their way among stones and tough, hardy shrubs scattered like spots over the hillside pelt of summer-gold grass. He would not be approaching the colony; his job was both more dangerous and much simpler.

He reached the foot of the hill and opened his senses. He smelled nothing but the sharp scent of spice bush and the musk of a fox, heard only the rustle of fleeing mice and the distant cry of a hawk. As long as he traveled by the sun, he was not likely to be detected by the Opir colonists, whose own powerful senses would be muted by their retreat into daytime shelter. As for the human serfs, they might as well be blind and deaf.

That left only the dhampires. It was not a matter of if they were coming, but *when*.

And he would be ready.

Chapter 2

The person, whoever or whatever it might be, was coming closer.

Flashing the hand sign that meant he was about to circle around behind the approaching stranger, Michael left Alexia to watch and wait. It was morning—the third since they'd left the ferry—so Alexia knew the one they were about to meet couldn't be a Nightsider. Silent as they were, even vampires couldn't move very quietly bundled up in the kind of protective gear they had to wear in daylight.

No, this was either human or one of the others. And while the stranger was making no particular attempt to sneak up on them, his "noise" was about as loud as the sound of a feather landing on a down pillow. Humans just didn't move like that, not even the most highly trained agents.

The one coming toward them could be only one thing: a Daysider. And whatever he or she intended...

He, Alexia decided, breathing slowly through her nostrils. Definitely male.

She checked the VS120 strapped to her pack and adjusted her grip on her assault rifle. He couldn't be stupid enough to think he could just stride up to an Aegis operative and dispatch her after all but announcing his presence. Not that agent deaths on either side were acknowledged by the respective governments, but that hardly meant they didn't happen. Enclave agents had been operating in and around the Zone too long not to have a very respectable reputation, even among vampires.

But if the Daysider wasn't planning to attack…what *was* he planning?

All Alexia's muscles tensed as the thicket of toyon bushes in front of her rustled, the slightest movement of leathery leaves that might have heralded the passage of a rabbit or some other small animal. She aimed the XM30.

The man who walked out from behind the bushes was tall, lithe and yet imposing. That was the first thing Alexia noticed as she drew a bead on his chest directly over his heart. Then she looked up into his face, knowing that an enemy's eyes—even a Daysider's—would give him away before he made the slightest movement.

The Daysider looked back at her without a trace of concern. His features were quite extraordinary…. That she had to admit, in spite of the situation. He was one of the most beautiful things she'd ever seen. Not beautiful like a woman, but in the perfect harmony of his features: the strong chin, straight nose, high cheekbones, expressive lips.

And his eyes. They were dark…not maroon like those of a Nightsider, but the deepest sapphire imaginable. The pupils almost swallowed up the blue. His short hair was not white, like most vampires', but a hue somewhere between brown and gold, and his skin was richly tanned.

Alexia swallowed. She had met her first Daysider at last, and he was so much…*more* than she had expected.

The Daysider glanced down at the assault rifle. "There is no need for that," he said mildly.

His English was unaccented, bearing no hint of the ancient language all Nightsiders, whatever their origins, spoke among themselves. His voice was a pleasant baritone.

Alexia's finger hovered over the trigger. "Put your hands up," she commanded.

He did so, slowly and without alarm. "I am not here to hurt you," he said.

She scanned him again the way she should have done the first time, looking for telltale bulges in his tan-and-brown uniform. She could identify no weapons, but if all she'd heard of Daysiders was true, they were just as good at concealing whatever they needed as the agents of Aegis.

"I am no threat to you," he said.

Alexia didn't even bother to reply. "On your knees. Hands clasped behind your head."

He obeyed, each muscle working in such perfect harmony that suddenly he was on the ground without her having even noticed how he got there.

"You see," he said in that same reasonable tone, "you have nothing to fear from me. It's generally accepted that Half-bloods are only a little inferior in strength and skill to my kind, so you seem to have the adva—"

The butt of a rifle slammed into the Daysider's temple, and he slumped to the ground. Michael turned the gun around and aimed it at the Daysider's head. He was already stirring, only temporarily stunned by the blow.

"Are you crazy?" Michael demanded, glaring at Alexia. "Chatting with a Daysider as if he wouldn't bite your throat out the second you blinked?"

Alexia knew she had no call to be angry with Michael. He was right. She'd let her curiosity about her first Daysider dangerously compromise her training. And her sense.

"Shoot him if he moves," Michael said, crouching behind

the enemy operative. He unfastened a pair of steel cuffs from his belt and bound the Daysider's hands behind him. Then he rolled the man over, patted him down and removed a wicked-looking knife and a small pistol of a type unfamiliar to Alexia. He tossed them into the bushes, pushed the agent back onto his stomach and jabbed the muzzle of his XM30 into the Daysider's spine.

"Sit up," he said.

The Daysider rocked to his knees and blinked as a thin trickle of blood dripped from his forehead into his left eye. In a few more seconds the bleeding had stopped, the small wound closed by the accelerated healing powers dhampires and Daysiders shared, and the agent was studying Alexia as if nothing had happened.

"That wasn't necessary," he said. "I have come to offer a truce."

"A truce?" Michael scoffed. All the good nature he displayed at home, the charm that drew so many women to him—even the human ones—was lost in hatred. The very emotion Director McAllister had warned *her* about. "You?" he said. "*You* have the authority to make a truce for your masters?"

Not by the slightest flicker of expression did the Daysider acknowledge that Michael could sever his spine at any moment. "Not for Erebus," he said. "For myself."

Alexia stared into those remarkable sapphire eyes and had to fight off a shiver. "Explain," she said harshly.

"We have both been sent on the same mission," the Daysider said. "If your people were not aware of the colony, you would not be here, so close to the Citadel's border. We both know that the settlement is illegal under the Armistice, and that human serfs are being held within it, but the Council has no desire to see new conflict break out between our peoples. They have assigned me to observe the colony for Erebus and gather information that will help them determine what should be done to prevent such hostilities."

The Daysider was so straightforward compared with the average leech that a normal human might actually have been taken in by his story.

Michael wasn't. "'Hostilities,'" he said mockingly. "Your leaders should have thought of that before you broke the Treaty."

"*They* did not," the Daysider said. "That is why it is necessary to—"

"Liar," Michael snarled. "Freak. You were sent here to kill us."

The Daysider tilted his head as if he were listening to Michael, but his gaze never left Alexia's. "I had the discretion to kill you if it would have served my mission, but you know as well as I that your unexpected deaths in the Zone would likely be counterproductive." He paused. "I think we all want the same thing, and that is to maintain the peace."

Michael spat into the brown grass at his feet. "There will never be peace until every last one of you is—"

"Carter," Alexia interrupted. Michael glanced at her, took a deep breath and calmed down. She didn't know what had gotten into him, but his uncharacteristic loss of control didn't exactly make either one of them look strong in the eyes of the enemy.

She and Michael were at least going to have to pretend they were considering the truce the Daysider had offered. Just as she would continue to act as if she didn't despise this leech even more than Michael did. And despise *herself* for feeling nearly overwhelmed by his sheer, undeniable masculine power.

His. She didn't want to know anything more about him than she absolutely had to, but it was going to be damned inconvenient to keep thinking of him as "the Daysider."

"What is your name?" she asked him.

He inclined his head as if to acknowledge her civility. "Damon," he replied.

Appropriate, coming as it did from the ancient Greek word for "demon." But what interested her more was that he had no Sire-name to indicate which Bloodmaster or Bloodlord claimed his vassalage.

It was true, then, what Aegis taught…that Daysiders lived outside the strict hierarchy of Nightsider society. No one in the Enclaves was completely certain of how they had come into being. The ongoing question was whether or not they had "awakened" years ago along with the regular Nightsiders, or if they had been created since.

"I'm Agent Fox," she said, "and this is Agent Carter."

"Ms. Fox," Damon said, arching a brow. Alexia wondered how close he was to comparing her to her animal namesake. What did he remind *her* of?

A leopard. Sleek and swift, well-defined muscle sliding under golden skin and mottled olive-brown uniform, dappled with shadow.

"*Agent* Fox," she corrected him. "Let's not waste any more time. What exactly are you proposing?"

Damon moved his shoulders as if he were stretching against the pull of the cuffs. It almost looked as if he could snap the reinforced steel like the thinnest plastic.

"I propose that we work together," he said, "pool our skills and our knowledge. Learn what we can about the colony without engaging the colonists, and then go our separate ways."

"That's insane," Michael burst out.

Alexia was inclined to agree. But she also wasn't too blinded by hatred to see the possibilities inherent in Damon's suggestion.

"Why would you encourage your enemies to learn more about a settlement founded by Nightsiders?" she asked him bluntly. "Wouldn't that be against your handler's best interests?"

"Since Aegis will eventually obtain the information in any case," he said, "it is my judgment that our working together would be very much to the Citadel's advantage."

Michael spun to face Alexia. "Can't you see he intends to lead us along the garden path and annihilate us at the end of it?" he said.

Alexia let his anger pass over her. "Why should we trust you?" she asked Damon.

The Daysider's eyes, already so dark, grew darker still. "Your partner wants to destroy me," he said. "I am in no position to stop him. There are two of you, and I am alone. Yet I am offering this truce because I know that the distraction of fighting each other will lose us valuable time." He leaned forward. "You understand the delicacy of the situation. Even the smallest misstep—"

"Are you trying to tell us that your Council didn't encourage this colony from the beginning?" Michael interrupted.

"Yes."

"And your masters don't see this setup as a way of getting a foothold in the Zone, or provoking a new war they think they can win?"

Damon blew out his breath in a brief sigh. "Your agency is well aware of the way my government is organized," he said. "The Expansionists have minority status at this time. I serve the Council as a whole, which wants to keep the balance just as it is."

"So you say," Alexia murmured.

The corner of his mouth quirked up. "If your agency believed the Expansionists were in ascendance, this new settlement would be the least of its concerns."

He made perfect sense, Alexia thought. Too much sense, in fact.

She rose, keeping the rifle leveled at Damon's head. "My partner and I will have to discuss this privately," she said.

"Of course." Damon shrugged his shoulders again. "It's unlikely I'll be going anywhere."

"I'll make sure of that," Michael grunted. "Lie on your stomach."

Damon did as he commanded, and Michael made quick work of cuffing his ankles. Maybe the Daysider could break free of them eventually, but Alexia didn't plan to be away more than a few minutes.

She and Michael retreated into the brush, backing away with their weapons still fixed on Damon. Once they were a good thirty meters away, Alexia pressed the skin of her throat over the subcom implanted beside her larynx and adjusted her earpiece.

I think we should do it, she said, speaking soundlessly through the subcom.

Mike touched his own highly sensitive earpiece, which picked up their subvocalizations as if they were spoken aloud. *He'll kill as soon as our backs are turned.*

You think I don't hate him as much as you do? she asked. *But we have to find out how much he knows, if he's really working for the Independents.*

Independents, Michael repeated, the scorn evident in his words. *You know even they would enslave or slaughter all of us if they could find an excuse.*

So let's not give them one, Alexia said. *Look, there are useful things we can learn just by observing him. Maybe he'll slip and give us a clue about his real agenda.*

Then you're assuming he's lying, too, Michael said.

We don't have to trust *him. He may be stronger and faster, but we're pretty well matched in acuity of smell and hearing—and there are two of us. One can stay with him while the other keeps watch from a distance. That way we'll have someone free to report back if there's any treachery.*

Forget it, Michael said. *We stay together. That's Aegis policy, and—*

We can break policy if we judge it necessary. And I think it is, Mike.

He gave her a look she'd never seen on his face before, one uncomfortably like mistrust. But when he spoke again, there was only resignation in his expression.

Okay, he said. *Who do you propose stays with him?*

I will, she said without hesitation. *I'm better at hand-to-hand, and you're the better marksman.*

Once we split up, he'll know what we're doing, Michael said.

Then he's not likely to try anything, is he?

After a long moment of silence he nodded, briefly and not at all happily. Alexia frowned. It just wasn't like him to be so grim. *I guess the best thing to do is pretend to have an argument,* she said.

Michael pulled a face. *He'll never fall for it.*

Probably not, but he'll be even more suspicious if we don't try to make it sound convincing.

Michael signaled agreement, and they switched back to audible voice, still whispering to make it seem as if they were trying to prevent Damon from listening in. Michael was extremely persuasive in his refusal to go along, and Alexia found it easy to work up the appropriate anger. She'd already been troubled by Michael's open protests before, and Damon wasn't likely to think their exchange this time any worse than the previous one.

Once Michael had "stomped" off, vowing to let her learn from her own mistakes, Alexia returned to Damon. He was sitting up again, head cocked as he watched her approach. He wasn't smiling, but she could feel his amusement at her and Michael's little game.

"It seems your partner doesn't agree with your decision," he said.

She crouched a safe distance from him, her gun loose in her hands, and met his gaze. "We work together, but we're not chained at the ankle. He'll see reason eventually, and until then you won't be able to complain that we aren't on equal footing."

Damon's eyes reflected a shaft of sunlight breaking through the rustling canopy of oak leaves above them. "I don't remember complaining," he said, "but I'm gratified that one of you has seen the benefit in my proposition."

Something in the way he said the words, the way he looked at her, made Alexia feel unaccountably warm. He was so damned *agreeable* that she found she had to remind himself what he was and whom he worked for.

And she didn't dare make the mistake of believing that this mild behavior wasn't just a cover for savagery that would reveal itself the instant she let him think she trusted him.

"I don't expect you to trust me," Damon said, as if he'd been reading her mind—an ability she was pretty sure not even full vampires possessed. "But we can do nothing if you don't release me."

Alexia wasn't in any hurry to follow his pointed suggestion. "First I want to know exactly what you plan to do."

He shifted as if he were trying to make himself more comfortable, but Alexia could see the tension in every line of his hard, lean body—tension that belied his easy manner. "I suggest we approach the settlement together," he said, "and once we're close enough to observe the colonists' activities, we'll separate. At the end of a set time we rendezvous and pool our information."

Too simple, Alexia thought. *Much too simple.* "Why do you think we'll come up with different information?" she asked.

"Because *we* are different, you and I."

She knew that technically that wasn't as true as she wanted it to be. Over the years Aegis had determined that Daysiders and dhampires were much alike in their speed, strength and senses, with one or the other holding slight advantages in a few areas. Neither was as strong and fast as a Nightsider, but both held the advantage of being able to move freely in daylight without suffering the deadly burns that afflicted full vampires.

The only comfort Alexia took from the comparison was that dhampires were, without exception, on the side of law and decency, while Damon's kind served an evil, corrupt society of unrepentant killers. And while *they* lived on blood like their masters, no dhampir would ever give way to that sick, unnatural hunger.

"Yes," she said coldly. "We are very different."

He stared into her eyes again, and she felt as if she could fall right into that spellbinding blackness and never come out again. "But not so different that we cannot understand each other," he reminded her. "And in one way we are very much alike."

"What way?"

"We are both outsiders in our worlds."

Alexia wasn't about to admit how true that was, but Damon had freely offered information that seemed a little too personal to share with an enemy. It had to be part of a plan to get her off guard.

"Have you ever met a dhampir before?" she asked.

"I have only observed from a distance."

Once again his candidness surprised her, though he could, of course, be lying.

"You don't allow the birth of my kind in Erebus," she said, testing him.

"Such matters are the province of the Bloodmasters."

"Do they kill my kind when they're born, or before?"

"Such conception is forbidden."

"Funny how that didn't stop vampire males from impregnating human females during the War. But then again, *they* didn't have any part in raising the children they created. None of our mothers had much choice about conceiving, but at least they didn't discard us." She paused, remembering to breathe. "We have a unique place in the Enclaves, and a purpose. What about you?"

"If I had no purpose, I would not be here."

"So even though you're an outsider, you're loyal to your masters."

"As loyal as you are to yours." His expression, previously so mild, went cold. "Tell me, how much choice did you have in becoming an agent of your city, risking your life every time you leave it?"

"How much choice were you given to be what *you* are?"

They stared at each other. Eventually Damon shook his head.

"I have suggested a course of action," he said. "Do you intend to release me?"

Alexia shouldered her gun and crossed the space between them, every sense alert. She used her own key to unlock the cuffs. The moment he was free she jumped well out of his reach. He stretched his long legs and rubbed his wrists just as if he could feel pain and discomfort as much as any human being.

"What about your partner?" he asked, gathering himself to rise. "Do you expect him to rejoin us, or is he likely to move on his own?"

"If you mean will he attack you, no. He won't endanger me." She watched him intently as he got to his feet, her eyes drawn once more to the litheness of his body and the assurance of every move he made. Why, in God's name, wasn't she feeling the disgust and contempt she should have felt at the mere sight of him?

Because it was something else she was experiencing, both physically and emotionally. Something she couldn't begin to understand.

She hated it.

"What about your people?" she asked before her emotions could escape her rigid control. "Do you expect me to believe that Erebus hasn't sent more than one operative to observe the colony?"

"It seems likely," Damon said, "but as we generally work alone, I would not know the nature of their assignments." He brushed the dirt from the front of his pants. "I would advise you to tell Agent Carter not to compromise your mission by approaching the colony alone."

"You know wireless communication is forbidden in the Zone," she told him.

Which wouldn't have made any difference to agents from either side, except that both the Enclave and the Citadel scrambled all signals outside their borders. She might be able to get through to Michael, but the odds were against it. He'd have to find a way to keep close enough to help her if she needed it, but far enough away to avoid making Damon too nervous.

"May I collect my weapons?" Damon asked.

Back to that damned politeness. Alexia jerked her head in permission, though every instinct was screaming in protest. Damon searched among the bushes, found the knife and pistol, returned the knife to a sheath at his back and tucked the pistol into some inner pocket of his uniform jacket.

"That's it?" she asked, narrowing her eyes. "You must have other weapons." He straightened and zipped up his jacket, though the weather was warm and he probably didn't react to changes in temperature any more acutely than she did.

"I left them some distance from here, along with my pack," he said. "I will retrieve them on the way to the colony."

"I assume you know the way?"

He stood facing her, unmoving, legs braced slightly apart. "Don't you?" he asked.

Now he was testing *her*. "Let's not play games. You've tried to make us believe that your Council hasn't known about the settlement all along, but that's a little difficult to believe given that it's less than two klicks away from the Citadel's western border. It's not exactly hidden, is it?"

"I see you do have some information already," he said, deflecting her question. "Perhaps Aegis has sent other operatives before you."

"You haven't answered *my* question."

"The first concrete intelligence on the colony was provided to the Council by an operative less than a month ago." He hesitated, frowning with what appeared to be uncertainty. "It *is* possible the Expansionist Faction were aware it existed before that time."

Alexia didn't believe for a moment that he hadn't rehearsed that line very carefully. "Hasn't it occurred to you the Expansionists also set it up right under your Council's noses?" she said.

"No. This was done quietly, by those who did not expect to be noticed. Or missed."

"Like your Freebloods and the cast-off human serfs no one in Erebus wants. But you've admitted the Council has been aware of the colony for a month, and they still haven't done anything about it."

An inscrutable look flitted across his face. "The first agent was able to tell us very little. He died soon after he made his report."

"That's unfortunate," she said with false regret.

"He was fatally injured in the Zone by an unknown assailant. The one who attacked him was a professional and used a weapon forbidden in Erebus."

Alexia stiffened. "What are you suggesting?" she asked. "That one of *our* people killed him?"

"The weapon was the one you call 'Vampire Slayer,' such as the one you carry strapped to your pack," he said, his eyes locked on hers.

"The killing of hostile agents isn't permitted except in cases of self-defense," she retorted.

"Yes," he said with a wry twist of his lips. "We are only spies, after all, tasked to make certain the buffer zone is maintained. But it would not be the first time an agent of either side has died between the Borders."

Not the first time, Alexia thought, and certainly not the last. There had been at least one dhampir fatality in the Zone each year since the Treaty had been signed, the latest Michael's former partner. Such facts could not be openly acknowledged by either side. But dhampir agents were hardly a renewable resource, and they weren't casually sent on missions to assassinate enemy operatives for no good reason.

"Even if I believed one of ours did it," she said, "I wouldn't tell you."

"I wouldn't expect it," he said. "Just as you won't expect to learn anything from me that my superiors don't want you to know."

So he was confirming that everything he said to her was calculated to achieve a certain goal. Not that she'd ever doubted it.

She smiled back at him, baring her teeth. "I guess we understand each other," she said. "After you…"

Without a word he turned and set off north, moving almost soundlessly now that he had no need to be heard.

Alexia followed close on his heels. He was giving her the chance to shoot him in the back, but nothing in his posture suggested that he was worried. She kept half an ear out for Michael, but he must have decided to stay out of range of her senses, or Damon's. Just as well.

They traveled quickly over once-occupied land that was gradually reverting to its original state, hiking up and down oak-studded hillsides and avoiding the valleys with their decaying suburbs and open streets. Damon picked up his rifle and pack after they'd gone a few miles, securing the weapon to the back of his pack as a sign of "good faith." There was no further sign of human or vampire presence until they reached the summit of a hillside overlooking what had once been known as the Bennett Valley.

Most of the fields and vineyards below had long since become overgrown with native grasses, shrubs and scattered trees, but there wasn't any mistaking the nature of the several green rectangles that marked out the deliberate cultivation of crops. They had not been created for Nightsiders, who had no need to rely on such food sources, but for their human "property." At the opposite side of the valley, tucked up against the foot of the low Sonoma Mountains, stood a high, rectangular wall guarding a compound of buildings— twelve or thirteen according to Alexia's count, suggesting the presence of as many as a dozen Nightsiders and perhaps three or four times as many humans.

The sight both chilled and infuriated her. She glanced at Damon, who crouched beside her with his own binoculars in hand, almost as if she expected the same reaction from him.

Of course that was ridiculous. He was from Erebus. What disgusted her would be perfectly natural for a leech. This was only a job to Damon. There was nothing personal in it.

She couldn't afford to make it personal, either. Not if she wanted to keep her head…and her life.

Alexia pulled off her pack, and Damon did the same. "How do you want to do this?" she asked him. "If we split up here, you can go around from the north and I'll approach from the south." She glanced up at the sky, noting the angle of the sun. "We don't have much daylight left. Let's rendezvous tomorrow morning at 0900 hours on that hill directly east of the colony, by the rock formation. Whoever gets there first will wait for the other. Agreed?"

Damon lowered his binoculars. "Agreed," he said. He met her gaze, his own unreadable. "I trust you'll keep your partner from killing me if he rejoins you?"

"I already told you. He won't do anything rash, unless you—"

The report of an automatic weapon cut her off, and she flung herself flat on the ground. Damon was down beside her a second later. Bullets whizzed over their heads and struck the tree trunk just behind them.

"Someone," Damon said, "does not want us here."

Chapter 3

Alexia smothered a cynical laugh. "Whatever gave you that idea?"

As much as he detested his own feelings, Damon couldn't help but admire her. He had done so from their first meeting, when she'd played it so cool in the face of her partner's intransigence.

All feigned, of course. Not her courage—he had no reason to doubt that—but certainly Carter's fury. No trained agent of Aegis would be so flagrantly emotional when facing the enemy. It had all been an act for his benefit.

Just as *he* was putting on an act for the dhampires, doing his best to make them believe he didn't hate everything they stood for.

But not Alexia herself. Lying so close beside her, he could inhale her scent, both floral and spicy, without the distraction of other smells. He breathed in deeply, tasting the air around her: the heat of her skin, the unique signature of the blood pulsing through her veins, and the faint female tang that stirred his body in a way he wanted very much to ignore.

Once again, as at the beginning, he was captivated by her beauty, her natural grace, the harmony of her movements. Not even the bulky camouflage fatigues could conceal how extraordinary she was. Her sleek, slender figure, strong and utterly female at the same time, was as perfect as that of the most beautiful Opir female. Her hair was the color of her namesake's fur, her skin honey-warm in the light of the dying sun, her green eyes with their oval, almost catlike pupils vivid and fearless.

If it hadn't been for all those compelling qualities and a hundred more uncounted, he might have continued to forget that he had once been capable of wanting a woman. But she had made it impossible for him to take any further comfort in that denial. Or in the solitude he had learned to embrace over the past two decades.

Lifting his head a little, Damon peered in the direction from which the shots had come. The shooter wasn't in the valley; Damon estimated that he or she must be hidden somewhere in the hills on the other side.

"Do you see anything?" Alexia whispered, unslinging her rifle from her shoulder.

Once again he found himself focused on her instead of the danger confronting them. He remembered the first time he had met her gaze, the brief flash of uncertainty and surprise he had glimpsed in her eyes. It had been obvious that she, unlike her partner, had never met one of his kind before.

He had been careful to watch her reaction when he'd told her about the dead Council agent, hoping she would slip and reveal some knowledge of a previous Aegis mission to investigate the colony. In spite of her defiance, he could tell she knew nothing.

Perhaps she and her partner *were* the first. But he wasn't foolish enough to believe she wouldn't use her time with him to augment her agency's knowledge of the Council's activities in the Zone.

That was good. As long as Alexia was asking questions and he kept her satisfied with vague answers, she would be less likely to realize what he was doing. The fact that her partner had broken away was a problem, but not an insoluble one. Not as long as Damon kept his head.

And kept himself from feeling.

"Our would-be executioner is firing from the east," he said, belatedly answering Alexia's question.

"A single sniper," she said. "From the colony?" She looked sideways at him, eyes narrowed. "It's still light. Do they have any Daysiders down there?"

Damon was genuinely surprised at the question, though he had no intention of offering the real reason why that was virtually impossible.

"Unlikely," he said.

"But a Nightsider would be taking a chance emerging so early," she said, watching him out of the corner of her eye. "Even protective gear doesn't ease most vampires' fear of sunlight."

She waited for Damon to answer, but he held his silence. She shifted her weight and rested her chin on her forearms.

"It wouldn't be one of the colony's humans unless he or she is under the direct control of a Bloodmaster," she said. "You suggested the Nightsiders who founded the settlement were the kind who wouldn't be missed leaving Erebus. Are you sure there are no Bloodmasters down there?"

"That is what I am here to find out," Damon said.

A second round of shots pierced the air above them, almost close enough to graze Damon's scalp. He grabbed Alexia and rolled them both down the slight incline behind them, fetching up against a clump of scrub oaks with Alexia's chest and hips and legs atop his, her rifle trapped beneath him.

She lay panting in his arms for a moment, obviously surprised by his sudden action, and he felt the thumping of her heart through her clothing and the rush of her breath on his cheek. He was holding a woman in his arms, a woman like no other, and his body woke to furious life.

Damon had engaged in sexual intercourse with only three females in his brief three decades of memory: one a Bloodmistress named Jocasta, with whom he'd had a clandestine, lengthy affair; the second a human female "given" to him by the Council as a reward for good work; and the third the Darketan woman with whom he had shared the only happy year of his life.

The first relationship had begun because the Bloodmistress had been intrigued by the Darketans' outsider status and their reputation for sexual prowess, and it continued so long because she had been pleased with his performance and he had been content to sate her considerable appetite. There had been little affection involved. The second had been a matter of some shame to him and had never been repeated. But the last...

It had begun as a means of easing loneliness, two equals coming together for mutual comfort in a world they could never fully be a part of. But it hadn't stayed that way. Damon had learned what it was to feel as the Opiri claimed no Nightsider could, a way no Daysider dared.

Eirene had returned his feelings, but she and Damon had been forcibly separated, and the Council had sent her on a solo mission to the Border. He had never seen her again.

From that day forward, Damon had been numb to his body's sexual demands. But now the protective distance was gone, and so was his control. Every hair on his body was standing erect, and his heart seemed to thunder like the vast generators beneath Erebus.

As if she sensed—or felt—his arousal, Alexia rolled off him with a sound very much like a growl, yanked her rifle from under Damon's back and dropped into a crouch two meters away. Damon got to his knees and raked his fingers through his hair, dislodging twigs, dun-colored grass and last autumn's brittle leaves.

"Don't do that again," Alexia said.

"You mean save your life?" he snapped, struggling to regain his equilibrium.

They stared at each other, confusion and hostility warring for dominance in Alexia's remarkable eyes. Oh, she'd felt it, too, that searing physical awareness, but she didn't want to acknowledge it any more than he did.

He looked away. "We'll have to fall back," he said, "and find a way to lure the shooter into a trap so that we can question him. If he's from the colony, he can give us valuable information."

"And what if he's not? You admit the Expansionists may have known about the colony before the Council did, even if they didn't actually help found it. Maybe your war party has sent its own agents to stop you from reporting back."

"Impossible," Damon said. "All operatives answer to the Council, not to individual factions."

"Are you so sure? Every government has its dissidents, those who work secretly against the ruling party."

Of course she was right. But he *knew* that was not the case here, and even to consider that the Expansionists could send their own operatives into the field and so blatantly attack legitimate agents would suggest that the Independents' hold on the Council was dangerously weak. If he believed that, anything he did now would ultimately be meaningless.

There was a part of him that wanted war with the Enclave. They had slaughtered thousands of Opiri, including his fellow Darketans. But he had made a promise to Eirene. *"Work for peace,"* she had said just before their final parting. *"For peace, and freedom."*

He met Alexia's gaze. "You seem to be overlooking one

other possibility," he said. "The shooter could be your partner."

Alexia drew herself up, her shoulders rigid. "No," she said. "I've already told you why that couldn't happen. He would know he'd be as likely to hit me as you."

Her denial was just a little too vehement, and Damon wondered if she thought it was possible...if Michael Carter had really been as angry and bitter as he had appeared. Angry enough to risk his partner's life.

If he could encourage her to believe the worst about Carter, Damon could keep her off balance and make sure she never even considered the truth.

"It seems there is more than one possibility here," he said, retrieving his pack, "and we won't know which one is correct until we catch the shooter. If he wants us dead badly enough, he'll keep firing and we can track his position."

"That wouldn't be too bright of him," Alexia remarked, keeping low to the ground as she pulled on her own pack.

"It depends on how desperate he is and what his orders are, if any," Damon said. "If he's from the colony, he won't want to be cut off from it."

"*If* he's from the colony, he probably isn't the only one guarding it. They must know we're coming. That'll make it a little tricky getting close enough to observe."

Naturally, Alexia would regard that as a serious problem, but to Damon it meant that everything was proceeding as planned. "Are you giving up?" he asked.

She grinned, revealing her very white incisors. "I'll give up when you do."

"Then I suggest our primary goal now should be to catch the shooter and stay alive in the process."

Alexia studied him a moment longer, green eyes slitted like those of a deceptively lazy cat. "All right," she said. "Let's go."

They started back down the other side of the hill, Alexia

taking the lead. There were no more shots, no sound but the typical movements of small mammals and leaves sighing in the evening breeze. The sun was beginning to set, and soon, Damon knew, he would have to rely on Alexia's superior ability to see in the dark. Darketans were by no means night-blind like humans, but Opir-like night vision was one of the few advantages dhampires had over his kind.

But his advantages over *her*—greater speed and strength—would come into play sooner or later, if they remained together. And he would make sure they did.

Perhaps it was time for a little reinforcement of Alexia's decision to work with him. He would do so by telling her part of the truth.

As they turned south, hiking parallel to the valley, Damon caught up with her.

"There is something I should have disclosed earlier," he said.

She stopped abruptly, her hand moving to the strap of her rifle. "What is it?"

"It was not my idea to join forces," he said. "I was instructed to contact and work with any Aegis agents I encountered in the area of the colony."

Her hand remained on the strap. "The Council ordered it?" she asked, frowning. "Why?"

"For the same reasons I gave you when we met. I would not be surprised if your own agency had some part in it."

Her frown deepened. "We were given no such instructions."

Damon had never thought they had, but he had succeeded in planting the idea in her mind.

"Would it shock you to learn that Aegis and the Council were already in contact regarding the colony?" he asked.

"Yes," she said without hesitation. "As much as it would shock me if you defected to our side."

A palpable tension vibrated between them, in some ways

not unlike what Damon had felt when she had lain in his arms. Her words were a challenge, one she didn't expect him to take up, and yet there was an undercurrent beneath the flatness of her voice that hinted of a strange, almost wistful regret.

As if, secretly, she wished he would shock *her* by saying yes.

"You're right," he said, setting off again with a long, ground-eating stride. "It's impossible."

She caught up with him, matching his pace in spite of her smaller frame and shorter legs. "What gave you the idea they might be working together?" she demanded.

"It was only speculation," he said. "And perhaps a little hope."

"Hope? That your Council would want to work with my people beyond the bare minimum necessary to keep the Armistice? Why would that matter to you?"

He glanced down at her. "We should be quiet now, Agent Fox, unless we wish to tell our shooter we're coming."

Alexia offered no further conversation, but Damon sensed that she was thinking through what he'd told her. She would be wondering if her own government was, in fact, secretly conferring with his own without the knowledge of their citizens, their operatives, or those who would gladly revert to a state of war.

It might even be true. Damon was too far from the circles of Opir power to know for certain, and the Council had no earthly reason to confide such matters to a Darketan. Their business concerned him only so far as it affected his work. And his promise to Eirene.

But he didn't think it *was* impossible. And if there was some new rapprochement over the illegal colony, the Council would never allow the Enclave government to learn any secrets that would endanger Erebus.

The humans would know that. Just as Alexia did.

Listening intently, Damon slowed his pace as the sun sank behind the hills to the west. Alexia took the lead again. The landscape darkened, the details blurring in Damon's sight. Alexia moved with assurance, certain of her path as they descended into a narrow hollow between two low hills.

But it was Damon who sensed the attack. The snap of a single twig beneath a booted foot warned him an instant before the bullets began flying.

He was just a second too late to push Alexia out of the way. Several bullets tore into her shoulder in rapid succession, spinning her to the ground. She went limp, curled on her side with her red hair fanned around her head.

Swallowing a howl of protest, Damon knelt beside her, broke the strap of her rifle between his hands and brought the weapon into position, spraying the hillside above them.

A drift of unfamiliar scent behind him sent him skidding around on his knees to take aim at the second shooter, but he got off only a dozen shots before a single large projectile struck him full in the chest. He continued to fire, ignoring the black burst of pain that filled his lungs with blood and flame. He heard a faint grunt that told him one of his bullets had found a mark, and then the gunfire ceased.

Gasping for air, Damon crouched over Alexia and pivoted on his feet, doing his best to cover every possible angle of attack. None came. He and Alexia would have made easy prey, but their enemies were leaving them alone.

It would have made perfect sense, all part of the plan, if the ones he'd expected hadn't tried to kill both him and the dhampir agent he was supposed to keep by his side.

Something was very, very wrong. And Damon's ability to grasp what had happened was rapidly fading. One of his lungs was collapsed, and there was blood filling his chest cavity. He could recover in healing stasis, but it would take time, and once he was unconscious he would be unable to protect Alexia.

And he *had* to protect her. He couldn't risk being held responsible for an Aegis agent's death when the situation was so precarious. At another time, he might have let her die.

So he told himself.

With the last of his energy, he shrugged out of his pack, bent over Alexia and tried to assess the damage. She was rapidly losing blood, and her eyelids fluttered in semiconsciousness. Fighting off waves of nausea, Damon removed her pack, worked her jacket off and fumbled inside his pack for the field dressing every Darketan carried in the Zone. He tore open the waterproof packet and applied the treated bandage to her wound, fixing it in place with the attached strip of fabric.

He was forced to lift her body to remove her bandage, and it soon became apparent that the dressing wouldn't be sufficient to stop the bleeding. There were still bullets inside her, and though they would eventually be pushed out by her healing flesh, she couldn't afford to lose too much blood or she wouldn't be able to heal. He rooted inside her pack, found her med kit and unwrapped her field dressing.

Hardly able to catch his breath, Damon applied the second dressing. Alexia's blood soaked through it almost before he had finished. He yanked the tail of his shirt from the waistband of his pants, tore the bottom half of the shirt into wide strips and folded them together, pressing the makeshift bandage over the soaked field dressings. He knew he wouldn't be able to maintain the pressure once he was out, so he lay across Alexia's slender body, using his own weight to hold the bandages in place.

"Hold on, Alexia," he whispered. "Hold on."

Then the last of his air ran out.

Alexia woke to throbbing agony that centered in her right shoulder and numbed her arm all the way down to her fingertips. In a flash she remembered the attack, and the bullets that had slammed into her flesh. She knew she had fallen, shocked by the blinding pain and the impact, and then there had been some kind of movement, a voice.

Then nothing. But now she was awake, and alive, and someone was lying on his belly beside her, his cheek pressed against a rough patch of dirt.

Damon. It had been his voice she'd heard, his hands working over her body and tying the bandage that had stanched her wounds. Now the bleeding had stopped, and though she was still very weak, she knew she wasn't going to die.

But she couldn't tell from her position if Damon had survived the attack. Her heart lurched. She rolled over on her right side, pressing her hand to her bandages, and watched for signs that he was breathing.

He was. She closed her eyes and sank onto her back again, sick with pain but too grateful to care. She didn't understand *why* she should be grateful; Damon was still the enemy and had probably been lying about nearly everything he'd told her to advance his own agenda.

But he'd quite possibly saved her life by giving her body a chance to repair itself. He was probably in stasis himself, letting his own body do its work to heal whatever injuries he had sustained.

Hissing through her teeth, Alexia tried to sit up. It took her three tries, but she finally managed it, taking care not to risk damaging the tissue still knitting under the bandage or jog the bullets working their way out of her back. She scanned the hollow where they lay and the slopes of the hills to each side, but there was no sound, smell or sight of the enemy… whoever they had been.

Not Michael, she thought with relief. Not that she'd ever believed he was capable of turning on her. There had been at least two shooters this time, maybe more, and they had to be either Daysiders or leeches. Damon had denied there could be Daysiders in the colony, and given that their numbers were believed to be very limited, the shooters would almost certainly be vampires.

But were they from the colony, or Erebus? Damon had also dispelled the notion that the Expansionists had their own agents, but even if *he* believed that, she had no reason to take his word for it.

Alexia crawled over to Damon and touched his back. It rose and fell steadily. There was a hole in his jacket that marked where a large-caliber bullet had pierced his body. Carefully she rolled him a little to the side and felt the front of his torn shirt. There was another hole that matched the first. A through-and-through, then. Thank God for that.

She shivered, quickly realizing that the state of her body, and Damon's, left them both more vulnerable to the chill of the early autumn night. Getting to her feet, she retrieved her pack and jacket, which Damon must have taken from her after the attack. She draped the jacket over her shoulders, removed the tightly wrapped blanket from the pack, laid the blanket over Damon's back and picked up the rifle lying about a meter away. It had recently been fired, and she was pretty sure Damon was the one who had done it. With luck, he'd taken down at least one of the shooters.

Her Vampire Slayer, however, was gone. That didn't surprise her. But if the shooters had gotten so close and intended to do so much damage, why in hell had they left her and Damon alive?

She sat beside him and sipped from her canteen, drawing her knees up to her chest to combat the chill. There was no question of leaving him. They had become partners of a sort, and no field agent abandoned her partner.

Except Michael *had*. He'd gone far enough away from her that he hadn't known she was being attacked.

Not good. Not good at all.

She dozed a little, chin on knees, unable to help herself. Some time later she jerked awake again, aware for the first time of another ache she hadn't noticed before, camouflaged by the greater pain of her shoulder. She removed her jacket, wincing at the stabs of pain radiating out from her shoulder, and touched her left inner arm. Her shirtsleeve was crusted with dried blood.

Suddenly alarmed, she unbuttoned her shirt, pulled it open and slid it down behind her shoulders. There was a thick scab under her arm where her patch should have been.

It was gone. Someone had dug it out in a hasty, brutal attempt at surgery, leaving it to heal over.

Leaving her without the drugs she needed to survive.

Chapter 4

Alexia closed her eyes, breathing deeply to control her panic. *Calm,* she told herself. *You have choices. Think.*

But she really didn't have choices at all.

Damon shifted slightly, a low groan catching in his throat. That was a positive sign…the only good news she had to cling to at the moment, aside from the fact that she could feel the bullets in her shoulder emerging from the skin of her back. She loosened the bandage and ran her hand across the exit wound, dislodging the nearly scoured bullets and brushing them off like dead ticks.

She moved the bandage back into place and rose to her feet, determined to stay awake. She paced the little hollow, measuring out its width from the base of one hill to the other. By the time she sensed the coming dawn, her legs would barely carry her.

It wasn't just lack of sleep and her body's need to heal. The effect of the drugs in her bloodstream would already be diminishing. She'd be able to get through a few days—a week, maybe, if she was lucky—before she began to starve.

Dropping down beside Damon again, she took one of the bags of field rations out of her pack and withdrew a dense nutrient bar. She ate it slowly as misty light crept into the hollow. Soon her ability to digest solid food would be seriously compromised, and so she had to use all her rations while she could.

She had just finished her third bar when Damon opened his eyes. He looked at her through slitted lids and tried to lift himself on his elbows. Her blanket slid from his back.

Alexia hurried to his side, intending to tell him that he was moving much too soon. But he was already pushing his body up, though stiffly, and rolling onto his knees. He grimaced and sat there with his hands braced on his muscular thighs. His skin was still extremely pale, almost as light as a Nightsider's. Even though he was recovering from a serious wound, the change in color seemed almost unnatural, considering the darkness of his tan the previous day.

He spoke before she could. "You're all right," he said, his voice rasping with pain. "How long have I been out?"

"I don't know," she said, crouching to hand him his canteen. "I remember going down almost as soon as we were attacked. That was around sunset. Considering it's almost dawn, I'd say we were both dead to the world all night."

Damon drank with a nod of thanks, set down the canteen and raised his hand to pluck at the front of his bloody shirt. Alexia realized for the first time that the garment was in tatters, the hem ripped off almost to the level of his pectorals.

"They shot me soon after you fell," he said grimly. "I didn't know if you had—"

"I'm fine," she lied. "The shooters haven't come back."

Damon nodded and dropped his hand from his chest. "They let us live."

"Yes. Considering how badly they wounded us, that's a little surprising. Any idea why?"

"None."

"You didn't see anything? Recognize any scents?"

"I could not identify them. But I don't think they are the same as the first shooter."

"What makes you say that?"

"A feeling." He said the word almost mockingly, as if he recognized how ridiculous a reason it was. "Did they take anything?"

"One of my weapons." She hesitated, wondering how much she should tell him about her real state. She knew what she had to do to survive: abandon the mission and return to the Border.

But there was something else at stake besides her life. Someone—vampires, either from Erebus or the colony—had stolen her patch. Aegis had always assumed that the Nightsiders didn't know about the inherent weakness in a percentage of Enclave agents, or they would have exploited it long ago.

Apparently Aegis had been wrong. The shooters had obviously known what to look for. That meant the Nightsiders must already be aware of the patches and that they had some essential purpose, even if they'd never been able to get their hands on one before.

Maybe Damon knew about them as well. If he did...

Keeping her face perfectly still, Alexia reconsidered what she'd assumed about his motives. He had outright admitted that the Council had sent him to join her. Sometimes telling part of the truth was more effective than an all-out lie. Had their "partnership" been part of the plan to get her patch? Had he lulled her suspicions just enough to leave her vulnerable?

Had they caught Michael and done the same thing to him?

She examined Damon's face covertly, feeling such a conflicting jumble of emotions that she could hardly think straight. She had almost begun to trust him, forgetting all her rigorous training, because he'd sounded so reasonable. And, if she were honest with herself, because she had felt drawn to him in ways that defied logic. In the brief time she'd known him, they had forged enough of a bond that she'd been sick with worry that he might be fatally injured, or already dead.

That was all in the past now. She wouldn't make the same mistake twice. But the question remained: If Damon had been assigned to take her where the Nightsiders could get to her, why would they try to kill *him?* Or had they deliberately aimed their shot so that he would be able to heal?

Somehow she had to find out what he was up to. The colony wasn't her only priority now; she had to discover just how much the Nightsiders—including Damon—knew about the patch and the drugs in it.

Since she had no way of knowing when she'd meet up with Michael again, she had to proceed on the assumption that she would be working alone. And if she didn't succeed very quickly—quickly enough so that she could still make it to the Border in a condition to report whatever she'd learned—she would die here in the Zone.

In the meantime, she would have to pretend she accepted whatever Damon chose to tell her. That they were still on the same side.

"Which weapon?" Damon asked.

She shook herself, realizing she had been silent for an uncomfortably long time and he must be wondering why.

"My VS120," she said quickly, unwilling to dwell on the subject. She rummaged inside her ration kit and pulled out the last nutrient bar.

"You'd better take this," she told him. "You need nourishment to heal properly."

He stared at the bar, and she sensed he was aware that her offer was another test. Aegis knew that Daysiders could go for long stretches without blood—much longer than a Nightsider—but they weren't certain if the Citadel operatives could digest "human" food as dhampires could. That would be an extremely useful thing to know.

After a long period of silence, he shook his head. "You keep it," he said. "I had sufficient nourishment before I left Erebus."

Of course, he'd lie anyway if he knew what he'd taken in Erebus wasn't enough to fuel his healing. But if his job was done…

All the anger she'd been suppressing burst like a suppurating wound inside her chest. "I suppose if you need more, you'll take it from me?" she asked.

"No," he said firmly. "Never."

"Why not? It's not as if you'd have to kill me."

"We are partners, Agent Fox," he reminded her. "That makes us equals, does it not?"

"And I wouldn't be your 'equal' if we weren't? What if I were human? Would that make me fair game?" She leaned toward him, her breath fanning his neck. "Tell me…does it work the same with Daysiders as it does with leeches? Could you make me do whatever you want? Would I become your serf?"

Damon's expression hardened, but Alexia almost didn't notice. As the first beams of sunlight pierced through the trees on the hill above them, touching Damon's face, his skin began to darken. Within a minute it had returned to its previous tan, transforming like the pelt of a leopard that had suddenly changed from black on gold to gold on black.

If Damon had glimpsed her surprise before she concealed it, he didn't give any sign. "Fishing for information, Agent Fox?" he mused with a faint, ironic smile.

She returned the smile. "Didn't you hope you'd gain useful intelligence from working with an Enclave field agent?"

He inclined his head, acknowledging her point. "But I would not have you constantly worried that I might tamper with your mind," he said. "Only some Bloodmasters and

Bloodlords are capable of what you suggest, and Darketans can't do it at all."

"That's comforting," she quipped.

"As is the fact that we seem to have very similar healing abilities."

"You're telling me Erebus didn't have that information before?"

"Did Aegis?"

She snorted and bit into the ration bar. "I didn't know a Daysider's skin changes color with the light." Damon rubbed his jaw. The shadow of a beard had darkened it overnight. That was a very human characteristic, one that male dhampires shared.

"Aegis must be aware that Darketans have a natural adaptation that makes the melanin content of our skin alter in accordance with the level of illumination." He dropped his hand back to his knee.

"What is 'Darketan'?" she asked. "I've never heard the word before."

"That is what we call ourselves." He climbed carefully to his feet. "It's a name from ancient legend."

"What legend?"

Instead of answering, he bent to retrieve her blanket, folded it neatly and handed it to her. "Thank you for keeping watch," he said.

"Should I thank *you* for saving my life again?"

"Since I was ordered to work with you, it would hardly appear to my advantage if I were to let you die."

"Of course."

And that was that. She hadn't expected him to answer any differently, though part of her had hoped…

She cut off that line of thought and focused on her own body. Though it was early yet, she was just beginning to feel a faint crawling sensation under her skin, a twitching of certain deep muscles, an ache in her bones. It wasn't likely to get much worse for some time, but she had to conserve her strength, and she needed sleep.

But she also wanted Damon to reveal his plans. "What do we do now?" she asked.

"You need rest," he said. "I'll watch."

Alexia had to remind herself again that there was nothing remotely personal in his concern. "We can't stay here," she told him.

Damon scanned the hollow in every direction. "I think the shooters are gone, at least for the time being."

"Then you don't think they'll attack again if we move?"

He cast her a probing glance, undoubtedly wondering why she was asking him what he couldn't possibly know.

"There's only one way to find out," he said. "If you want to risk it."

Gingerly, Alexia shrugged into her pack and secured her rifle. "We'd have to leave sooner or later," she agreed. "No reason to sit around healing if we're going to die, anyway."

His dark, piercing gaze continued to hold hers. "We are not going to die," he said.

She nodded without comment as he removed his jacket, rummaged in his pack for a fresh shirt, and put on the new one. She quickly turned away from the sight of his bare, muscular chest and started up the hill to the south. There were no more bullets, nor did Alexia sense anyone else, vampire or otherwise, in the vicinity. It seemed the shooters had, indeed, accomplished their mission. With or without Damon's help.

She was panting by the time they reached the third hilltop. Damon took her arm and herded her into the shade of a large, stately oak.

His touch seared her skin, but all at once the crawling sensation was gone. She worked her arm loose from his grip and sank onto the patchy grass among the oak's thick roots.

"Rest now," Damon said, helping her remove her pack.

"We're at a good vantage point, and I'll know if anyone approaches."

Alexia didn't want to sleep with Damon standing over her, but she wouldn't last even twelve more hours without it. By the time she woke up the shakes could be worse, and it would take concentration to keep Damon from seeing them.

Maybe, when she was well rested, she might even figure out why he thought he could keep her alive if he had any idea just how desperately she needed the patch.

Maybe he doesn't *know,* she thought. *Maybe Erebus is still in the dark...for now.*

"Sleep," Damon said, his voice soft with what almost sounded like concern. "I'll wake you when it's time to go."

She was trying to figure out what he meant when her bone-deep exhaustion carried her away.

There was something wrong with her.

Damon crouched over Alexia as he had when she'd lain injured in the hollow, the same unbidden emotions crowding his chest and filling his throat.

It wasn't just her injury. Soon after she'd fallen asleep, he had carefully checked her wound and found it nearly healed under the bandages, enough so that he was able to remove most of them to let her skin breathe.

Yet in spite of the healing, he had seen her get subtly but steadily worse since they'd begun hiking again, though she did her best to hide it. The smell of dried blood was still strong on her clothing, but there was another scent now, a mingling of chemical odor and the scent of illness that any Opir—or Darketan—could detect from a kilometer away.

Damon had no idea what it was. He had never come closer to a dhampir than shooting distance; though he wouldn't have disobeyed an order to kill any Enclave agent who stood in the way of an assignment, he had been forbidden those missions that might involve such acts.

Now that he wanted to keep a dhampir alive, his ignorance about Alexia's kind was no longer a minor inconvenience. The Council had provided no information about dhampir illnesses; that was no surprise, since the breed was believed to be as hardy as Darketans. Perhaps this was something that also afflicted humans, but his instincts told him otherwise. Even a mild sickness might become deadly to one as weakened as Alexia was.

And though he'd told her that he didn't think the shooters would attempt another assault, he knew nothing of the kind. Either the original plans had drastically changed, or some other party had been involved.

After the first sniper's attack, Damon had been quick to deny any possibility that the opposing faction might send operatives to stop him and the Enclave agents. The gunman had been a good shot, too good to miss unless it was deliberate. Damon could well believe he had been carrying out his or her part of the mission as planned.

But these last shooters had been out to kill or incapacitate Damon and Alexia—or send a powerful warning. They could have been colonists. That still seemed by far the most likely possibility.

If the attack had been meant as a warning, it might explain why the shooters hadn't killed him and Alexia. Murdering sanctioned operatives would be making a move too provocative to be ignored by the Council or Aegis. Surely the shooters would realize that.

Just the attack alone was provocation enough.

Damon rose and paced back and forth under the gnarled branches of the grandfather oak. Once again he was faced with a crucial decision: leave Alexia under cover while he tried to find the shooters, or stay with her and wait until she was recovered enough to continue. He couldn't imagine her agreeing to stay behind; she'd drive herself into her grave first.

He stopped to gaze down at her, wondering if it was his imagination that her breathing was much more labored than it had been even an hour ago. She had become steadily weaker since the attack, and he could easily overpower her if he had to.

But then he would have to tie her down, and she'd be helpless. With a curse Damon began to circle around the oak, noting every detail of their location: the number of nearby trees and shrubs, the various angles of potential attack, the approaches and avenues of escape.

Still no sign of the shooters. But that didn't mean they weren't there, just beyond Damon's senses.

Making his decision, he knelt beside Alexia and carefully gathered her up in his arms. She moaned as he carried her to a thicket of low shrubs just outside the circle of shade and laid her down again under the entangled branches. He searched her pack and found the small, thin blanket she had covered him with before, laid it over her, and then began to gather twigs, fallen branches, rotting leaves—anything he might use to camouflage her while he was gone. When he was finished, he knelt beside her and touched her shoulder. Her skin had become so feverish that he could feel the heat through her shirt and jacket.

"Alexia," he said.

Her lips parted, soft lips that seemed to beckon him now that they were no longer stiff with suspicion. Her eyelashes fluttered.

"Damon?" she murmured, lifting one hand toward him. "What is it? Is it time to go?"

She sounded like a child, innocent and trusting, certain that the one who loved her would make sure everything was all right. *It must be the fever talking,* he thought. A delirious, fever dream.

"Not yet," he said gently, taking her hand in his. "I have

to leave for a short time, to make sure we're safe here. I need you to stay under cover while I'm gone."

Her eyes opened, searching for his as if she couldn't quite make out his face. "I'm going with you," she said.

He stroked her fingers, aware of a painful and inexplicable wave of tenderness that threatened to dissolve the foundation of everything he had worked so hard to build since Eirene's death. "You aren't in any shape to help now," he said. "The best thing you can do is rest until I return." He laid her hand on her chest, picked up his canteen and held it to her lips. "Drink."

Alexia did as he asked without protest, though she wouldn't take more than a few drops. Her eyelids grew heavy again.

"Don't leave me," she pleaded. A small vertical line had formed between her arched brows, suggesting an inner struggle of which she was hardly aware. Damon smoothed it out with his thumb.

"I'll be back soon," he said. "Promise you'll stay here."

"I…" She shivered and subsided, the muscles of her neck and shoulders relaxing. "I promise."

Then she was asleep again, and Damon covered her with the assembled leaves and twigs until she resembled no more than a pile of forest debris blown against the bushes by a gust of wind. He hesitated long after he was finished.

He didn't *want* to leave her. Not even for a minute. And that was all the more reason he had to.

Moving almost soundlessly, Damon began to work his way down the other side of the hill, weaving back and forth to and from any small cover he could find. Once he'd reached the bottom of the hill, he walked around it, pausing to listen every few steps. Then he climbed very slowly, circling as he went.

Still nothing. It seemed their attackers really had left them—completed their task, whatever it was, and gone on their way.

Or they were lying in wait somewhere between here and the colony.

Damon reached the top of the hill, assured himself that Alexia was still safely hidden, and then continued to canvass the area, placing each step with infinite care as he turned northeast toward the colony.

He'd gone about four hundred meters and was descending the last of the hills overlooking the valley when the shots came, pelting the underbrush around his feet and shredding leaves overhead. He ducked and fell to his stomach, rolling sideways until he was behind an outcrop of rock thrusting out of the slope.

A heartbeat, two, three, ten. No further attack. Damon rose to his knees, waited, and then got to his feet. Silence. He took a step back, in full view of whoever was doing the shooting. Still no shots. But when he took a step forward…

The bullets tore a very clear line in the ground three centimeters from the toes of his boots.

He backed away, staying well back from the invisible line, and made his way a little farther to the north. When he moved east again, the bullets erupted again, tracing out that very distinct line between him and the valley.

It was a clear and unmistakable boundary. This was as close as he and Alexia would be allowed to approach the colony. But that still didn't tell him who was doing the shooting, or even if these gunmen were the same as in the last two attacks.

None of this made any sense to him yet. But as long as the snipers didn't go any further than trying to keep him and Alexia away from the colony, he could still carry out his mission. In fact, considering that the two of them had been left alive, the current circumstances would make his task even easier.

Provided there really *wasn't* anyone out to kill them.

Damon retraced his steps toward the temporary camp. No

bullets assailed him. He was back at Alexia's hiding place in less than an hour. She was still there, still safe.

But the mild shivers he had noted earlier had become so violent that she'd shaken off most of the leaves and branches heaped around her body. He dropped to his knees beside her and felt her forehead. It was no longer hot, but icy cold and clammy to the touch.

"Alexia," he whispered. "Can you hear me?"

She thrashed her head from side to side, muttering words he could barely understand.

"Garret," she cried. "No. Don't…" Her teeth began to chatter. "I won't let them take you."

Damon leaned closer, his lips nearly brushing her cheek. "Who is Garret, Alexia?"

Tears broke from beneath her lids and slid across her temples. "I can't…I can't stop them." Abruptly her eyes opened, and for a moment they fixed on Damon's so directly that he was certain she was fully aware again. "You'll save him, won't you?" she said. "You're the only one who can."

He stroked her auburn hair away from her forehead. "Save whom?" he asked softly.

"He didn't deserve it. You must see that."

"What did he do, Alexia?"

Without warning she flung off the blanket and reached for him, locking surprisingly strong arms around his neck and pulling him down to her. Her lips brushed his, her tongue feathering over his mouth like moth's wings.

Then she kissed him. There was no doubting her intent, or her will. It wasn't sickness he smelled now on her skin and in her breath, but Alexia's living blood, relentlessly tugging at him like a full moon at the tide.

The blood of a dhampir.

Damon pulled back, clinging to his rapidly fragmenting thoughts. Alexia was no human serf, or a Bloodmistress who deigned to let him taste the nectar that flowed through her veins.

Alexia was his peer. His *equal,* as much as anyone from the Enclave could be, though they were enemies and kept themselves alive by different means. He'd said he would never take her blood, and he had meant it.

But now it was as if he were falling under the influence of an addiction, one that had once ruled his life and been forgotten until this moment.

And Alexia was the drug.

He stared down into her half-open eyes. He saw hunger in them—physical lust and the craving for pleasure, almost as if she, too, were experiencing the euphoric effects of some unknown narcotic agent.

She wasn't herself. He *knew* it, and he was ashamed of his own forbidden thoughts, his own struggle to maintain discipline and self-control that should have been second nature to him…and had been, until now. But Alexia held him there, demanding, refusing to let him go, and he forgot she was ill—forgot he could feel nothing for her—forgot his mission.

He worked her mouth open with his and slipped his tongue inside. She sucked him in eagerly, grinding her hips into his pelvis, stabbing her fingers into his hair. Her small incisors grazed the inside of his lower lip, and he felt a brief stab of pain.

She'd bitten him. He jerked back, probing the tiny wound with his tongue. He knew that dhampires were forbidden to take blood of any kind. That they were taught to loathe the very taste of it, even though it could sustain them as well as it could any Opir or Darketan.

Yet she had bitten him. Had she forgotten who and what she was? Was she reverting, becoming something a lifetime among humans had suppressed?

She pulled him down again, putting a quick and decisive end to Damon's speculation. This time she used her own tongue to tease his into her mouth. He felt the sensation of it all the way down into his belly, and his cock swelled until the ache exceeded anything he'd suffered in the hollow when he was fighting to survive.

Alexia couldn't have missed the pressure of his groin in the cradle of her thighs, but she didn't stop. She lifted her legs and wrapped them around his waist, rocking and thrusting as if they were both naked and she was begging him to enter her.

Damon groaned. This couldn't be happening. Nothing about this was sane, or right. But the more desperate his need, the less rational he became.

It was instinct, pure and simple. This couldn't end until he was inside her, thrusting deep, hearing her gasps and moans of pleasure. And surrender.

As if her own thoughts had merged with his, Alexia began to tear at his shirt. She managed to unbutton it without ripping it to shreds and clawed at his undershirt, seeking flesh. Her fingers brushed his chest, scraping him with her nails as if she wanted his heart, as well.

Damon took more care with her shirt, some remnant of sense guiding his hands, but Alexia wouldn't allow it. She tore it open herself and ripped her close-fitting tank from neckline to hem, baring her breasts.

They were perfect, like the rest of her, but Damon was too hungry to admire them for long. He bent to take one nipple into his mouth. Alexia arched upward, letting her head fall back, gasping as he suckled her, hard and fast, with no attempt at gentleness. His teeth grazed her tender flesh, accidentally drawing her blood as she had drawn his.

It was sweet. Incredibly sweet, like the taste of her mouth or the way he imagined the rest of her would be.

But he had not forgotten his vow never to take her blood. A vow that seemed increasingly impossible to keep. For it was as if, somehow, a part of his blood already flowed through her veins.

No, not *his* blood. He had never taken dhampir blood before, and it was to be expected that its signature would be utterly different from anything with which he was familiar. But this was much more subtle than the unique amalgamation of strains that came of her mixed heritage. It was so muted that he couldn't identify it, but it had the effect of releasing the last, pitiful scraps of his reason.

He moved to her other breast, licking and nipping, raising himself high enough to work his hand under her waistband. He found her undergarment, damp with perspiration, and reached beneath.

She was wet and hot and ready, pushing up against him with an uninhibited boldness that took his breath away in spite of all she'd already done to him. He stroked her, distantly aware of her moans of pleasure as she found his cock and rubbed it through his pants, tracing its contours and molding it with her fingers. He closed his eyes and groaned when she began to unzip him. Only moments now. A few quick movements to free themselves of their clothes, and then—

The muzzle of a gun barrel came up hard against the side of Damon's head.

"Get off her," Michael snarled, "before I blow your frickin' bloodsucker brains out."

Chapter 5

Alexia heard her partner's voice as if through muffling layers of gauze that seemed to fill her head and keep her thoughts from comprehending what was truly happening. Her body throbbed—not with pain, but pleasure—and her breasts ached as if she had scratched them on the sharp little branches of the manzanitas growing nearby.

She opened her eyes. It took her a moment to recognize what she was seeing: two faces, both male and as pitiless as the Court that had condemned Garret to a lifetime of servitude.

"Cover her up," one of the men said—Michael, his blond hair mussed and his face smudged with dirt. The other man, the one whose scent still bathed her skin, laid something on top of her…his jacket, still warm from the heat of his body.

"Alexia," Michael said, staring down at her. "Are you all right?"

No. Not all right. The pleasure was beginning to fade, replaced by a sense of something profoundly wrong with her body. She began to remember what had happened since Damon—yes, *that* was the other man—had left her alone, hot and shivering and barely aware that he had gone away.

Then there had been brief moments of lucidity between much longer spans of darkness, the consequences of the illness raging inside her body. When Damon had come back for her, she had been half out of her mind. More than half. She had known she needed something, something important, that only Damon could give her.

Garret. She had said something about Garret. And then she'd forgotten about her half brother, forgotten everything, and...

She felt frantically under the borrowed jacket. Her uniform shirt and undershirt were torn wide open. The bandage was gone, and her shoulder wound was nothing but a patch of puckered skin, cool to the touch. She brushed her lips with her fingers. They were bruised and sore.

God. What had she done? What had *he* done?

"I can kill him now if you want me to," Michael said, his voice ringing with hatred. He held the muzzle of his gun to Damon's temple, just as when they'd first met. Damon looked steadily at Alexia.

She tried to sit up, but a surging tide of dizziness forced her back down. The borrowed jacket slipped to the ground, and she pulled her own jacket closed over her breasts as she fought to clear her mind.

"No," she said, as steadily as she could. "It wasn't what you thought, Michael."

"Then what was it? It looked to me like he was about ready to tear your chest open."

Was that what he'd seen? Which would be worse—his believing that Damon meant to take her blood or that they were having sex in the middle of a dangerous mission?

Sex with a Daysider. And she'd been willing. More than willing.

"He didn't hurt me," she insisted. "It wasn't his fault."

Mike scowled at her, contempt in his eyes. Not only for Damon, but for her. Judging her, even before she had a chance to get him alone and explain.

How could she ever do that when she didn't understand it herself?

"Where were you, Michael?" she asked.

He shifted his weight and looked away. "Scouting. I didn't leave you, Alexia. I—"

"Did you know Damon and I were attacked?"

He blinked at her sudden question, hearing the anger in her voice. And she *was* angry. At him, at Damon, at herself most of all. Herself, and the sickness that was stealing her mind and will and body bit by bit. Her bizarre behavior had tempted the predator in Damon, Darketan or not. If he looked chastened now, if there was any regret in his eyes, she doubted that it had anything to do with shame.

Had he taken her blood? She could find no sign of it, but then again a small enough bite would heal quickly, and chemicals in Nightsiders' saliva both sterilized and closed the small incisions created when they fed.

A vague memory of tasting blood hovered on the edges of Alexia's mind, and she nearly gagged. *I couldn't have,* she thought. *It isn't possible.*

"We were shot at by unknown assailants," she said, forcing the image out of her mind. "Possibly from the colony. You didn't hear the gunshots?"

"No." Michael's skin had paled beneath the dark smears across his face. "Were you injured?"

"How does it appear to you?" Damon asked him scathingly.

Michael made a threatening gesture. Despising her vulnerable position, Alexia tried to sit up again. Damon reached for her. She flinched away, and Michael's finger twitched on the trigger.

"I'm fine," she said, pretending to ignore Damon even though her flesh felt as if a million tiny circuits were sending bursts of electricity racing through every nerve. "But because of the attack, we haven't been able to get close to the colony."

"It's worse than that," Damon said quietly. "They've set up a defense perimeter between us and the settlement. We aren't getting anywhere near it now, not without a fight."

"Then the colonists saw you," Mike said, glaring at Damon.

"Or they were expecting intruders," she said.

Damon craned his neck to look up at Michael, forcing the rifle's muzzle away from his cheek. "How did *you* get through?" he asked.

"Shut up," Michael growled.

"It's a good question," Alexia said, wondering why, after what had just happened, she could take Damon's side against her partner's. "Were *you* able to observe the colony, Michael?"

"While I was reconnoitering, I discovered that there was another enemy agent in the vicinity."

"Nightsider?" she asked, trying to sit up again.

"He was wearing heavy clothes, so that's a good bet." Michael nudged Damon with the rifle again. "You didn't say anything about other Erebus operatives running around out here."

"He told me it was likely there were," Alexia said, "but he didn't know who or what their assignments would be."

"That's convenient." Michael said, staring down at Damon. "Think any of them could have been sent out to get rid of us while you were keeping us distracted, leech?"

"I would have been informed were that the case," Damon said.

"Oh," Michael said, sarcasm turning his words almost sickeningly sweet. "That's all *right,* then."

"What happened to the Nightsider you were following?"

Alexia asked, cutting in before Michael could work himself into another rage.

"I tracked him most of the night, but he never went anywhere near the settlement."

"He didn't hear you?"

"No." Mike's voice turned defensive. "I thought seeing what he was up to was worth my staying away a little longer. Obviously I made a mistake."

More than you know, Alexia thought grimly. "Why did you stop?" she asked.

"I lost him. He could be anywhere right now."

"And we can't assume he wasn't one of the shooters." She raised her hand to forestall Damon's protest. "We can't eliminate *any* possibility. He could have been from the colony. We need to get through that perimeter to find out what's going on. Now that you're back, Michael, we can work out a plan to create a diversion so that one of us can get closer to the settlement."

"Are you including *him* in this plan?" Michael asked, prodding at Damon's neck.

Damon's next move was almost too swift to follow. He literally turned on himself, striking Michael's gun aside as he twisted his body in a way Alexia wouldn't have believed possible. In three seconds he had Michael pinned to the ground like a rabbit between a leopard's paws.

"The question," Damon said through his teeth, "is whether or not *you* can be trusted."

Michael heaved against him, but Damon easily held the agent down with his hand around Michael's throat and one knee pressed to his chest.

"Damon!" Alexia said, climbing to her knees. "Let him go!"

He continued to stare into Michael's eyes. "Maybe he stayed away because he *knew* we were going to be attacked."

"That's insane," Michael said, wheezing the words through his constricted throat.

"Stop it!" Alexia shouted. "How do you think he would have known that? Are you accusing him of working for the enemy?"

"No. Only of cowardice."

Michael made a noise of pure fury and clamped his hands around Damon's wrist. Damon tightened his grip. Alexia gathered her legs underneath her, stiffened her muscles and stood up. She managed to stay on her feet for five seconds before she began to sway.

Damon snapped his head toward her. "Sit down!" he commanded.

"Alexia!" Michael croaked. "What—"

"She's ill," Damon said to Michael, showing a glint of his right incisor, "and it's because of *you.*"

Michael ceased his struggles and tried to look at Alexia. "You said you weren't hurt!"

"She was lying," Damon said. "She was badly wounded in the attack. She recovered from that, but something else is wrong with her. Some kind of illness. You're going to tell me what it—"

Alexia's legs collapsed beneath her. Damon leaped up and caught her before she hit the ground. Michael was at her side a moment later.

"What's wrong?" he demanded as Damon gently lowered her to the ground. "Alex, what's going on?"

"My body's still healing," she said, her teeth chattering. "That's all."

Damon cupped the side of her face, sliding his thumb over her cheekbone.

"Get your hands off her," Michael said through his teeth, grabbing Damon's wrist.

With hardly a glance, Damon broke free and pushed Michael back, shoving him onto his knees.

"Stop!" Alexia gasped. "He saved my life, Michael!"

Michael resumed his previous position, carefully avoiding Damon's eyes. He didn't try to interfere as Damon unbuttoned Alexia's jacket and peeled it back behind her shoulders. When it was out of the way, Michael pushed the torn edges of her shirt and undershirt aside and touched the place above her right breast where the bullets had hit.

"It's already healed," he said. He lifted one of her eyelids. "Hyperemia," he said. He took her wrist. "Rapid heartbeat. Has she had a fever?"

"I'm still here," she said testily. "You can ask *me*."

"Have you?" Michael asked.

"The best thing you can do is leave me alone and let me heal."

Michael ignored her and pushed her shirt open over her left shoulder. She tried to stop him, but she wasn't strong enough, and Damon didn't interfere. Exposing the underside of her upper left arm, Michael cursed.

"Your patch," he said. "For God's sake, Alexia, what happened?"

She glanced at Damon. His gaze jerked from the unhealed wound to Michael's face, and his eyes narrowed.

Don't say anything, she begged Michael silently. She didn't want to know if Damon had made it possible for someone to take the patch. If she was going to die anyway…

"What happened?" her partner repeated.

She closed her eyes. "When I was wounded," she said slowly, "I was out for several hours. Damon was shot after I fell unconscious. He managed to bind my wounds before he went into healing stasis. He was still out when I woke up, and that was when I found out that someone had cut the patch out of my arm."

"Someone," Michael spat. He turned on Damon. "Where is it?"

Damon met his accusing stare without reaction. "I don't know what you're talking about," he said.

Bunching his fist, Michael swung at Damon. Damon ducked easily and rocked back on his heels.

"That's enough!" Alexia said. "If you two don't behave yourselves, I'll—" A cough rattled in her chest, swallowing the impotent threat. She settled back again, sensing how close she was to sinking into a morass of despair from which she might never emerge.

It was too late now. Too late to pretend. She rolled her head to the side, meeting Damon's eyes. She glimpsed something in them she hadn't seen before.

Fear.

"Did you?" she asked hoarsely. "Did you have something to do with this?"

He stared at the exposed wound, his expression gone cold. "No." His gaze returned to her face. "Why didn't you tell me you had this other injury?"

"You *knew* about it," Michael said, jumping to his feet. "This is what you were after all along, wasn't it? You don't give a damn if she dies."

Damon rose to face him. "Why should she die?" he asked. "What is a 'patch'?"

"I'm not dead yet," Alexia said with asperity. "I'd appreciate it if you wouldn't talk over me as if I were."

Both men looked down at her. Mike had tears in his eyes. He glanced back in the direction of the bushes where Damon had tossed his rifle.

Damon moved before he did. He covered the space in two strides and swept up the gun, aiming it squarely at Michael's chest.

"Tell me what this is about," he said, his voice deadly quiet, "and perhaps I won't kill you."

"Frickin' leech," Michael gasped. "She *trusted* you."

Damon stalked toward Michael like the big, tawny cat

Alexia had imagined, coming to stand toe-to-toe with his enemy. He jabbed the rifle into Michael's ribs.

"Take off your pack."

Michael obeyed with a sneer and tossed the pack, VS120 still attached, toward the bushes.

"Your other weapons," Damon said.

Her partner removed his pistol and combat knife and threw them after the pack.

"Now," Damon said, "talk."

"*I'll* tell you," Alexia said softly. "Look at me."

He looked, though every muscle in his body was tense with readiness to attack should Michael make the smallest attempt to break away.

Alexia held his gaze. "A percentage of dhampires, like me," she said, carefully watching his face, "are born without the ability to digest normal food. We wear patches that deliver certain drugs directly into our bloodstream, which allows us to eat like humans. Without it—" She shrugged, though the movement sent needles of pain into her arm.

There was nothing in Damon's expression to indicate his emotions, but his eyes told a different story. In a human or dhampir, she would have called them stricken. Horrified.

It was possible that he was feigning the reaction. She would be wise to make that assumption. But she could still feel his warm breath on her face, his lips on hers. And though she despised her lack of control and his willingness to take advantage of her body's mindless urges, she couldn't make herself believe that he had led her into a trap.

"I didn't know, Alexia," he said quietly.

"Liar," Michael said. "You were with her when you were attacked, and someone who knew what to look for took her patch. Pretty convenient, isn't it?"

To Alexia's relief, Damon ignored her partner and addressed Alexia again. "We considered the likelihood that the gunman who attacked us the first time—"

"The *first* time?" Michael interrupted.

"—after Carter left us," Damon went on with a severe glance at Michael, "was from the colony, attempting to drive off intruders. That still seems the most likely explanation for the second attack. Though I knew nothing of this patch or its importance, it is quite possible someone in the colony did."

"And why would *they* take it?" Michael asked. "I can see why Erebus would want anything that they could turn into a weapon against us, but an illegal settlement wouldn't have the Citadel's resources. Were your friends planning to trade it to Erebus in exchange for being left alone?"

"The colonists are not my *friends*," Damon retorted. "I am here to—"

"Do you have any proof that the colonists did this?" Michael asked, thrusting his face closer to Damon's as if the rifle weren't jabbing him in the belly. "Or did you make sure there was no evidence to find?"

Damon bared his teeth. "I've had enough of your accusations," he said. "If you say another word, I'll put a gag in your mouth."

"He didn't do it, Michael," Alexia said, her mind foggy with exhaustion. "They hurt him, too. He could have died."

"You really don't see it, do you?" Michael demanded, disbelief in his voice. "What in hell are you thinking, Alexia? Who screwed who?"

With a grunt of rage, Damon hit Michael on the side of the head. Michael staggered and fell to his knees. Alexia rolled onto her stomach and crawled over to him, grabbing his arm as much for support as to protect him.

"Kill me first," she said, looking up at Damon's stony face. "I'm going to die, anyway."

"No," Damon said. He tossed the gun back into the bushes. "Tell me what must be done."

"There's nothing to be done," Michael said, rubbing at

his temple. "Not unless I can get her back to the Border and into a hospital."

Alexia tried to laugh. "*That* isn't going to happen," she said. "I thought about it. But I'm a lot weaker than I expected to be at his point."

"What else?" Damon asked Michael as if she hadn't spoken. "There must be another way."

Mike stared straight ahead, his jaw working. "I might be able to reach the Border in time to get her another patch."

"Then that is what you must do."

Implacable hatred still burned in Michael's eyes. "Why do you care? What have you to gain? Another chance to screw her while she's helpless? Drain her dry?"

"Michael!" Alexia said, jerking on his arm to silence him before Damon decided to do it himself. "It doesn't matter. I won't let you risk it. We've been shot at twice, and at least one unknown Nightsider is probably still at large in the area. You'll be killed."

"But the defensive perimeter was clearly established to prevent us from going near the colony," Damon said, staring at Michael with death in his eyes. "They would surely allow a retreat." He backed away, letting Michael get up. "You will return to the Enclave and acquire one of these patches. I will provide cover in the event that you are attacked. Are we agreed?"

Michael glanced down at Alexia, and she knew exactly what he was thinking. What she didn't understand was why he was still acting like an untrained novice who hadn't learned to keep personal emotions out of the job.

And that was why she had to let him go. Her own emotions told her to protect him, but he had to get back to Aegis, not for her sake, but to tell them about the patch. There was nothing else she could do to keep him from harm or prevent him from attempting what she knew he had in mind.

"Agreed," Michael said to Damon, avoiding her eyes. "You'll have to return my weapons."

Damon waved his hand. "Take them." He bent to help Alexia to a sitting position, but Michael got between them and did it himself. He rested his hand possessively on Alexia's "good" shoulder and faced Damon with head high and shoulders drawn back in defiance.

"Are you sure you can't make it, Alexia?" he asked without looking at her. "You *know* you can't trust him. Even if he didn't have any part in stealing your patch, he'll still do whatever his masters tell him to. You don't have the strength to fight him now. If they tell him to kill you, he will."

"They gave no such orders," Damon said, holding Alexia's gaze.

"But you'd destroy anyone who stood in the way of your mission," Michael said. "Even if it meant your own death."

"And we would do the same," Alexia said before Damon could answer. "I'm not afraid, Michael. Not of Damon, and not of dying."

Michael swore and walked away. He retrieved his weapons and returned to set his VS and a box of ammunition on the ground beside her.

"Take this," he said. "And take care of yourself, Alex." He cast Damon a scathing glance and strode to the other side of the oak to wait.

"Alexia," Damon murmured, kneeling beside her.

His nearness set her nerves to jangling again. She had to be tough now. She couldn't afford any vulnerability when she was completely in his power and sick enough to lose her head the way she had just before Michael's arrival.

"If you're going to go, go," she said, struggling to pull her jacket up again.

He helped her, though she shook him off once the jacket was safely closed over her chest. "If I had known—" he began.

"Do you think I'd admit that kind of weakness to an enemy?"

She could have sworn he flinched. "I would never harm you," he said softly.

"Don't lie for my sake. Michael was right. We may have worked as a team and saved each other's lives for the sake of expedience, but you'll kill me if you thought it was necessary to protect your people."

"But it is not," he said. "Quite the contrary." He picked up his jacket and pulled it on. "You are being irrational. As I told you before, if I'd been sent to kill you, you would be dead. As your partner must know, if he could look beyond his hatred."

She met his gaze again. "Don't you hate us just as much?"

"My personal opinions are hardly relevant."

"I know what hate is, and I see it in your eyes when you look at Michael. I'd say that was pretty personal."

His mouth tightened. "My judgment of your partner changes nothing. I won't let you die."

"You might not have any choice."

He leaned over her, bracing himself on his muscular arms. "I forbid it."

"I'm not one of your harem serfs." Her face grew hot, and she hardened her will. "Or do you think we have some…connection because of what happened before Michael showed up? That was my sickness, not me."

"*I* was not ill," Damon said huskily.

"But you have your instincts. You may be an outsider among your own people, but you're still a predator under your civilized exterior, just like the rest of them. I was vulnerable, and you thought you could take advantage of that, one way or another."

"And you wanted something from *me,* Alexia," he said, "or was that your sickness, as well?"

"I was crazy. If you think I wanted to have sex with you—"

He drew back, his expression going blank. "I will not trouble you again."

Because I'll kill myself first, Alexia thought, though her cheeks burned under his gaze. She took herself in hand and released her breath. "Do you really intend to get Michael to safety?"

The light flickering between the oak's branches shifted, pulling new shadows from Damon's face. "I wasn't lying."

"But you have an idea what losing the patch can do to a dhampir, and you can guess the likely consequences once Aegis finds out that Nightsiders have one, colonists or not. If you work for the Council and they want to keep the peace, you might think it would be better not to let Michael make his report."

Damon's pupils constricted to pinpoints, lost in a deep and turbulent sea of blue. "If I killed him, I would have to kill you."

"Yes. Because if I live, I'll eventually make the same report. But if you kill *him,* I won't survive, anyway."

Something happened to Damon then, an unfurling of the rage she had glimpsed once or twice before when he'd sparred with Michael, but multiplied a hundredfold. His eyes narrowed, his lips drew back and his body seemed to expand and broaden like the hood on a striking cobra.

She knew that was illusion. But what she saw in his terrible gaze was *not,* and suddenly he was far less human than animal—some kind of animal she didn't recognize, a creature neither Nightsider nor Daysider nor dhampir.

Because there was no rationality in that stare, in that expression, only pure, raw emotion. Whatever moved him now was nothing like what anyone dealing with vampires had ever reported before. Mindless savagery turned his face into a caricature of a man, lost to reason or even the leeches' twisted morality.

The face of a killer that no rules, no weapons, no will

could stop. A monster she had somehow awakened with her careless words, her bitter accusations.

It wasn't some kind of act meant to scare her. It was terrifyingly real. Damon was going insane before her eyes, and she didn't know how to stop it.

Chapter 6

"You—" Damon growled, panting between each word he forced out of his throat. "You—will—not—die."

A brown leaf shook free from one of the oak's down-curving branches, brushing against the coarse bark and drifting to lie among the handfuls that had fallen before it. Michael stood just out of sight behind the tree, utterly unaware of the danger.

Danger Alexia didn't know how to define. Or fight. All she knew was that Damon wanted her alive, and that might be the only way to reach through his madness.

"If it matters so much to you," she said calmly, hoping he could still understand her, "I promise I'll stay alive as long as it takes. *If* you make sure Michael gets well away from the shooters or anyone who might attack him."

Damon squeezed his eyes shut, breathing sharply through his nostrils. She could see him, *feel* him struggle to find words amid the chaos of a mind that was no longer wholly his own, ruled by a brutish, alien consciousness that was hungry for something it had never possessed.

"I—" he gasped.

"It's all right, Damon. Whatever is wrong, I'll help you."

He bowed his head, shaking violently. "I will…not…"

"You won't kill Michael."

"No."

"No matter what he does?"

She knew she was taking a grave risk, but it paid off. Damon's eyes opened again, and there was a glint of real comprehension in them. He heard her. He understood.

"Won't…kill," he said.

"Even if he tries to kill you first?"

Abruptly Damon leaped to his feet, moving with sinuous, deadly grace. His whole body shivered as if he were emerging from icy water. He stalked in a circle around her, shoulders hunched, and came to a stop in front of her.

"Promise…" he said. "Stay alive."

Alexia understood, without knowing how, that he would believe her if she did what he asked…that somehow her promise could bring Damon back from this strange and terrible darkness.

"I promise," she said.

With a low moan, Damon flung back his head, clenching his fists at his sides. A violent shudder took him, and for a moment he seemed to go boneless, staggering and almost falling before regaining his feet. When he looked at her again, he was sane.

Alexia sighed. It had worked. But now she was faced with another problem. Because all she saw in Damon's eyes at that moment was bewilderment, as if he had just awakened from an ugly dream.

He didn't know what had happened. Alexia was sure of it, though she had only her own instincts to tell her so. His gaze was completely devoid of shame or horror or the kind of satisfaction that came of tricking an enemy into surrender.

Had this been some kind of psychotic break, a madness born of an abnormality in Damon's brain or a trauma in his past? Was it an illness, a vampire or Daysider affliction no other agent of the Enclave had ever witnessed? Or something else she couldn't begin to imagine?

And what had triggered it? He had changed right after she'd told him she would die if he killed Michael. Could it happen again? Could she make it happen, just with certain words and phrases?

Why should he care so much if she lived or died?

She couldn't even attempt to understand any of it until she was sure he hadn't known what had happened to him.

And there was only one way to find out.

"You'd better go," she said, as if they had been having a normal conversation. "Michael's going to come looking if you wait any longer."

Damon searched her eyes. "You aren't getting any worse?"

A normal, rational question. No trace of the savage he had been only moments before.

"I said I'd hang on as long as necessary," she said. "You just get Michael safely to the Border, as we agreed."

He frowned a little, reached inside his jacket and withdrew the small, unfamiliar pistol he'd been carrying when they met. He bent to set it down beside her.

"Take this," he said. "It was meant to be used only as a last resort, but it's more powerful than it appears."

"Michael already gave me his Vampire Sl— His VS," she amended quickly.

"It will not hurt you to have both."

She picked Damon's pistol up and weighed it in her hands. The model wasn't like anything Aegis had manufactured, not even for its agents.

"Your own version of a VS, huh?" she asked lightly.

"As I said, a last resort."

"Thanks."

Abruptly he scooped her up in his arms and carried her back to the scanty shelter of the bushes. He covered her with the blanket again, pushing leaves and twigs and dirt up around her and sifting a few handfuls of debris on top of her for good measure.

"I'll be back soon," he said. He stood, no longer graceful but oddly mechanical, as if he had forgotten how to use his limbs. "Don't move from this place. Remain still and quiet. Fire only if you have no other choice."

She curled her lips into a wry smile. "I'm not one of your harem slaves, remember?"

An echo of the savage gleamed in his eyes, a change so subtle that she never would have noticed if not for his recent and much more dramatic transformation. "Darketans do not *have* serfs," he said, and walked away without looking back. In five minutes he and Michael were out of range of her senses.

Exhausted beyond her ability to resist, Alexia let her muscles go lax and allowed the sickness she'd been fighting to claim her, pulling her down into fever again.

And she remembered.

"You'll be all right," the voice whispered. It was comforting, full of gentle concern, and Alexia felt almost safe even though she felt so sick she could hardly breathe.

She didn't remember how she'd come to this place, dark and cold as it was, or why the nice lady had come to help her. She only knew that when the lady had talked to her, she felt ever so much better.

"There, now," the lady said, stroking Alexia's hair. She rolled up her sleeve and held the underside of her wrist near Alexia's mouth. "Don't be afraid. You need to bite. Just a little blood, and you won't feel so sick anymore."

"But I'm not supposed to," Alexia whimpered. "Mommy told me never to bite anybody. Blood is bad for you."

"Not this blood. It will make you well."

Alexia met the lady's eyes doubtfully. They were different from hers, or Mommy's, but so kind. And she felt so awful, worse than she ever had. She bent her head and brushed her lips against the lady's skin. It smelled very sweet, and it was easy to open her mouth and let her teeth graze right where the blood beat so strongly.

It was like nothing Alexia had ever tasted before. She felt a twinge of guilt, but the hunger was too strong. She knew the lady was right. This *would* make her well.

She sipped just a little before the lady took her arm away. But it was enough. She felt better already, and with every breath she took she felt better still. She began to remember running away after Mommy had taken her to the big building with the very serious grown-ups who asked her so many questions. She remembered darting into hallways like long, dark tunnels and falling down stairs, hurting and crying for someone to find her.

That was when the lady came. She picked Alexia up and carried her outside, where it was nighttime, moving like a cat chasing a mouse, whispering for Alexia to be very quiet.

Alexia didn't remember how long they walked. Sometime during the night the pain came, cramps in her stomach and the feeling that she wanted to throw up. Then she began to feel very hot and shivery, and she started to see ugly things, monsters with bloody teeth and red eyes who chased her and chased her and wouldn't let her get away.

That was all she could see until the lady woke her up and told her she'd be all right. And now she was.

The lady took her by the hand. "We need to get you home now," she said, sadness in her voice.

Alexia looked up. "Are *you* going to take me?"

"Yes." The lady gave her a smile that wasn't a smile, and she led her out of the dark room into the sunlight.

When they got back to the big building, Mommy was waiting for her. She was crying, and the very serious people looked more serious than ever. The lady took Alexia to Mommy, said something very soft that Alexia couldn't quite hear, and went away with the serious people. She looked back once at Alexia, and Alexia stared at her for a long time after she disappeared inside the big building, memorizing her face.

Then Mommy took her to a place where other serious people made her undress and put things in her mouth and listened to her chest. When she went home again, she had to start taking two red pills every day. She still got sick a lot, and she always wished the lady would come back to make her well.

But she never saw the lady again.

Alexia jerked awake, the woman's face as clear in her mind as it had been all those years ago.

The eyes. Daysider eyes, blue that was almost black.

She sat up, shoving the blanket aside. She had forgotten. All through the painful years of her childhood, the long spells of illness before they had developed the drugs for the patch, she had lost the memory of something that should never have left her consciousness.

Trembling, Alexia pressed the heels of her palms against her burning eyes. She understood now what it had all meant, or at least she could make a very good guess. She had run away from the Examiners at Aegis who had been conducting tests on her suitability as a future agent, as they had done with all the dhampir children born during or right after the war. Somehow she'd come upon a Daysider, who had known or guessed the nature of her first bout of blood-sickness and temporarily "cured" her.

Then the Daysider had taken Alexia back to Aegis and—

Alexia dropped her hands, staring unseeingly at a jay hopping from branch to branch among the oak leaves. Things that hadn't made sense two decades ago looked very different in light of her years of training and experience. She'd been only six then, born the same year as the signing of the Treaty. The "nice lady" could have been anywhere from twenty to one hundred years old; no one could be sure of the age of any adult man or woman of vampire heritage.

Regardless of the Daysider's age, she shouldn't have been in the city. The Treaty specified that her kind, like Nightsiders, were forbidden within Enclave territory. That meant she could have been some kind of spy, an operative from Erebus, which had been completed just the year before. Somehow Alexia had stumbled into her hiding place.

But there was another possibility. If she *wasn't* an agent, she must have been there with the full knowledge of Aegis. And they would never have let a potential enemy run loose in the city.

What if the woman had been a prisoner? If Alexia had found her while she was in the middle of an escape…

Alexia shook her head in disbelief. It couldn't be. Under the Treaty, all prisoners were supposed to have been released. Never, in sixteen years with Aegis, had she ever heard so much as a rumor that the Nightsider captives might still be in Enclave custody.

Either way, spy or prisoner, the woman had returned Alexia and gone with the "serious people." Examiners, agents, security…it didn't matter. She'd given herself up. She could have used Alexia as a hostage, but she hadn't. She had cared more about Alexia than her own freedom.

What price had she paid for that compassion? How had Alexia's time with Aegis so completely erased the memory that even Daysiders were capable of kindness and self-sacrifice?

Because that was not what she'd been taught from the day, at the age of ten, when she had begun the intense schooling that would eventually transform her into the perfect operative. Every day the same lesson had been drummed into her head: Daysiders and Nightsiders were monsters without empathy, morality or anything resembling human emotion.

Evil.

The jay screamed a querying note, tipping its dark head to examine Alexia with one bright, dark-rimmed eye.

What did they do with her? Alexia asked the bird silently. *Did they set her free?*

It would have been difficult to keep the woman's presence secret all these years. But if they had killed her, there would be no need for secrets.

Battling her body's weakness, Alexia struggled to her feet and made her way carefully toward the oak, hands outstretched to catch her weight. She spread her palms on the knotted bark and pressed her cheek against it, breathing in the scent of its indomitable life.

The unknown Daysider woman had sacrificed her freedom, possibly her life, for Alexia. Just as Damon, who could have killed both her and Michael anytime if he chose, had saved her life and fought to keep her alive.

And Damon had said he wanted to keep the peace. If he was telling the truth, whoever had attacked them was working as much against him as her. Whoever had stolen her patch hadn't cared what might happen to her as a result.

But Damon did. She had very personally experienced his capability for loyalty, courage…commitment. How was he any different from the Daysider woman with her gentle voice and willingness to sacrifice herself for a child she had just met and would probably never see again?

Alexia laughed mirthlessly and bumped her forehead against the trunk. There was one major difference: Damon had most definitely been willing to extend their alliance to a more intimately physical plane. But he hadn't tried to force her, not in any way. He had treated her body like something worth savoring, receiving as well as giving pleasure. It almost seemed as if he genuinely cared about her.

No, he wasn't evil. Not even close. In her heart, she'd known it all along, even though she'd fought every minute to remind herself what his kind had done to her mother. To Garret.

But he wasn't a Nightsider, either. *He* hadn't made the rules that condemned human convicts to eternal slavery. Nothing could change what had happened to the people she loved. Damon was not to blame for the sins of those who could never fully accept him. Even if he was capable of becoming something savage and unpredictable for reasons she didn't understand, she knew she could never go back to hating him.

Michael hadn't experienced what *she* had. He still loathed Damon with every fiber of his being. If he did try to kill Damon—if he provoked the Daysider far enough—maybe he could provoke the shadow inside Damon, as well. She'd been a fool to think Damon could speak for that other side of himself. If it came to a fight, one of them would surely die.

However, she would do everything in her power to prevent that from happening. Neither blood-sickness, invisible snipers nor even Damon himself would stop her.

Lurching back to the bushes, she crouched to dig in her pack for a spare shirt and took off her jacket, wincing at the pain, and then put on the fresh shirt. She strapped the VS to the back of her pack and dragged it over her shoulders. Finally, she picked up the weapon Damon had given her and tucked it in her belt.

Inhaling a deep lungful of air, she set out after the men, praying she would reach them in time.

If there had been any other way, Damon would have taken it. For Alexia's sake.

But he had to know. And though he and Carter had made it well away from the area of the colony and over the hills to their western border without once being attacked, they both knew there would be no fond farewells between them.

And Carter was still prepared to fight. He moved fast against Damon the moment he had the chance, and his speed was almost enough to let him shed his pack and slip Damon's grasp. He managed to work his knife free during the struggle and slash Damon's arm before Damon got his hands around Carter's throat and slammed him up against the nearest large tree.

After that, it was as if the dhampir had given up. He let Damon remove his weapons and stood quiescent in his enemy's hold, breathing hard but offering no further resistance.

It was if he'd *wanted* to be defeated.

"What did you do?" Damon asked, staring into Carter's catlike eyes.

"I don't…know what you're talking about," the dhampir said without inflection.

"When you uncovered Alexia's other wound," Damon said softly, "you were shocked."

Carter gave a choked laughed. "She's my partner. What did you expect?"

"It was not your concern that was strange," Damon said, "but the way you expressed it."

"Naturally. Your kind doesn't have normal feelings. You wouldn't know a real one if it hung you up and left you out to dry."

Damon didn't rise to the bait. "I was trained to understand human feelings," he said.

"Funny. I'm not human."

"But in many respects you are as much one of them as if you had been born of two human parents. And I know you were overreacting. The way a man does when he isn't as surprised or shocked as he wishes to appear."

Carter spat. Damon dodged, and the shot went wide.

"There isn't much you wouldn't do to hide your own part

in this," Carter said, grinning like a death mask. "Just because *she* doesn't believe you betrayed her—"

"That is an interesting word, *betray*," Damon said, returning the operative's smile. "I had understood the loyalty between Aegis partners to be virtually unbreakable."

"And there's nothing you can do to change that," Carter said. "Alexia and I would die for each other. That's a concept you couldn't possibly comprehend."

"Perhaps. Unless your commitment has already been given to someone or something else. Or your hatred is too powerful to bind you to anyone."

Carter lunged against Damon's grip, but Damon held him fast.

"I was born to a mother who was abused and abandoned by a bloodsucker, like all of my kind," Carter rasped. "If we could find a way to wipe you out once and for all—"

"Again," Damon said. "Too histrionic, like your accusations against me. Even Alexia discounted your charges because you were clearly not rational."

"I saw you grunting on top of her." Carter pushed forward again, seemingly indifferent to the risk of strangling. "Whatever you did to her back there, it only worked because she's—"

"Weak?" Damon finished. "Too trusting? Yet, in spite of your mistrust of me, you were willing to leave her to my mercy."

For the first time Damon saw uncertainty in the slight twitch at the corner of Carter's mouth. "I didn't have much choice," he said. "She'll die for certain if I don't get another patch. But you always knew that, didn't you?" He displayed his teeth like a Bloodmaster challenging a rival. "I swear I'll come back and skin you alive if you hurt her."

Damon's heartbeat began to rise. "It would be foolish of me to tell you I'll hunt you down if Alexia dies, but I will do it, even if you spend the rest of your days cowering in the Enclave."

Carter's sandy brows lifted. "You're good," he snickered. "I admit you're almost convincing."

Bearing down on the pulse points in Carter's neck, Damon shoved the Enclave agent back against the tree. "I know you took the patch," he said evenly. "You were also one of those shooting at us." He pressed on the arteries until he could feel them begin to close off the blood supply to Carter's brain. "Who are you working for?"

Carter closed his eyes and began to wheeze. "I work…for Aegis. For *my* people."

"Tell me who took the patch, and I may let you go."

"If you…don't let me go," Carter grunted, "Alexia *will* die."

That was the ugly dilemma, and Damon knew he'd underestimated Carter's will to resist.

"How can I be sure you'll return with the patch?" he asked.

Carter's lips twisted in a grotesque grin. "You can't."

A pulsing shadow fell over Damon's vision. Alexia had said it was hatred, and he knew she was right. He could feel it trying to seize his mind with claws of iron.

Protect Alexia. That was everything. For the first time in his years of field work—here in the Zone, where he was free—he didn't know what choice to make. If he dared leave Alexia alone, he could go with Carter all the way to the Border and make sure the agent did what he said he would.

But if he left her, and she died…

His fingers loosened on Carter's neck. The dhampir jerked up his arms, striking Damon's with the stiffened edges of his hands. Ordinarily it wouldn't have been enough, but Damon had been off guard for a fraction of a second, and in that infinitesimal span of time Carter broke free and was sprinting in the direction of the Border, leaving pack and weapons behind.

He didn't go far. Half a dozen running strides away he faltered, came to a sudden halt and spun around. Damon nearly ran into him.

Carter scrambled just out of reach. "What is it?" he asked, his voice rising. "What's coming?"

Expecting some kind of trick, Damon tensed his muscles to attack. But then he smelled the thick, acrid odor and heard the tread of something neither animal, human nor Opir.

Lamia.

Chapter 7

The monster wasn't even trying to disguise its approach, and that was Damon's only advantage. He unslung his rifle and backed away, facing the unseen enemy. Carter dove for his own weapons.

The Lamia pushed out from behind a dense screen of scrub oak and lunged toward Damon. He got off four rounds, each one hitting its mark, before the thing reached him, swinging its distorted hands with their razor-sharp nails in wide arcs. Damon jumped back and swung the rifle like a club, striking the monster across its shoulder and the side of its grotesque, vaguely humanoid head.

It slowed, its red, almost pupil-less eyes glaring with hatred. Blood flowed over its leathery skin, but already the bullet wounds were beginning to heal. Its lips moved as if it were trying to speak.

Damon stepped back, leveling his gun to shoot again, but the Lamia came to a stop, nostrils flaring, and swung its long, almost skeletal face toward Carter.

The dhampir stood well out of the way, his rifle at his shoulder. "Orlok," he said hoarsely. "I've never seen one this close."

Orlok. That was the human name for the monsters who roamed the Zone, killing animal and human, dhampir and Daysider with equal relish. But the Opiri called them Lamiae after legends of child-eating demons, driven mad with hatred and grief.

Damon continued to retreat until he stood level with Carter. "The last report said they had moved out of this region," he said.

"I guess your report was wrong."

Perhaps fatally so, Damon thought. "Where there is one," he said, "there are usually many."

Breathing raggedly, Carter looked wildly in every direction. "Your bullets hardly had any effect," he whispered.

"They heal even more quickly than we do," Damon said. He watched the creature's face, seeking some indication of what it would do next. But its mouth continued to work, bringing forth low grunts and growls that almost sounded like words.

"It's trying to talk." Carter's face blanched. "What in hell—"

Damon fired again, but he was not fast enough. The Lamia charged past him, straight at Carter. The dhampir went down in a flurry of striking limbs and blood.

Aiming with swift precision, Damon peppered the Lamia's back with a dozen bullets in rapid succession. The creature barely seemed to notice. It bent over Carter, its serrated teeth at the dhampir's throat.

Damon threw his rifle aside and drew his knife. He flung himself at the Lamia, stabbing down between the creature's shoulders. It shook him off without even turning around. Damon tried again, grabbing hold like a tick on a dog's back and bringing the knife around to the Lamia's throat.

The blade bit into tough flesh, and the Lamia hissed in pain. For a moment it forgot about the dhampir sprawled beneath it and twisted around to claw at Damon's head and shoulders.

Holding fast, Damon adjusted his grip and pulled the blade across the Lamia's throat a second time. With a gurgling roar, the creature fell away from Carter and rolled onto its back, nearly crushing Damon beneath it. In a matter of seconds the Lamia would turn and tear him apart.

But Damon had something it didn't have: the ability to reason. He let himself go limp, waited until the Lamia had lifted itself to its haunches, and lunged up to drive his knife into the creature's chest. He felt the blade skitter against bone and drive deeper, reaching the heart at last.

With a hiss like air escaping a valve, the creature fell hard, flailing in its death throes. Only when Damon was sure it was truly dying did he crouch beside Carter, quickly checking the extent of injuries.

Carter was still alive, but barely. His throat had been slashed, and though his body worked to mitigate the damage, it could do little against the severing of veins and arteries except slow the loss of blood. Bright and dark, it pumped slowly out of his wound, and Carter stared at the sky without seeing.

Still with half an eye on the dying Lamia, Damon went after Carter's pack, tore it open and found the agent's field dressing. He knew it would only slow the dhampir's death, but there were things he still needed to know. Perhaps now Carter would tell him.

He pressed the bandage against Carter's throat. The dhampir tried to move his head, and his lips parted.

"Can you speak?" Damon asked.

Carter tried to grin. "What…do you want now?" he rasped.

"Who are you working for?"

"No time," Carter said. "Alexia…"

Red froth bubbled up from the agent's mouth. Damon bent his head close to Carter's face. "What about her?" he asked urgently.

"You can help her." Carter choked and tried to swallow. "The patch... Drugs were derived from Daysider blood. If you let her..." His breath rattled. "Let her drink, and she... may survive."

Damon pushed aside his shock. "Who has the patch?" he demanded.

But Carter's eyes were already glazing over. "If you care... about her," he said, "save her."

Then he closed his eyes, shuddered once and died.

Damon rocked back, remembered the Lamia and reached for the rifle.

The creature was gone. It had left multiple trails of blood, but somehow it had managed to skulk away on two feet, surviving its terrible injuries as Carter had not.

It would not be returning anytime soon. Unless it brought back others of its kind.

Damon looked down at Carter's body. He almost felt pity for the man. He had died an ugly death, and yet Damon's conviction that the dhampir had been partly culpable for the stealing of Alexia's patch hadn't diminished in the slightest.

Nor had his astonishment at Carter's claim about the nature of the drugs in it. The implications were staggering. The only way such a thing would be possible was if Aegis and the Enclave had had access to a Darketan after the War. It suggested that there could be some connection between dhampir and Daysider no one had ever suspected.

And it made perfect sense that someone from Erebus—Colonists, Council or Expansionists—would want to get their hands on the patch, since it could be used not only to increase Opir knowledge of dhampir weaknesses but as a foundation for sanctions against Aegis, setting off a potential wave of political consequences Damon couldn't begin to imagine.

But for the moment, for Damon, this knowledge meant that he wouldn't have to leave Alexia and go to the Enclave in Carter's place. Her partner's death didn't mean she would die, too.

Damon could save her himself. And he couldn't waste any more precious minutes brooding over what Carter had told him, certainly none to see to his body according to either human or Opir custom. If the Lamia returned to finish him off, so be it.

Retrieving Carter's pack, weapons and his own bloody knife, Damon focused on clearing his mind. He had to decide quickly how much to tell Alexia. The knowledge of Carter's death might further weaken her, but eventually she would learn the truth. She would wonder why he'd kept it from her, and any trust she might have begun to feel would—

"Michael!"

Gasping for air, Alexia stumbled toward Carter's body and fell to her knees, her hands hovering over her partner's face.

"Michael," she said, her voice breaking.

Damon started toward her. "Alexia! What are you doing here? I told you—"

"You told me?" She looked slowly up at Damon, the grief in her eyes turning to accusation. "You killed him."

Damon was utterly unprepared for her arrival and had no ready answer. He dropped the knife and began to move in her direction again, but she pulled the gun he had given her from her jacket and pointed it at his head.

"I didn't kill him, Alexia," he said. "And you should not have left camp."

"That's funny," she said. "I thought Michael would try to kill *you,* but I didn't really believe—" She swallowed and glanced at Carter's face. "I didn't think you'd go through with it."

"I didn't." Damon crouched some distance away, trying

to catch her eye. "We were both attacked by one of the creatures you call Orloks."

She met his gaze again, her body trembling with shock and anger. "Orlok? Are you telling me some monster did this?" She balled her other fist and punched at the ground. "Where is it?"

"It got away," Damon said. He indicated the area around him, where the creature had torn up the earth in its struggles and left trails of its blood. "It attacked me first, and then it went for Carter. I tried to stop it." He sighed, very much aware of the racking grief Alexia was trying so hard not to let him see. "I'm sorry."

"Are you?" she asked. "Do you still deny that you hated him?"

"His death was unnecessary, and it has caused you pain. That is enough to make me regret it."

"What about the Orlok?" She stared at him as if he were something far worse than Carter's supposed murderer. "We know they come from Erebus. Some believe they have been created and bred to hunt down and kill any human or dhampir they find in the Zone. Is that true?"

He shook his head vehemently. "They are monsters even to the Opiri. They cannot be controlled."

Damon felt her absorbing his words, taking him in, noting the fresh, blood-rimmed slashes that had reduced what was left of his shirt and jacket to tatters. It was not something Carter could have done, even with a knife.

"You have blood on your face," she said.

He lifted a hand to rub at his jaw. Dried blood flaked off in patches and fell to the ground like scarlet rain.

No wonder Alexia had assumed he had killed Carter. He could have ripped the dhampir's throat out almost as easily as the Lamia if the hunger was on him.

But it wasn't. And he still hadn't convinced her of his innocence.

"There was a great deal of blood," he said. "His jugular…"
He hesitated, unwilling to burden Alexia with the ugly details.

Alexia leaned over Michael again, the muzzle of her gun
beginning to drop, and she touched the bandage at Carter's
throat with her other hand. "You did this?" she asked, her
green eyes glistening with unshed tears.

"Yes."

"If I'd been here—"

"You could have done nothing," Damon interrupted. "And
now you risk your own life. Carter would never have wanted
that."

As if to prove his point, Alexia's fingers spasmed in pain.
She dropped the gun and made no attempt to pick it up again.

Damon stood. "You must lie down," he insisted, starting
toward her again.

Alexia raised both hands and leaned away as if to fend him
off, and he stopped. "Alexia," he said, "I did not kill him."

Tears slid from the corners of her eyes, and her shoulders
sagged. "Did he…say anything before he died?" she asked,
her voice breaking.

Once again Damon was faced with the dilemma of how
much to tell her. There was no good reason to assume that
only her partner knew about the origin of the drugs in the
patch; she could easily have been concealing that knowledge
from him just as Carter had.

But why would she, if she knew he could save her simply
by sharing his blood? No, he was certain her behavior toward
him would have been different if she'd known the source of
the medication that kept her alive.

Still, it now seemed much more significant that Alexia
had attempted to seduce him—if it could be called seduction, seemingly subconscious as it had been—and had tasted
his blood. True, she'd taken no more than a drop, if that, but

something inside her had known that in that blood lay something she must have to stay alive.

Alexia would have to be made to understand how important it was that they act on Michael's information immediately. But Damon still had no proof that Carter had betrayed her. Or *why* he would. Even suggesting such a possibility would be the surest way of turning Alexia against him once and for all.

Damon dropped to his haunches. "He told me how to keep you alive."

She looked up from Carter's still face. "There was only one way he could have done that," she said. "I would never have bought my life with his."

"Getting a new patch isn't the only way," Damon said. "He told me more about it. What makes it work."

"What does that matter now?"

"Because he said the drugs in the patch are derived from the blood of my kind."

She froze. Her muscles locked, and even the tears on her cheeks seemed to harden like crystal.

"*Your* kind?" she said. "Darketans?"

"Yes."

"My God," she whispered.

Her shock wasn't feigned. She was genuinely astonished, and perhaps even more than that—horrified.

"He didn't say where your Enclave obtained the blood," Damon added, "but if the patches have been in use for years…"

"Since ten years after the Treaty," she said, looking away.

She knew as well as Damon what that meant, though being from the Enclave, she might see some of the implications he had missed. Her face remained an expressionless mask.

"I don't understand how that is supposed to keep me alive," she said.

"Your partner suggested that taking my blood might save you."

She stood abruptly and headed back the way she had come, her legs jerking with every step. Damon glanced down at Carter one last time, gathered up packs and weapons, and followed her, watching carefully to ensure she didn't stumble or fall.

"Do you understand?" he asked, catching up to her. "You have a chance to live."

Alexia continued to walk without glancing in his direction. It was obvious that she was pushing herself to stay on her feet, and the farther she went the more she slowed down. Damon had to resist the compulsion to take her in his arms and carry her the rest of the way.

Moving at an extremely slow pace with many stops to allow Alexia to rest, they reached their camp several hours later. By then it had been dark for some time, and Alexia was walking with her arms wrapped around her stomach, her skin almost yellow and her body racked with wave after wave of severe tremors.

Ignoring the risk, Damon took her arm and forced her down onto the blanket. She resisted, but even in full health she was not as strong as he was. As soon as she was on the ground, she jerked her arm away.

Damon remained standing, trying not to loom over her. "You can't go on like this much longer," he said softly. "We will have to attempt it."

Her jaw set. "Forget it."

"Why? Have you no desire to complete your mission, if only for Carter's sake?"

She picked up a twig and scraped jagged lines through the dirt as if she were inscribing her refusal in some ancient, arcane language.

"The price is too high," she said.

The price. What price was worth more than her life? "You don't want to live?" he asked, hearing the anger in his voice.

She jabbed the stick into the ground with such force that it snapped. "We do not drink blood."

The very fact that she objected so fiercely confirmed Damon's belief that she had no memory of tasting his blood before. But he was not about to let the matter rest at that.

"Why not?" he asked.

"We don't drink it," she repeated, holding herself tightly as if she feared she might shatter into a million pieces.

"Because you refuse to acknowledge that you are half-Opir?" he asked, moving closer. "Is that what you were taught, to despise that part of yourself?"

"I *do* despise it," she burst out, struggling to her feet. "I hate that the man who forcibly impregnated my mother was a vampire. I hate that I was born sharing anything in common with your kind."

Her vehemence hit Damon with the force of a blow. He was not surprised by it; he had always accepted that the hatred her partner had so clearly expressed must be the prevailing opinion among their kind, even if Carter's willingness to let it interfere with his work put him on the extreme end of the emotional range.

But that Alexia hated *herself* so much…that was something he couldn't accept so easily. It wasn't that he didn't understand. There had been many times in his life, before he had accepted his duty, that he had hated what he was. Hated that he could never fully be part of Opir society, that the true-bloods would always consider him, and all his kind, almost as far below them as humans.

When he had told Alexia he was an outsider, it had been to gain her trust. But what he'd said was the truth.

"You have already taken something from one of my kind," he said. "And shared something much more personal."

"I told you that didn't mean anything," she said. "It was the illness."

"And now you have a chance to rid yourself of that illness. If you can set aside your prejudice."

"Prejudice?" She faced him eye to eye, passionate with defiance. "Your breed came into our world and ignited a war so you could make every human a slave to your needs. We were…are…cattle to you, and you expect us to regard you as anything but tyrants and murderers?"

"You may rest assured that I do not regard you as livestock, or an inferior."

All the fire in Alexia's eyes winked out as if his simple statement had smothered every spark of hatred in her heart. "It doesn't matter," she said wearily. "I can't do it. I won't."

She sank down again and lay on her side, turning her back to him. A furious desperation began to eat away at Damon's control. He had sworn he wouldn't let her die. Nothing had changed. If she wouldn't cooperate, he would force her to accept his help. Even if he had to tie her down, puncture his own flesh and drip his blood into her mouth.

"Is this it?" he demanded. "Is this all Carter's death means to you, that you lie down and surrender?"

"Better than drinking blood and becoming like you."

"Better to stay alive and fight for what you believe in."

She rolled over to face him. "Why do you give a damn, Damon? We're still on opposite sides. Why have you fought so hard to keep me alive?"

"Because I…" He stopped, knowing full well what he was about to admit aloud was the culmination of every forbidden emotion he had fought against since he had met her. Once he had spoken the words, there would be no going back. Not until his mission was complete and they were parted forever.

"I *care* about you," he said, forcing the words through gritted teeth.

As much as Carter's death and the revelation about the

patch had shocked Alexia, he had expected disgust, rejection, perhaps even derision. But she only gazed at him as if he had told her that the sun set in the west.

"I wouldn't believe you," she said quietly, "if you hadn't—" She broke off, biting hard enough on her lower lip to draw blood.

"Hadn't what?" Damon asked, trying to ignore his sudden and disconcerting interest in the crimson bead at the corner of her mouth.

"Behaved so…irrationally."

He winced. "It was not my intention to…to allow my reason to be compromised."

"Is that what you call caring about another person?" she asked with a sad, weary smile.

That she could smile at all was what humans might call a miracle. "I am surprised you think I am capable of it at all," he said.

She pulled herself into a sitting position. "I said I did, didn't I?" She took in a deep breath. "You said you wouldn't let me die. You practically *ordered* me to stay alive, remember? Not even Carter did that."

"You never thought I had a motive other than your personal welfare?" Damon asked.

"Of course I did. You said that was part of your mission, didn't you? I would have been crazy to think otherwise. But now…" She rubbed her hand across her face. "Part of me believed you really did kill Michael. I don't think that anymore."

Damon's heart began to pound under his ribs like heavy surf battering the shore. "And now that you do not," he said, "how *do* you regard me?"

Her frank gaze wavered and then fixed on his again as if she knew she couldn't escape the truth, no matter how unpalatable it was to her.

"I don't know," she said. "I don't know how to define what

I feel. But I have found some reason to admire you, to…recognize your good qualities."

"My 'human' qualities?"

Her lips twitched. "If you like."

"Yet you still insist what happened between us was meaningless?"

"I told you—" She sighed. "Even if I'd known what I was doing, it was only sex."

Damon's throat felt as if he had swallowed his own knife. "You have had sex before," he said.

She pulled the edge of the blanket up over her legs without any apparent realization that she was doing it. "I'm no virgin, if that's what you mean."

"Who?" he asked.

"Are you kidding?" She cast him a glance that was an uneasy combination of amusement and profound discomfort. "Making love is a normal part of human existence."

Her answer didn't release the knot in Damon's stomach. *"Making love,"* he said. "A strange phrase to suggest a sexual relationship. Is it such a casual thing among humans?"

She shrugged. "It can be."

"But what you call *love* is not."

Her expression changed, shadowed with thoughts she clearly found disturbing. "Why don't you tell me what it's like for Daysiders? Do you force yourself on humans the way your masters do?"

Memories of the single human he had taken in his youth silenced his protest. He hadn't forced himself on her. She had come to him knowing her duty, unafraid.

But not wanting. Not free. Just as he had never been truly free with, even though he had told himself their relationship was as much by his choice as hers.

"I can speak only for myself," he said. "I would never take a woman unwilling, no matter what her kind." He caught

Alexia's gaze, turning the tables again. "Did you have intercourse with Carter?"

"What?" She blinked at him, her expression transforming from surprise to outrage. "Carter was my partner. I cared about him, but I didn't sleep with him. Clear enough?"

Not clear at all, Damon thought. There were still too many things about human and dhampir emotions he didn't fully understand. But knowing Carter had never been with her that way...

Damon closed his eyes. The very thought of what might have happened if Carter hadn't interrupted him and Alexia sent a fierce shock of desire through his body. He imagined Alexia's breasts bared to him, his mouth on her nipple, his skin naked against hers. His cock stiffened, throbbing with a deep ache that could end only one way.

But if he ever gave in to that lust, he would drive Alexia away for all time. If he didn't lose her to her own stubbornness.

"What *is* clear," he said, "is that you promised me you would stay alive."

She turned her back on him again. "I think we've covered that topic."

"Evidently not thoroughly enough. You gave me your word. Are you breaking it?"

She sat up and met his gaze. "Do you remember my exact words, Damon?" she asked intently.

It was a strange question, but when Damon tried to recall the conversation he couldn't remember when or how she'd made her promise.

"Are you denying you said it?" he pressed.

Alexia heaved herself to her feet and reached down for her pack. "I have to go bury Michael. I'm not going to let scavengers tear him apart."

Damon blocked her path. "Carter is beyond caring what becomes of his body," he said.

"He deserves to be laid to rest."

"That is foolishness."

"I'll give him a proper burial." She pushed him aside with her healed shoulder and strode away. Damon went after her, seized her arm and swung her around to face him. He bared his teeth.

"Don't make me tie you up," he said. "I will if you try to leave."

"Then that's what you'll have to do."

Chapter 8

Without hesitation Damon herded her back to the blanket, compelled her to kneel and pulled his pack close with his free hand. He unfastened one of the outer pockets and withdrew a carefully bundled length of cord. In spite of its thinness, it was easily strong enough to bear a large Darketan's weight or keep a dhampir firmly bound.

Alexia struggled, but her excursion to look for him and Carter had taken a severe toll on her body. Damon pinned her down, caught both her wrists in his free hand and lashed the cord around them. He let her go just long enough to secure the cord and then helped her sit up.

There was nothing but cold contempt in her eyes.

"You won't like what happens when I get free," she snapped.

"I'll take my chances."

Alexia lapsed into silence, and after a while her chin began to sink to her chest as she gave way to her body's demands. Damon wasn't deceived. She might be too weak to resist him now, but he knew she wouldn't give in, even with her last breath.

So he waited her out, keeping watch over her and looking for any sign that she might be worsening. He removed the remnants of his shirt and undershirt, leaving his torn jacket spread over a bush to air out.

The night was cool and silent save for the usual animal sounds, and Alexia fell asleep sitting up within fifteen minutes. Gently Damon laid her down and pulled half the blanket over her. She didn't awaken at his touch.

He knew he shouldn't postpone the inevitable, not even for another hour. Yet when it came down to the decision of forcing her to drink his blood, he couldn't do it. She had to be willing.

As "willing" as she had been before? Or fully conscious of her choice?

He had no answer, and so as the long night dragged on, Damon paced the hilltop until he had memorized every twig, every rock, and every leaf on every bush. Still Alexia slept. A few hours before dawn he lay down beside Alexia, his back to her chest, and forced himself to relax. Even if he fell into the twilight sleep Darketans and Opiri used to regenerate, he would still be fully capable of sensing danger.

But sleep wouldn't come. He rolled over and studied Alexia's quiet face. Her features were soft again, revealing that strange innocence that her years as an agent had erased from her conscious mind. Her lips were slightly parted, and her lashes brushed her cheeks like fine strands of silk.

Slowly he reached for her, brushing his fingertips across her chin. She sighed and curled toward him.

Her body did what her mind could not. It trusted him.

Damon let his fingers trail across her lips, move up to trace her brows and brush back the hair that had fallen across her forehead. He couldn't bear it, this strange tenderness, this desire that was so much more than physical. How could he justify the way he had taken her dignity by trussing her like a steer bound for the serfs' table?

Rising silently, Damon walked around her and knelt to free her hands. He tossed the cord aside, settled her arms in a more natural position and rested his hand on her back. It was like touching a smoldering fire. A shiver worked its way through her body, and Damon knew she was sinking into fever again.

She would be vulnerable now, as vulnerable as she could ever be. But Damon knew he couldn't steal her will and dignity again.

Even if I must let her die? he thought.

No. He'd let her keep her pride until her body and mind failed, until there was no hope left. And then...

He stretched out beside her again, cradling her against his chest. Her breath hitched and released, but she was no longer shivering. Damon rested his face against her hair, breathing in the fragrant scent that days of hardship hadn't erased. He pressed his lips to her neck, feeling her thready pulse and the sluggishness of her blood. He nuzzled her shoulder, her ear, her jaw, drawn into a memory of Eirene lying in his arms on his narrow cot in the Darketan dormitory.

The image froze and Damon stopped, arrested by the recognition of a change in himself he had never expected. Until this moment, his thoughts of Eirene had been acutely painful, laced with hatred, grief and guilt he thought he would carry until the end of his days.

But suddenly those feelings had receded into shadow, driven away by the remarkable woman he held now. He could remember Eirene's smile, her courage, the warmth and gentleness even a Darketan's rigorous training hadn't diminished. He could remember and not despise himself.

It was almost as if he were free—not of the memories of Eirene's death, but of the blackness it had left festering inside him.

The blackness that would come roaring back to life when Alexia died.

But not yet.

"You would have liked Eirene," he murmured against Alexia's ear. "She was not afraid of what all Darketans fear most." He brushed his knuckles across Alexia's cheek. "She cared for me, and I lost her. But now…"

Alexia shivered again. "Now," she echoed. She pushed her back against Damon's chest, compelling him to loosen his hold, and rolled over to face him. The first, thin light of false dawn filtered through the darkness, deepening the shadows under her lower lids and beneath her cheekbones, but there was a kind of peace in her eyes. No fear, no anger, only acceptance.

"*Now* is all we have, you and I," she said. "It was all we ever could have, even if I still had my patch."

Damon berated himself for having spoken his thoughts aloud. He had never meant Alexia to know about Eirene, or anything else about his life in Erebus.

But it was too late to take back his confession. And what did it matter? Alexia was right. Even if she hadn't been condemned to a painful death…

"Yes," he said. "There could never be anything else."

Alexia bowed her head and examined her wrists, unbound and unmarked. "You let me go," she said. "Why?"

"I could not take your choice from you," he said. Hesitantly he touched the moisture gathering under her eyelids. "I didn't know that dhampires wept like humans."

She gave a husky laugh. "Don't rub it in." She scraped her palm across her cheeks. "Do Darketans? Cry, I mean?"

It was an absurd conversation under the circumstances, but he had already exposed the worst of his weaknesses to Alexia. One more would hardly make a difference.

"Yes," he said, keeping his expression carefully neutral. "Darketans are capable of it."

She searched Damon's face. "Who was Eirene?"

He reached for the canteen and offered it to Alexia. "Drink," he said.

Without taking her eyes from his, Alexia took the canteen from his hand. Her arm trembled so much that Damon had to help her lift the vessel to her lips. He watched her uneasily as she swallowed the stale water, half afraid she might choke, but she finished without difficulty and let him take the canteen away.

"Thank you," she said, brushing moisture from her cracked lips. "I've never been so thirsty."

Nor, Damon realized, had he. But not for water. A short time ago he'd seen Alexia bite her lip and tried to ignore his immediate reaction to the sight, dismissing it as a brief aberration. He had taken nourishment just before he had left Erebus, and that had been only been a few days ago.

But now, all at once, he began to realize that his lapse then hadn't been just a passing impulse. It seemed his need for blood had come on him far more quickly than it should have. If he concentrated, he could trace this new and unexpected hunger to the moment when he had tasted Alexia's blood during their interrupted embrace and had detected that "other" in its signature.

Whatever had brought it on, there was nothing he could do about it. Not without leaving Alexia.

"Tell me about her," Alexia asked softly. "Talk to me, Damon. I don't want to be alone in my head just now."

Alone in her head. How many times had Damon felt the same, knowing how few Darketans would understand?

Eirene had.

He rolled onto his back, staring up at the lightening sky. "She was Darketan," he said quietly. "One of the best operatives Erebus has ever known."

"You said she cared for you, and you lost her." She hesitated, her voice dropping to a murmur. "I'm sorry."

Damon didn't let himself respond to her gentleness. "It was long ago."

"Not long enough for you to forget." He heard her shift to lie on her back, sharing his study of the heavens. "What wasn't she afraid of, Damon? Emotion?"

It was impossible for Damon to answer. Not with *her,* in this place, at this time. Alexia accepted his silence for a while, but she wasn't finished.

"You aren't a Nightsider," she said. "We know they aren't capable of feelings as we understand them. You've proven that doesn't hold true for Darketans. Why do your people fear it?"

Damon clenched his fists, welcoming the bite of his nails into flesh. "Are Enclave operatives not discouraged from letting emotion interfere with duty?" he asked.

"Of course we are. But sometimes it can't be helped. I'm proof of that. So is…was Michael." She laid her forearm across her face as if she didn't want him to glimpse whatever might lie in her eyes. "I guess that's what makes us…" She sucked in a breath. "What makes us human."

And what had sent Carter rushing to meet his inevitable downfall.

"Eirene wasn't human," Alexia said, "but she wasn't afraid. And you weren't afraid to care for her."

"It was a mistake," Damon said flatly. "It cost her her life."

"How?" She lowered her arm and turned on her side to face him, her weight resting on one elbow. "How, Damon?"

The concern in her voice made it even more difficult for him to speak. "It is forbidden for agents to become personally involved," he said. "Sex is allowed, but only for recreational purposes. To go beyond that is a grave transgression that must be punished."

"The way Nightsiders punish their serfs for disobedience?"

Damon sat up, stung by her question even as he acknowledged how accurate it was. "If *we* were serfs," he said, "we would not be permitted to move freely in the Zone."

"They don't think you'll try to escape," she said.

"Why should we wish to?"

"You just told me why." She rested her hand on his thigh. "They *did* punish Eirene, didn't they?"

Her question lodged inside him like the projectile from a Vampire Slayer, sending tiny, razor-sharp slivers outward from his chest to sever his spine and slice through his brain.

No, he hadn't forgotten. Alexia hadn't quite driven the rage and hate and guilt away. Nothing could ever do that.

"They sent her on a suicide mission against the Enclave," he said. "She was reported dead within a week."

Alexia's fingers tightened on his leg. "I'm sorry," she repeated. "I…know what it is to lose someone."

Damon met her gaze. Her eyes were laced again with tears that he knew were more for him than herself. "Who was he?" he asked gruffly.

"My brother. My half brother." She drew her hand away, and he knew she was going to change the subject even before she spoke again. "What did they do to *you?*" she asked.

"Nothing," he said, clenching his jaw against any further explanation.

"They didn't have to, did they?" Alexia said. Her gaze grew distant, as if she had been claimed by her own painful memories. "You loved her, and—"

"Love," he said harshly, "is a word even Darketans have no use for."

He thought for a moment that she flinched, but when he looked again she was as still as before. "Of course not," she said. "There is a Zone of difference between caring and love."

"Have *you* loved, Alexia?" he said, trying and failing to hold the question behind his teeth.

"I loved my brother, my mother, my stepfather," she said. "I loved Michael, as a friend and comrade. But you wouldn't understand that, would you?" Her breath caught, as if she was finding it increasingly difficult to fill her lungs. "Your kind doesn't have parents…or brothers or sisters. Only Sires and fellow vassals. What could actual love or loyalty mean in a society where there is no compassion, power and ruthlessness determine rank, and the weakest are kept as chattel?"

Contempt thickened her voice, but there was challenge in it, as well. Was she expecting him to agree with her, to admit that his people were no better than savages?

"The Opiri consider your society decadent and unfit to survive," he said.

"Is that really what *you* believe?"

"I can judge only by what I have observed."

"And what exactly *have* you observed, Damon? All you've ever seen of humans in Erebus is your beaten-down slaves. You said you've never dealt with dhampires before. How many times have you met free humans?" He felt more than saw her lean toward him. "You know only what you've been taught, the propaganda and prejudice of Erebus and every Citadel like it."

He met her gaze. "The Enclave killed Eirene."

"How?" Alexia lifted herself higher on her arm, the lines around her eyes deepening in distress. "You said the Council sent her on a suicide mission. What was she sent to do, Damon?"

"Eirene was no assassin, if that's what you mean." He looked away, swallowing his grief as he had done a thousand times before. "She was captured by your agency. It was reported that they tortured her before she died."

"I don't believe it," Alexia said. She got to her knees and caught at his arm, compelling him to look at her. "*We* don't torture, Damon," she said. "We have laws."

"Laws that send every condemned criminal in your city to Erebus." He turned his arm to grab her wrist, feeling the pulse beating fast under the soft skin of the underside. "*You* make the serfs as much as Erebus does."

Alexia twisted her arm, but he refused to let her go. Her

nostrils flared and her eyes narrowed in an expression that must terrify any human she turned it on. She and Damon stared at each other, neither willing to give ground.

But when she began to slump and her breathing grew constrained, Damon let her go, cursing himself for upsetting her when she had so little energy to spare for pointless argument.

Alexia sank back on her heels. "Do you think I don't know that?" she whispered, the heat of anger draining away with her sigh. "It was part of the Treaty, a system developed so the leeches wouldn't be driven to raid and kidnap citizens to feed their hunger. Can you justify the way Nightsiders live?"

Damon could hardly bear the raw pain in her voice. He understood that in spite of Alexia's hostility toward the Opiri, the hatred she had expressed for their way of life, she believed in something better than the fragile Armistice that kept Opiri and humans from each other's throats. Her sincere question was a revelation to him, an admission of hope.

Hope Eirene had shared.

"You and I," he said thickly, "can have no effect on the decisions of those we serve. It is beyond our power."

"Is it?" She placed her palm on his chest. "Why *do* you still serve them, Damon? You hate what they did to Eirene. From what you've said, they'd do the same to any Darketan who cared for another. Why doesn't all your kind leave and start your own society?"

"Like the illegal colony?" he asked.

"No. It would be different, because *you* are different." Her eyes were no longer dull with illness or dark with anger. They shone with the reflection of excitement, as if she could see what she envisioned as surely as she could see his face. "What if there's a way to create what you need, the same way the Enclave used Darketan blood to create the drugs?"

He looked down at her small hand, so delicate in spite of its strength, wondering if she could feel how hard and fast his heart was beating. "Even if that were possible," he said, "why do you think any Darketans would wish to leave?"

"If they're like you—"

He pulled out of her reach. "You don't know me, Alexia," he said harshly. "Eirene *was* different. But most of my kind would never consider what you suggest. It wouldn't even occur to them. They know only one way to live."

"*You* could teach them. Damon—"

"We would never be allowed to leave Erebus permanently."

"Because they're afraid of you," she said, as if she had finally understood some great mystery.

"The Opiri have nothing to fear from us," he said bitterly. "But we are rare mutations, so—"

"Mutations?"

"You didn't know?"

"We've all heard the rumors and theories, but if Aegis knew, they didn't see any reason to tell us." Her mouth tightened. "How does it happen?"

Damon closed his eyes. "During the Awakening and the War after," he said, "when the Opiri were converting many humans to become their soldiers, it sometimes happened that the process failed to complete. It was believed to be a result of an allergic reaction to Opir blood, which resulted in unforeseen genetic changes."

"*Was?*"

"It happens rarely now, since few humans are permitted to convert."

She leaned toward him again, reaching out to stroke the tense muscles under his ribs. "How long ago were *you* converted?"

The distraction of her intimate touch almost robbed him of his ability to speak. "I don't remember," he said, his voice roughening. "Loss of memory is another side effect of an incomplete conversion."

Her fingers worked into the waistband of his pants. "The

eldest Nightsiders claim they were always on Earth, even before humans," she murmured. "But *you* were human once. And now you're something else, with insights and abilities they don't have. That's why they're afraid of you, and why you have to leave Erebus, go far beyond any vampire's reach."

Flattening his hand, Damon pressed his palm over her fingers and held them still. "That would be to the benefit of the Enclave, would it not?" he said. "They would be pleased to see the Darketans abandon the Citadel."

"You're right," she said. "But you know that's not why I said it."

"Would the Enclave welcome us if we went to them?"

She lowered her gaze and didn't answer. Damon hardly noticed. His desire for her was devouring him, a forbidden temptation that made him crave not only her body but her spirit, the unique spirit he had met in only one other in all the course of his existence. It was all he could do to keep from pulling her into his arms, forgetting her bizarre ideas and existing only in the "now" Alexia had spoken of before this pointless discussion.

But he couldn't. He respected her too much. He began to rise, but Alexia gripped his pants and pulled him back down. She slid her hand up to his collarbone and curled her fingers around the back of his neck.

"When I'm gone," she said, "I want you to promise me to think about what I've said. It's almost all I have to give you."

Despair and defiance rose like a tempest in Damon's chest. He caught Alexia's face between his hands. "I said I would not let you die."

Her smile was sad. "You're not a god."

"There must be something—"

"Let's not talk about it now," she said. "There are other things we could be doing...."

Sires help me, Damon thought. "Let me go to the Enclave," he said. "There is still a chance—"

"You'd never make it in time."

"Then I'll track down the Opir your partner was following. He may have the patch, or know where it is."

Alexia put a finger to his lips. "I want only one thing of you, Damon. Let's finish what we started.

Make love to me."

Chapter 9

The fire rose hot in Damon's eyes, and Alexia knew she had won.

Not her life. That she had already lost. But something almost as precious, something she could take with her into the darkness, the memory of becoming one with the man she—

No. That word meant nothing to Damon, or to her. She held his gaze, asking him again with her silence.

"It isn't safe," he said hoarsely.

"No one has come near us since you went on recon," she said. "If they'd wanted to come after us, they would have by now."

"And the Lamia?"

"I'm willing to risk it, if you are."

Maybe it was asking too much of him after all. He was so still that she thought he was going to refuse. But then the fire in his eyes claimed his body, and he pulled her to him, seizing her mouth with his.

Alexia had been kissed before. Not often, because of what

she was; there was nothing to prevent dhampires from having relationships with each other, ranging from casual sex to cohabitation, but few humans felt comfortable in an intimate relationship with them. The few dhampir lovers Alexia had taken had been friends, no more; her one human lover had left her when he couldn't cope with her vampire blood, even though she never so much as grazed him with her teeth.

With Damon, none of that mattered. For the first time, as his lips claimed hers, she felt a barrier between them crumble, one so deep inside her that she hadn't even realized it existed. It wasn't just because of the closeness of their bodies, or how they would soon be closer still. It was more than mere emotion. It was oneness with another being, for the first time in her life.

She opened her mouth to welcome his tongue, feeling his hand work its way down her side to the waistband of her pants, tugging the tail of her shirt free and sliding his palm over her stomach. He rubbed her skin with slow, almost lazy strokes and began to explore the rest of her face with his lips: brow, cheeks, chin, jawline. He suckled the lobe of her ear, provoking shivers that began at the top of her head and ended just below his caressing hand. He grazed her with his teeth, just for an instant, and licked along the ridge of her collarbone.

At the same time, he had managed to undo nearly all the buttons of her shirt and was working on the last as he kissed her lips again. He rested his hand on her right breast, cupping it through the thin fabric of her undershirt. Alexia gasped as he began to massage her, rolling her nipple between his fingers without baring her skin.

Then his mouth was on her breast, wetting the fabric with his tongue while his fingers found the fly of her pants. When he had unbuttoned her pants and unzipped them, he pushed her undershirt up above her breasts and resumed kissing and suckling them with a hunger she knew was as potent as her desire. He flicked his tongue over the tips of her nipples and then kissed his way down, between her breasts and below the arc of her ribs. He pushed the waistband of her pants down to her hips, and she arched her body so that he could pull the pants all the way off.

Then he stopped.

"Damon?" she whispered, lost in a haze of pleasure.

His eyes, when they met hers, were almost those of a stranger. But not a dangerous one, not like what he had been before he had left with Michael.

The emotion was there, yes—passion laced with lust and bewilderment, as if he had as much trouble believing this was happening as she did.

"It's all right, Damon," she said, pulling him down again. "I'm all right, and I want this. I want it more than anything I've ever wanted in my life."

Whatever had made him hesitate, her words broke the spell. He bent to kiss her navel and continued below, working toward the powerful ache that only he could cure. He reached her tight nest of curls and slid his tongue into the tender depression beneath.

Alexia moaned as he tasted the soft, moist flesh, stroking and exploring. She tangled her fingers in his thick hair, urging him to drink deeply. He licked his way to her entrance and dipped in, just for an instant, before working back up to her clitoris. He took it between his lips and sucked, drawing Alexia to a nearly unbearable pinnacle of need. Pleasure became pain, pain pleasure. She began to throb and tremble, balancing on the brink of a fall that would never end.

But when she stepped over the edge, Damon was there to catch her. She felt herself pulse wildly against his mouth, felt him lick the moisture from her swollen lips as if it were the only sustenance he would ever need.

But he wasn't finished, and almost as soon as it was over

she felt a renewed ache between her thighs—an overpowering need to be filled with everything Damon could give her.

He licked his lips, savoring the sweet taste of Alexia's body. He was not ignorant of the many flavors of a woman, but never had he experienced it this way before. Not even with—

He pushed the memories away. Alexia deserved everything he had to offer her, and he needed to be inside her as much as he needed blood to stay alive.

Positioning himself over her, he unzipped his fly, too impatient to remove his pants. She spread her thighs wide to accommodate him, and he settled between them, his cock briefly resting between her stomach and his. Then he lifted himself, shuddering as her hand found him and guided him in.

His need was too intense to control. With a long, slow thrust he entered her, listening to her gasp of surprise and moan of pleasure as she felt him begin to move. She was tight and very wet, and he knew for all her casualness about sex that she hadn't been with a man for a long time.

But she didn't ask him to be gentle, and for all his efforts to move slowly, his hunger continued to drive him. He thrust deeply and pulled out, thrust hard again, and all the while Alexia gripped his shoulders and urged him on. Her head rolled back and her eyelids fluttered. She cried out his name.

When she finally came again, pulsing hard around his cock, he followed her quickly, pumping fast to fill her with seed that could never create life. He released his breath and buried his face in her neck, still tucked inside her, reveling in the scent of her perspiration and the hot femininity of her sex.

But this wasn't only about his pleasure, his need. He lifted himself up again so that he could see her face. It was flushed and relaxed, but when her eyes opened and her lips parted to display her teeth, he knew she wasn't really seeing him. She wasn't aware what was happening when her incisors grazed his neck, pressed gently down and pierced the skin. She had no idea that she was saving herself as she licked up the blood and sucked it from his veins, but for him it was pleasure even beyond pushing deep inside her body, and he knew it was the same for her.

He wasn't forcing her. Her own body was doing what instinct told it to do. She was keeping her promise to him, and he wasn't going to stop her, not even if she hated him afterward.

A strange feeling overwhelmed Damon, and it was so unfamiliar that he didn't recognize it until he heard his heart beating in time with hers.

It was joy. And as he felt Alexia's tongue trail over his skin and his blood flow into her mouth, he knew this moment, this emotion, would never come again. When she jerked again beneath him in a third orgasm, her thighs locking around his waist and her gasps of pleasure mingling with his, he thanked whatever gods might be that they had found each other for this brief moment in time.

When Alexia woke, everything had changed.

She felt it first in her heart, beating strong and steady for the first time since her patch had been stripped from her skin. Next she noticed that the pain under her arm was gone, and when she felt the wound she found it cool and dry to the touch, hardly even a trace of a scab remaining. Her whole body hummed with energy and an inexplicable happiness.

Breathing in a lungful of late-morning air, Alexia realized that all her senses had been renewed, sight and smell and hearing, as if she had taken one of the illegal drugs that were said to create a sense of oneness with the world that could change a human's experience for a lifetime.

But the only drug she had ingested was her joining with the man beside her, sleeping the sleep of utter exhaustion, his expression so relaxed that she realized just how much he had suffered trying to protect her and keep her alive. Here he had no masters, no ugly memories…only peace, for a few precious hours.

She had new memories now—*good* memories of lying beside Damon, quivering with excitement as he found all the most sensitive spots she'd forgotten, tasting her breasts and farther below, where his tongue had searched out the very center of her need.

And she remembered him moving inside her, fitting so perfectly that she could imagine it was her first time, her first lover, and there could never be another. She remembered her own moans and cries as he thrust deeper, harder, carrying her into a white-hot sun of pleasure beyond description.

After that…Alexia sighed, closing her eyes as the warmth of the rising sun, creeping over the hills to the east, bathed her face and shoulders. There had been those few moments of utter bliss at the end, an explosion of sensation that had blotted out all thought and consciousness, everything but that eternal moment of ecstasy. She could still feel her body humming with it.

Had Damon felt the same thing? Did it really matter? They had comforted each other, giving and taking in equal measure. That was all anyone could ask.

More than *she* had ever asked for. Or could ever expect to come again.

Unwilling to wake Damon, Alexia rose silently and went for her pack and canteen. Her balance had returned, along with the strength in her legs. She knelt to pick up the canteen and realized it was nearly empty. So was Damon's. Almost certainly he had given her most of the water when she'd been ill, but she was pretty sure even Daysiders needed to drink something other than blood.

There was a creek within two kilometers of their current location, but it lay at the foot of the hills to the east, at the edge of the very same valley where the illegal colony stood.

Even though she and Damon had been left alone for over twenty-four hours, Alexia had no illusions about the risk they would be taking just to replenish their supply of water.

The very idea that she could be thinking of taking a hike through the hills startled Alexia. She paused to take stock of her body again, listening to the even throb of her heart, the clean feel of air in her lungs, the healthy hunger that reminded her how long ago she'd eaten.

Her first thought had been right. It was exactly as if she'd taken a drug. The most powerful drug anyone could imagine.

The canteen dropped from Alexia's hand. She touched her mouth. The taste was faint, almost imperceptible, but it was there.

Blood.

She shook her head fiercely, but the idea would not be dislodged. Surely it was impossible. She couldn't have done it without being aware of it.

But she hadn't been fully aware the first time she had offered herself to Damon, when she'd been too ill to know what she was doing. And there was that blank spot in her memory at the very pinnacle of the night's lovemaking.

Could sex with Damon have so completely erased her inhibitions, everything she believed in?

How many other things you once believed have you abandoned? she asked herself numbly. Would it be so incredible that her body, in a state of ecstasy and abandon, should seek what it needed…especially if the one who could fulfill that need was not only willing, but eager to give it?

She turned to look at Damon, struggling with the urge to shake him awake and demand an answer. His face was still peaceful, as innocent as any Daysider's could be. Almost content.

Was he content because he had finally gotten her to do exactly what he wanted without forcing her? Had he taken something else for himself in the process?

Probing her neck and shoulders with her fingertips, Alexia could find no tenderness that would indicate the presence of a bite. No, Damon hadn't bitten her. But that didn't mean *she*—

Alexia dropped her head into her hands. Maybe she was wrong. Maybe she wasn't really one of the forty percenters after all. Her illness had been temporary, and she would have recovered, anyway.

But she knew in her heart that wasn't true. Because of the "nice lady," who had saved her life so long ago.

Recognizing the danger of letting herself fall into her own dark thoughts, she pulled on her pack and considered what she had to do. She couldn't afford to forget that the shooters were probably still out there, even though they'd left her and Damon alone all night. But if the Daysider was right, the colonists would attack them only if they approached the settlement.

As long as she could walk and fire a gun, she would finish this mission, no matter how hard it was to accept what she had done to keep herself alive. What Damon had let happen.

And she could finally see Michael to his rest.

For a few moments she watched Damon intently. She could see he was sleeping lightly now, and that meant he would be able to smell or sense any enemy who intruded on the camp. She had to trust he would be safe. She untied Michael's VS130 from her pack and set it down at Damon's side along with the pistol he had given her the previous day.

Turning away with a heavy heart, she picked up the faint trail she had followed yesterday, working her way back to the place where Michael had died. The scrapes in the ground that marked the struggle were still there, and so were the spatters of blood, now crusted over and disintegrating into the soil.

But Michael's body was gone.

Alexia shrugged out of her pack, dropped it at her feet and rushed to the place where her partner had lain. There were more marks in the soil but no additional blood, no indications that someone—or some*thing*—might have dragged his body away. No sign that the Orlok, or others like it, had returned to finish off what it had killed.

She sank onto her haunches and ran her fingers through the dirt, blinking away the tears that had come without warning or purpose. Michael was dead. What happened to his body didn't matter, not to *him*. But the hideous image in Alexia's mind made her bend over with the dry heaves. She fought the nausea and got to her feet.

Damn Damon for not letting her bury Michael. Her partner would have been safe if he'd had the decency to allow a brave man a little dignity.

But anger wouldn't help her, or Michael. Maybe she could find something he had carried—some token to return to his kin in San Francisco. She knew he had an uncle, a cousin, people who would want something to remember him by.

And maybe there would be enough of him left to bury.

Clearing her mind of all distracting thoughts and emotions, Alexia searched for a trail. She found one among the dense thickets of scrub oak to the north. It smelled like Michael and traces of blood, and another stench that made her choke on her own breath—the same smell that had left its traces where Michael had died.

Orlok.

Alexia forged ahead, though her stomach cramped with horror. *Surely there must be some trace,* she thought. *That thing couldn't have—*

A glitter of metal caught the late-afternoon light, and Alexia moved under cover to search for the source. Nothing else moved, so she advanced slowly to the tree limb where the metal hung suspended from a cord or strip of something she couldn't quite make out.

It was leather. The metal was a buckle. Michael's buckle, the one he had bought on impulse at a street fair, back when he had seemed so lighthearted and carefree. The buckle had been cast in the shape of a grotesque parody of a Nightsider, more devil than leech, with a long, narrow face, slitted red crystal eyes, and protruding fangs.

Alexia pulled the belt from the branch and clenched the buckle in her fist. The edges bit into her palm. Dry-eyed, she tucked the belt into her pack and kept going.

She found bits of her partner's clothes as she went on, boots here, shirt there, the small pieces of gear he had carried close to his body. The stench of Orlok grew stronger, yet she saw nothing of the creature or Michael's remains.

Still she went on, tireless, grim with purpose. It was just past sunset before she began to sense that someone was following her.

She turned, carefully unslung her rifle and lifted it to her shoulder. But when her pursuer came into view, she nearly forgot the weapon was in her hands.

The thing was neither human nor Nightsider. It was lean and nearly hairless, bulging with muscle and tendon beneath pale skin, its face nearly as long as the creature on Michael's buckle. One of its long-nailed hands was pressed to its chest, the other curled into a fist at its side. It opened its mouth, and she glimpsed rows of serrated yellow teeth.

Then she met its eyes, and she saw something she recognized.

No. Alexia swallowed and backed away, the rifle pointed toward the ground. There were two kinds of dhampires: those who needed the patch and those who didn't. The ones who didn't could be converted by a vampire's bite. That was why Aegis always sent out teams consisting of both subtypes, so that one would survive in almost any situation.

Michael was of the second type. He hadn't been bitten by a Nightsider. An Orlok had attacked him, supposedly killed him. But he hadn't died, despite his terrible wounds. He had changed…into one of *them*.

Aegis had never been sure of the Orloks' nature or origins;

it was believed they were directly connected to Erebus and Nightsiders because they were, essentially, creatures of night that lived on blood—thus the name "Orlok," taken from the old tale of the grotesque vampire Nosferatu.

That was exactly what this creature—this man—appeared to be.

"Michael," she whispered.

The thing who had once been her partner swung its head from side to side, advancing on her slowly. She continued to retreat, unwilling to shoot even to wound.

But the Orlok didn't attack. It—*he*—stopped several meters away, still swaying, and opened its mouth. Sounds came out, sounds almost like words.

He was trying to talk.

Alexia's heart wedged in her throat. "Michael," she breathed. "Do you know who I am?"

His head bent ever so slightly. A nod. A moan of pain and sorrow. He moved closer, a purpose in his eyes she couldn't mistake.

"You don't want to hurt me, Michael," she said, speaking low and steadily as if she were quieting a cornered animal. "We were…*are* friends. We've risked our lives for each other." She lowered her rifle farther and held out one hand. "I want to help you."

The creature's mouth twisted in something like the old grin. He continued to advance, and Alexia braced herself. If it came down to killing or being killed, she knew which one she had to choose.

But Michael stopped again, just within reach, and lifted his fisted hand. He opened his long, distorted fingers and showed her what he held within them.

At first she didn't know what it was. The device was about the size of a large earpiece, but almost featureless. When Michael held it closer to her face, she recognized the tiny mic.

A communicator, but nothing like the one she carried, or like any she'd seen before.

Was it some new model Aegis had devised? And why had her partner been carrying it? Electronics seldom functioned well in the Zone, and she'd known nothing about it.

With a grunt, Michael seized her wrist with his free hand and dropped the device into her palm. His touch sent shudders of revulsion through her body, but she didn't break away, and after a moment Michael retreated. He gestured at the communicator, his mouth working.

Coming.

Alexia jerked. Michael hadn't spoken. The word had appeared inside her head. She stared at his contorted face, wondering if she were beginning to hallucinate.

Signal, the voice in her mind said. *Attack.*

Pressing the heel of her palm to her temple, Alexia tried to force the voice out through sheer strength of will. But Michael—what had been Michael—was still there, half civilized, half savage. And sinking quickly.

Warn, the voice said. *War.*

Warn whom, about what? What signal, and what attack? Was he asking her to send a signal to Aegis with this device? Was he telling her that war was coming?

There was no way to know, because all at once the voice went silent, and Michael shuddered again. It almost seemed to Alexia that his body was changing before her eyes, bending, writhing, slowly losing the last vestiges of humanity. She tried to approach him, but he backed away, shaking his head from side to side like a dog with a burr in its ear. Then, without warning, he loped off into the night-shrouded wood.

Alexia pushed the communicator inside her jacket and ran after him. She knew in her heart she couldn't save him, but she couldn't let him go down alone.

She was so intent on finding him that she nearly tripped over the man on the ground before she realized he was there.

Damon, she thought, wild with fear.

But it wasn't Damon, nor Michael. Her nostrils filled with the scent of Nightsider, and she stumbled back, pulling her rifle from her shoulder.

The Nightsider moved slightly, his pale, unbound hair fanned across the ground, his ascetic face drawn in pain. He didn't seem to be armed, and he was clearly injured; she knew Michael might have attacked him, but there were only a few tiny spots of blood on his clothing.

Then she recognized what was wrong with him. He had been in the sun. Blisters disfigured what would have been handsome features, and his once-dark eyes were milky with cataracts.

"Get up," she said, gesturing with the rifle.

The Nightsider's blind eyes turned toward her. "I am... not your enemy," he rasped.

Of course not. And he hadn't been roasted alive.

Alexia glanced past him in the direction Michael had gone. She could either continue to follow him or deal with the Nightsider. The vampire at her feet might easily have been among those who had shot at her and Damon, the one Michael had been tracking, or both. He was dangerous, even in his weakened state, and leaving him here could lead to serious consequences later.

"Where did you come from?" she demanded.

The Nightsider lay very still, well aware of what she would do if he tried to rise. "I am not what you think," he said, his voice a mere thread of sound. "I want what *you* want."

"Where are you from?" she repeated, lowering the rifle's muzzle to poke at his chest. "The colony? Are you one of the ones who have been trying to kill us?"

He blinked several times, as if even the emerging stars gave off too much light. "Where...is Damon?"

Alexia wouldn't have believed it possible that her heart

could beat any faster. "Why?" she asked sharply. "You aren't going to be able to hurt him now."

"The colony is not what we believed. I was to…report back, but I am dying. The others want to…" He took in a sharp breath. "They want to destroy it."

"Destroy the colony?" she asked. "*Who* wants to destroy it?"

"Our enemies, of course," someone said behind her.

Chapter 10

Alexia swung around, bringing the rifle to bear on the new arrival. He grinned, a flash of bright teeth in a pale, handsome face. His hair was drawn back in the traditional Nightsider style, framing his features like a crown of snow and starlight.

"Put down your weapon," he said. "I mean you no harm."

"Don't…trust him," the first vampire warned. "It is *their* doing. Tell Damon…the colony, the drugs—"

He cried out as the blast hit him square in the chest, leaving a smoking hole where his heart had been. The second Nightsider holstered his weapon and shook his head.

"Traitors to the Council must be eliminated," he said. He regarded Alexia with great interest. "Why are you alone, little Half-blood? The Zone is a dangerous place. Where *is* Damon?"

Alexia didn't answer. She had been stunned by the sudden killing, but her thoughts were clearing rapidly. And once she could think again, she was extremely grateful that Damon wasn't with her.

For whoever this leech was, he exuded a threat that utterly belied his words. It wasn't just that he'd murdered the other vampire so callously. Nightsiders often killed each other; they were vicious, amoral creatures, predators without compassion, constantly maneuvering for rank and power.

But now two Nightsiders had appeared in the area very soon after someone had tried to kill her and Damon. That couldn't be coincidence, and both of them obviously knew she and Damon were working together.

This vampire clearly meant to imply that he was with the Council, at least nominally on Damon's side of the fence. Damon had admitted there were probably other Council agents in the area; maybe one of the two Nightsiders, the living or the dead, was working for the same faction he was.

But it wasn't as if the leeches openly advertised their internal conflicts to their enemies.

And why would any Nightsider so blatantly slaughter one of his own kind right in front of an Aegis operative?

Alexia could think of only one good reason. And that was because he had to stop the "traitor" from telling her something he didn't want her to hear.

She had to be very, very careful. Careful to show suspicion and mistrust, but not enough to seem as if she wanted to kill him.

"Who are you?" she asked the Nightsider coldly. "Why did you kill this man?"

He clasped his hands behind his back as if he meant to show just how harmless he was. "As I told you, he was a traitor."

In spite of her resolve, Alexia's fingers twitched on the trigger. "'The colony is not what we believed,'" she recited. "'They want to destroy it.' What was he talking about?"

"You don't know?" he asked, eyes narrowing. "Have you not been observing the colony?"

"It has been a little difficult with someone trying to kill us," she said.

"Indeed?" the Nightsider said, lifting both brows as if he were genuinely surprised. "There are, unfortunately, many who would do anything to prevent cooperation between our peoples."

As hard as he tried to express sincerity, the Nightsider couldn't pull it off. She was dead certain he had already *known* someone had tried to kill them.

"We assumed it was the colonists who attacked us," Alexia said. "They must have known we were watching."

"They have protected themselves well enough so far," the vampire said. "But then again, certain parties in Erebus would wish to prevent anyone from providing the Council with intelligence that might create obstacles to their plans."

"What plans?" she asked, pretending ignorance. "Whose?"

The Nightsider glanced down at the body. "*He* meant to put you off your guard by confusing you, but there was much truth in his words. He merely twisted them around so that it seemed he was referring to others instead of himself."

He met Alexia's eyes again. "The colony is not, indeed, what any of us believed. This traitor *did* intend to report back to the Expansionists. We believed him to be one of our operatives, but in fact he was a double agent, as I recently discovered. I am certain he was hoping to persuade you to kill me when I caught up with him, and then eliminate you before returning to his true masters."

"So he worked for the Expansionists," Alexia said, continuing to play along, "and you work for the Council, like Damon."

"Didn't he tell you? The Council would hardly make the mistake of sending only one operative on such a crucial mission. And now that I know you have been attacked, the wisdom in that policy is apparent."

"What did this man mean when he said 'they' wanted

to destroy the colony? Why would the Expansionists turn against the settlement when extending the Citadel's reach into the Zone is exactly what they're after?"

The Nightsider sighed. "This traitor," he said, "was about to tell you that the colonists, whom his masters secretly hoped to control, were determined to keep their independence and refuse to cooperate with any party in Erebus."

His candidness caused Alexia an uncomfortable moment of doubt. Would he admit all this if he was with the faction most hostile to the Enclave?

He might if he planned to kill her after *he* made her think he was on her side. "Why would the colonists' lack of cooperation be enough for the Expansionists to want the settlement eliminated?" she asked.

"They will brook no possible threat to their ambitions," the Nightsider said. "They could create considerable trouble if they attacked the colony, and turn that trouble to their advantage. Of course, the Council would wish to prevent any action that might suggest bad faith in their dealings with Aegis."

All very tidy, Alexia thought. But this Nightsider had said that his victim hadn't yet made his report to the Expansionists. How could he, *or* the double agent, be so sure what the Expansionists intended to do *after* they received that report?

Because they already knew. The supposed "traitor" was going to tell the Council that an attack was coming.

Was that what Michael had been trying to tell her when he'd given her the strange communicator and spoken those few, ominous words?

Coming. Signal. Attack. Warn.

War.

Instinct told her to run on the chance she might actually escape and get the message to Damon. But she knew she had to keep the vampire talking in case he carelessly revealed the nature of the Expansionists' plans. And what the other vampire had meant about the "drugs."

"That makes sense," Alexia said belatedly, lowering the rifle. "But how did your double agent get caught in the sun?"

The Nightsider shrugged. "Once I learned what he was, I detained him. He escaped and was severely burned, but obviously not enough to prevent him from trying to provoke your sympathy and catch you off guard."

Alexia kicked at the dirt with the toe of her boot. "Considering that Damon and I have been attacked several times by Nightsiders, why are you so sure I would have believed *he* was on our side?"

"Because both you and Damon have strong prejudices that would make you inclined to believe exactly what this one told you. The Expansionists want war, and they despise Daysiders more than any other faction in Erebus."

"And that's enough to make Damon discard his training and all common sense?"

"Perhaps you have observed that he is of a passionate nature, not unlike humans or your kind. He also has an inordinate amount of pride."

"Like Opiri?" she asked.

The vampire ignored her mockery. "He is even more driven by irrational impulses than most of those you call Daysiders. That is the very reason he was sent to work with you. But it also makes him, shall we say, more apt to act according to emotion rather than intellect."

"And to believe a man who tells him what he wants to hear. But you still haven't told me what that is."

He hesitated very convincingly and sighed. "The colony," he said, "was founded by a Bloodmaster named Theron. Theron's *philosophy*—" he nearly spat the word "—encouraged the concept of full equality among all citizens of Erebus, from Bloodmaster to the lowest vassal. It seems he has put this idea into practice."

"And that's the *real* reason the Expansionists want the settlement destroyed."

"Perhaps," he said.

She wasn't going to push him. He'd given her a great deal more information than she'd expected to get already.

"That sounds like internal politics to me," she said. "Once I get back to the Enclave, I'll advise that we should continue to observe from a distance unless it becomes imperative that we interfere."

"You 'advise' your superiors?" he asked mockingly.

"My opinion, as well as my partner's, counts for something, yes," she said. "In fact, I was on my way to rendezvous with my partner when I stumbled over this man."

"I will gladly stand by to protect you until he arrives."

Sure you will, she thought. Now that it was down to the wire, she had very few choices about what to do next.

"I've been wondering," she said idly, as if she were reluctant to end a pleasant conversation, "how do you think the Council will stop the Expansionists?"

"I am not privy to their decisions. In any case, you and your partner need no longer be involved." He reached inside his sleek black jacket. "When I located Damon, I was to present him with his new assignment, which is to escort you back to the Border and return to Erebus for further instructions."

His new assignment? This guy said he'd just found out about the double agent and had been chasing him, but he'd had time to return to Erebus and get new orders for Damon before Damon had reported back himself?

She frowned slightly and met the vampire's gaze. "I think you'd better come back to camp and repeat all this to Damon," she said. "You wouldn't want him working in the dark."

The Nightsider grimaced at her weak joke. "Of course," he said, bowing like a courtier.

"It's that way," she said, pointing east.

He hung back with a knowing smile. "Please. A lady should always go first."

"I didn't know women had any special privileges in Erebus," she said.

"I merely defer to your human customs," the Nightsider said, pressing his hand to his heart as if he had wounded her. "We regarded males and females as equals long before your kind dreamed of giving your women the right to vote. Equals," he said, showing his teeth, "in their freedom to compete for rank and power."

"And you really think that we humans—"

She broke off, sensing Damon long before the Nightsider was aware of his approach. She didn't know why her senses were so much keener than a full vampire's, but she wasn't about to question her unexpected advantage.

Unfortunately, Damon made no attempt to sneak up on them. As soon as he walked out from between two bigleaf maples with her VS in hand and saw the Nightsider, he began to run toward Alexia. He stopped between her and the vampire, his anxious gaze raking up and down her body. He glanced at the dead Nightsider and turned to face the living one, head slightly bent and shoulders tensed to repel attack.

The Nightsider didn't move. "Damon," he said.

"Lysander." Damon's voice was so utterly cold that Alexia could almost feel ice crystals form in the air between him and the vampire. "What are you doing here?"

Lysander looked at Damon's ragged clothing, his bare chest under the dirty jacket and the shadow of a beard on his jaw with unconcealed contempt in his deep purple eyes. "The same thing you are," he said.

"I doubt that very much." Damon glanced again at the body. "Who is this Opir? What happened to him?"

"Lysander killed him," Alexia said.

Damon's jaw clenched, but he didn't seem surprised. "Why?"

Alexia spoke before Lysander could answer. "He said the

man was a traitor, a double agent working for both the Expansionists and Independents."

Damon's eyes narrowed. "But to *whom* was he a traitor?" he asked.

"The ruling faction, of course," Lysander said, glaring at the Vampire Slayer. "Put that abomination down, Damon. You know such weapons are forbidden in the Zone."

Damon set the VS on the ground, still within easy reach of both him and Alexia. "I never heard that you'd gone to work for the Council," he said.

Lysander shrugged, a consummately human gesture. "You do not hear everything," he said. "Or do you think you should be consulted in every matter that comes before the Council?"

"If it enables me to complete my mission, yes." He stared into Lysander's eyes. "You knew what I was sent to do?"

"Of course."

"How long have you been out?"

"I left Erebus soon after you did," the vampire said.

"Have you been in contact with the others?"

Shifting his weight ever so slightly, Lysander managed a sneer with a fractional twitch of his upper lip. "So many questions. I have not seen the others since I left with *him*—" Lysander gestured at the body "—and discovered he was working for the enemy. I was tracking him when this female—"

"Her *name* is Agent Fox," Damon said sharply.

"*She* was nearly taken in by the traitor's lies. I put an end to the conversation." Lysander raked Alexia with another disdainful glance. "I was told you had been shot at."

"You didn't know?" Damon asked, nearly growling.

"It was not in my purview to watch over you," Lysander retorted. "You should have been prepared to deal with any opposition." He smiled with some secret satisfaction. "Or have you become so incompetent since Eirene died?"

Eirene. Alexia flinched on Damon's behalf and watched tensely for his reaction. But Damon didn't move a muscle.

"You said you were with *him,*" Damon said, indicating the dead Nightsider. "Council agents work alone. Or are you an exception?"

"He was already under suspicion. I was to observe him until he made a mistake and revealed himself for what he was."

That wasn't what he'd said before, Alexia thought. "*He* wasn't suspicious?" she asked.

"He was not as clever as he believed himself to be," Lysander said.

Neither are you, Alexia thought. "Lysander was very surprised to hear about the attack on us," she said to Damon, emphasizing the adverb.

Some subtle change in his expression convinced her that he had picked up her hint. "He must have been very intent on his work to miss the noise," he said.

"Yes," Alexia said with a glance at Lysander. "We assumed the shooters were from the colony, but Lysander suggested they could have been Expansionist agents." She shook her head. "And *you* thought that wasn't possible."

"It makes little difference now," Lysander said with obvious impatience. "You will be pleased to know that neither of you will be at further risk."

Alexia felt the abrupt change in Damon as ice melted and nascent fire took its place. Anger was more than a description of an emotion to dhampires. She could taste it, smell it, sense it in a way indescribable to humans. Damon's hatred overwhelmed her senses.

"It would not have been a good thing if Ms. Fox had been killed," Damon said, his muscles so tense they were almost trembling.

"But she *is* alive," Lysander replied. "And now we can

move to prevent the Expansionists from destroying the colony."

She could see Damon's mind racing behind the unnatural stillness of his face. "Why would they do that?" he asked. "We know they secretly support it. Its establishment furthers their agenda, and they hate the Enclave. Destroying the colony would only please Aegis."

"Ask the little Half-blood," Lysander said.

Damon glanced at Alexia without letting his attention waver from Lysander's face.

"It *wouldn't* please Aegis," she said, wondering why Damon had even suggested it. "Any precipitous action in the Zone could be considered an act of hostility against the Enclave."

"Then perhaps they want to *start* a war," Damon said, bringing up the same possibility he and Alexia had so thoroughly discussed before.

"That isn't the motive Lysander suggested earlier," Alexia said, addressing Damon as she carefully watched Lysander's expression.

She told him about the vampire's claims that the colony had chosen not to cooperate with the Expansionists as they had expected…and that the colonists wanted equality for all Nightsiders, no matter what their rank.

Damon's eyes flashed with genuine surprise, but he didn't let the emotion cross his face. "How do the Expansionists plan to attack?" he asked.

"Their plans are no longer any concern of yours." Lysander's jaw flexed. "I have new orders for you. You are to escort Ms. Fox to the Border and return to Erebus."

"Indeed?" Damon said through his teeth. "When did you receive these orders?"

"You question *me?*" Lysander asked, his deceptively thin body drawing taut with offense.

"You're an operative and a Freeblood, not a Bloodmaster."

Lysander stewed silently for a moment and then seemed to relax. "I told you I had left Erebus soon after you did. The Council reconsidered its original orders and planned to recall you soon after you were gone."

"Why?" Damon asked.

"Your only duty now is to obey. You are to leave immediately."

"But *I* haven't received any new orders," Alexia said, moving up beside Damon. "I'm— We're not going anywhere until we can make a full report to Aegis."

She could see Lysander assessing her statement, comparing it with her earlier, more cooperative attitude. "That would be most ill-advised," he said. "The dangers of remaining are too great."

"I doubt that either Agent Fox or her partner will consider that sufficient reason to abandon their mission," Damon said.

"That is *your* problem." Lysander removed a folded sheet of paper from inside his jacket and offered it to Damon, careful not to touch his fingers.

Damon opened the sheet and read the brief sentences with a frown. Alexia could just make out some of the words of the Nightsider's script before he folded the paper again.

"Clear?" Lysander asked.

"Very clear." Damon tucked the orders inside his jacket. "You make an excellent messenger, Lysander."

The Nightsider smiled tightly. "See that the Half-bloods return safely to their territory. And you had better move quickly. You will need blood soon, and you would not want to rely on *them* for nourishment."

Damon took Alexia's arm in a firm, possessive grip. "Watch your tongue, Lysander," he said. "She is not a serf."

"I *take* it that you have an attachment to this Half-blood that is not only foolish, but forbidden," Lysander said. "I would have thought you'd learned your lesson." He smiled condescendingly at Alexia. "But she *is* a pretty thing. And spirited. Just like Eirene."

Damon's bone-deep trembling passed from his fingers into Alexia's arm, through flesh and muscle and nerve. Her body shivered in answer. Damon had disregarded Lysander's previous comment about his former lover, but Alexia knew Eirene was somehow at the heart of Damon's all-consuming hatred of the Nightsider. Had Lysander had something to do with Eirene's last mission and eventual death?

"Did you know, Agent Fox," Lysander said, turning to her with a vicious smile, "before the Armistice your breed were considered the finest prizes an Opir could obtain? I wonder how much a Bloodlord or Bloodmaster in Erebus would give to own you?"

Before Alexia could ask him what he meant, Damon had released her and thrown himself at Lysander. The Nightsider staggered back, too startled even to put up his hands.

Damon lost no time. Ignoring the knife at his belt and the VS130 at his feet, he slammed his fist into Lysander's face and pummeled him to the ground, hitting and kicking with a fury meant not to disable, but to kill. Alexia saw just enough of Damon's face to realize he was no longer in control of his reason.

In a matter of seconds, Damon had reverted back to the volatile creature he'd been before he had left on his mission with Michael. That time he had reacted to her lack of will to survive, but this wasn't the same. It wasn't *her* words that had ignited him. Now that simmering animal rage had become a weapon whose only purpose was to destroy.

"Damon!" she shouted.

He didn't hear her. He had Lysander on the ground and was locking his hand around the Nightsider's throat, his incisors exposed in a violent grin.

But Lysander had begun to fight back. He hurled Damon off and leaped after the Daysider before he could regain his footing. Lysander drove Damon down, his greater strength evident in the relative ease with which he held Damon pinned to the earth. The Daysider bucked and twisted, clawing and striking every part of Lysander's body he could reach. The Nightsider opened his mouth, stretching his jaws so wide that every tooth in his mouth was exposed.

Whatever reason Lysander had had for presenting Damon with the supposed "orders" from the Council, regardless of his original intentions, he was obviously ready to kill Damon without the slightest qualm.

Alexia lunged for the Vampire Slayer and brought it her shoulder. "Stop!" she shouted. "Get off him, or I'll kill you!"

The Nightsider barely glanced at her. "Remove all your weapons and throw them out of reach," he said, "or I will drain every drop of blood from the Darketan's body."

Chapter 11

With a wordless snarl, Damon worked one arm free and went for his knife. Lysander caught his wrist and bent it back at an unnatural angle. Something cracked under Damon's skin, but his mask of blind rage never faltered.

"Do it now!" Lysander shouted, sinking his teeth into Damon's neck.

Alexia almost shot him. Once she wouldn't have hesitated to sacrifice an enemy agent in order to eliminate a murderous leech. But Damon was no longer just an enemy agent, and the risk to him was too great. She threw the VS as far away as she could, took off her pack and kicked it away, and then removed her knife and pistol and did the same with them.

"Let him go," she ordered.

Lysander raised his head and laughed, his teeth stained with Damon's blood. "I never said I would let him go, only that I would not leave him a bloodless husk." He released Damon's wrist, grabbed his knife and ripped the sheath from Damon's belt. "You should run, little Half-blood, before I am tempted to sample the wares that make your kind so valuable to ours."

Damon howled and heaved under Lysander, gaining just enough space to jam his knee into the Nightsider's crotch. Lysander reared back and slashed his long fingernails across Damon's face, incising four deep gashes in Damon's cheek, jaw and chin. He bent and licked the welling blood from Damon's face. The Daysider's body began to jerk as if in a seizure, his eyes rolling back in his skull.

The odds had just gone from bad to worse, and Alexia was responsible. She moved closer to Lysander, spreading her hands as if begging a truce.

"The orders you gave Damon said that he was supposed to escort me back to the Border," she said. "Are you defying the Council you claim to serve?"

Lysander raised his head, Damon's blood glistening on his lips. "I have seen his strange affection for you, little Halfblood," he said. "I will merely be saving the Council the trouble of hunting him down after he turns traitor and defects."

"Defects?" Alexia laughed derisively. "He hates the Enclave as much as any of you."

"And he knew when he attacked me that I would kill him. Irrational impulses, remember?"

"If you kill him," Alexia said, "you'll have to kill me, too. And if you think Aegis won't investigate—"

"They will be too busy dealing with more important matters than the loss of one operative."

She took another step. "I don't think you work for the Council at all," she said. "I think *you're* the traitor."

Lysander curled his fingers around Damon's throat and dug his nails into the skin. The Daysider choked, and fresh blood soaked the collar of his shirt.

"Alexia," Damon said, his voice a bubbling whisper. "Run. Tell them—"

Alexia hurled herself at Lysander, less concerned about

doing damage than breaking up the lethal embrace. Without turning, Lysander batted at her as if she were an annoying insect and sent her flying. She rolled to her feet, sucking air into her lungs as she prepared to attack again.

But she'd broken the deadlock, and Damon was already moving. Blood spattered the ground and Lysander's face as Damon wrenched his arms up and broke the Nightsider's hold. Suddenly it was as if Damon had never been compromised at all, and Lysander was falling back, crouching with an incredulous expression on his face.

Then Damon was on him again, a whirlwind that could cut down everything in its path.

It was a ruthless, brutal fight, but the Nightsider was almost completely on the defensive now, quivering prey caught between the deadly claws of Damon's relentless predator. Each of Damon's blows was precisely aimed to do the most damage, and soon Lysander was scrambling away, intent only on survival.

Alexia knew they couldn't let him go. She ran to retrieve the VS and spun around to find Damon with his teeth sunk into Lysander's shoulder. The Nightsider screamed.

"Damon!" she shouted. "Get out of the way!"

He maintained his hold, biting harder, and Lysander began to flail like a madman, his eyes vivid with terror. Alexia knew Damon wasn't hearing her, wasn't feeling anything but the implacable need to kill.

And she had to stop him. She had no idea if Damon had ever killed anyone before, but this wasn't simply a matter of self-defense. This was the kind of bloodthirstiness Enclave soldiers and civilians had witnessed in rampaging vampires at the end of the War, when the leeches had finally realized they had lost their bid to enslave all humanity. Alexia knew in her heart that if Damon killed Lysander this way, like a beast—like an Orlok—he could never fully return to what he had been.

It was up to her to finish it. She was more than ready.

She advanced another meter, keeping the Vampire Slayer aimed at whatever part of Lysander she could see. "Damon," she said. "You've won. Let me take care of this."

Lysander rolled his eyes in her direction. "Stop," he gasped, blood foaming around his lips. "I will—"

Damon pulled back and struck the Nightsider across the face, and Alexia knew the only way she could stop him was to hurt him. She hesitated, holding the VS tight against her side, drew her knife and threw it directly at Damon's shoulder.

It bit through his bloodstained jacket into flesh, and Damon twisted to slap the knife away, his face streaked with blood like war paint. His eyes focused on Alexia, and she saw in him more than fury, more than hatred, more than the intensity of will that had driven him to keep her safe no matter what the cost.

It was the way Michael had looked at her the last time. The rage, the loss, the profound sorrow.

With a high-pitched scream, Lysander lunged up to clamp his teeth around Damon's neck. Damon felt behind him for the knife he had tossed aside, snatched it up and buried the blade in Lysander's back.

The two men broke apart, Lysander scraping his hand across his back in an effort to remove the knife, Damon shaking the blood from his throat and prepared to strike the final blow.

Alexia ran to the side, searching for a clear shot to Lysander's head or chest. Any other part of his body and the projectile might not kill him. But if she hit Damon instead—

Something moved on the edge of her vision, a tall, almost spindly shape that darted toward the combatants before she could alter her aim. It lifted Damon by his shoulder with one skeletal hand and tossed him a good three meters away. Then it grabbed Lysander and shook him as a terrier shakes a rat. Alexia heard the Nightsider's neck snap.

The Orlok met her gaze. *Safe,* it said in her mind.

She ran for Damon and dropped to her knees beside him. He was dazed and injured, but sanity was returning to his eyes, and when he looked at her it was with the bewilderment of a man who miraculously survived a fatal accident. His wounds, even the deep punctures and slashes in his neck and face, had stopped bleeding, and Alexia quickly returned her attention to the dead Nightsider and the creature that stood above him.

Michael.

The Orlok released its hold on Lysander's hair, red now rather than white, and started toward her. Damon scrambled into a crouch, moving stiffly as he put himself between her and the Orlok.

"It's all right," Alexia whispered. "He won't hurt us."

"He?" Damon asked, blinking the blood from his eyes.

She continued to hold Michael's gaze, so heavy with grief that she thought her heart would break.

Thank you, she thought, hoping Michael would hear her.

The Orlok inclined his head and began to shuffle backward, away from her and the Nightsider he had killed for her sake. And perhaps, even, for Damon's.

Don't go, she thought. *Let me help you.*

"Sires' blood," Damon swore hoarsely. "It *knows* you."

Michael's stare swung toward Damon. Alexia heard nothing, but suddenly Damon's face went blank with astonishment. He began to rise, but Michael melted away into the shrubbery, and Alexia knew he was gone.

Half stunned by the bizarre and violent turn of events, Alexia turned back to Damon, who was sinking down again.

"Hold still," she commanded. He obeyed, still staring after Michael, as she pulled his blood-saturated jacket away from his skin and helped him remove it, taking care not to jog his broken wrist any more than necessary. She knew he was completely back to normal by the way he winced, ever so slightly, at her gentle probing of his neck and shoulder wounds.

"What in the Human Hell just happened?" he asked hoarsely.

Alexia let out a long breath and closed her eyes. "What do you remember?" she asked.

"I was…fighting Lysander," he said.

Alexia almost laughed. She opened her eyes and found herself staring at Damon's neck. Even though the bleeding had stopped, the smell of blood—*his* blood—was ripe in the air, so strong she could taste it.

She swallowed and looked at Lysander's broken body. She could smell his blood, too, but it had no effect on her at all.

Damon's blood. God help her.

As if he had guessed the course of her thoughts, Damon raised a finger from his good hand to brush at the deepest wounds in his neck.

"Leave that alone," Alexia snapped, slapping his hand back down. "Let it heal." She swallowed again, trying to ignore the bitterness on her tongue. "What else do you remember?"

"Almost nothing, except he…threatened you," Damon said, spitting the last few words through his teeth. His skin began to flush with fresh anger. "Alexia—"

"Easy," Alexia said, lightly touching the uninjured part of his arm. "Do you remember how the fight started?"

"I…think *I* started it," he said. He covered his mouth with a bloody hand. "Something…went wrong. I should have forced him to tell us—" He broke off again and raised his head. "What *did* I do, Alexia?"

She didn't know how to answer the agony in his voice, the knowledge that he had to ask someone else what he'd done because his memory was a blank. He saw the blood on himself, on Lysander, and still he didn't realize how he had transformed, become something for which Alexia had no name or explanation.

"You kept him from trying to kill us," she said simply.

He glanced at her and quickly looked away, his torn face drawn with confusion and pain.

She needed him clearheaded after all this. *She* needed to be clearheaded, and it wasn't going to be easy. There were too many issues clamoring for her attention, including finding out where Damon's "spells" were coming from and what to do about them. If anything could or *should* be done about them.

"The Lamia," Damon said suddenly, catching her off guard. "Why did it kill Lysander, and not us? Have you seen it before?"

"No," she replied, lying before she could think about it.

"But it recognized you." Damon worked his body into a crouch that brought his face very close to hers. "How is that possible?"

Alexia knew she was going to have to tell Damon about what had happened to Michael and what he'd said to her, but not here. Not now.

"I don't know," she said, reaching down to help Damon to his feet. Still cradling his broken wrist close to his chest, he limped over to the double agent's body.

"Do you know him?" she asked.

"I may have seen him once in Erebus, but I do not recognize him as a Council operative." He turned his gaze to Lysander. "Few Darketans have ever attacked an Opir and lived, and none has ever killed one."

"But you *didn't* kill him," Alexia said, coming up behind him. "And anyway, this one deserved it."

His shoulders rose and fell in a heavy sigh. "I would have killed him if you hadn't interfered."

Alexia refused to take his words as a reproach. He couldn't be thinking straight yet.

She touched his bare shoulder lightly. "We should go now. We don't know who, or what, might be attracted to the smell of blood."

"Yes." He examined both bodies with a slight frown. "We will attempt to make it appear as though the Opiri were fighting each other," he said.

"They *were* fighting each other," Alexia said. "It was just pretty one-sided."

"Then we must hope that we do a convincing job of suggesting they were more evenly matched." He reached for Lysander's body with his good hand. Alexia got in his way.

"Maybe you should leave moving them to me," she said. "Your wrist is broken, and you've lost a lot of blood."

She was waiting for his response not only because she was worried about him pushing himself, but because she wanted to see if he'd react to her mention of losing blood. Lysander had suggested he would need nourishment soon, and that worried her greatly.

Damon hadn't reacted at the time, so maybe Lysander had been trying to scare her just for the hell of it, figuring she would be threatened by the idea of Damon taking her blood. And the Daysider hadn't made any attempt to actually drink any of Lysander's blood, which would have made perfect sense if he were in need.

"I'm fine," Damon said. "These wounds aren't as bad as they look." He smiled, a wry expression obviously meant to reassure her. "As long as I can avoid another fight within the next few hours, I will recover."

"Damon—"

He turned his back on her, and Alexia realized he wasn't going to accept her help, let alone admit that he needed rest and nourishment. While she gathered up her pack, the weapons and the scraps of red-dyed cloth shed in the battle, Damon arranged the bodies, wiped the handle of his knife on his pants and put the weapon in the first Nightsider's hand.

He stood up, scraping the back of his good hand across his face without taking notice of the still-raw gashes. "Anyone who comes is going to know an Orlok's been here, anyway," he said. He glanced sideways at Alexia. "That was unbelievable luck."

She didn't rise to the bait. "What about the clothes you're still wearing?" she asked, dropping the wad of bloodstained fabric at her feet. "They're saturated. If you think someone might find the bodies and come looking for us, you'll have to do something about them. You'll leave a trail even a human could find."

Immediately Damon went to work on his belt. Hard muscle bunched and flexed under the night-pale skin of Damon's arms, chest and ridged stomach as he stripped one-handed out of his trousers and underwear and bundled them into a loose ball, setting them on the ground beside the wad of bloodstained cloth Alexia had gathered. He bent to remove his boots, tied the shoelaces together—not an easy task with only one working arm—and placed his socks on top of the rest of his clothing.

"Do you have a lighter?" he asked.

Alexia bent to her pack and opened one of the many small interior pockets. She withdrew a pen-size lighter made to quick start a fire for cooking or any other use an operative might require in the field.

"Burn the clothes," he said.

"The smoke—" she began, trying not to look at his naked body in all its magnificent splendor.

"It isn't likely to make the situation more dangerous than it already is. Do you have any water left?"

"A little." She handed him her canteen, still averting her gaze, and crouched to set fire to the clothing. Damon had kept a relatively unstained strip of his pants, which he wetted down with the remaining water and used to wash the blood off his skin.

It was a hopeless task—there was too much blood and not nearly enough water. But when the fire was going and

Alexia glanced up again, Damon no longer looked like the walking dead.

She gripped the lighter tightly in her fist, doing her best to pretend Damon wasn't there at all. After everything that had happened since she'd woken up to find she'd taken his blood, when she'd been so angry with him and so disgusted with herself, she shouldn't have been capable of admiring the powerful symmetry of Damon's body, the way even his slightest move evoked the grace of a hunting beast in its natural environment.

He had been a beast, all right. She ought to remember that, and not be thinking of how much she wanted to touch that body, soothe his injuries, press up against him and feel his big hands on her—

"We'll have to get fresh water soon," Damon said, gazing in the direction of camp as if he were totally oblivious of her stare and the thoughts behind it.

"When we know we're not being hunted," Alexia said, watching the flames consume Damon's clothing.

He tossed the cleaning rag into the fire. Alexia rose, brushing dirt off the knees of her pants.

"Do you have a spare set of clothes?" she asked.

He picked up his boots and slung the tied laces over his shoulder. "In my pack back at camp," he said.

Busying herself with her own pack, Alexia clipped on her empty canteen and made sure everything was in place again. Then she kicked the ashes of the fire, mingled with blackened scraps of cloth, into the dirt and thoroughly covered both. The burned smell did a good job of obscuring Damon's scent, and hers.

If only disposing of all their other problems could be so easy. How this was all going to end—how she was going to settle things with Damon, and with herself—she didn't know. The only thing she could still be sure of was her duty to protect the Enclave, its people and all humanity.

And perhaps she could be certain of one other thing: Damon's commitment to her, which she could no longer deny. But just how deep was hers to him? When it really came down to it, how could she deal with his violently unpredictable shadow-side, and the knowledge that he refused to consider turning on his Opir masters in spite of his treatment at their hands?

If—when—they found themselves on opposite sides again…

"Are you ready?" Damon asked, glancing back at the bodies one last time.

"Wait a minute," Alexia said. She pulled her own spare shirt out of her pack and rigged it into a sling, gingerly slipping it over Damon's shoulder and easing his broken wrist into the cradle of cloth. "That should hold you until it heals." He looked at her hand lingering on his shoulder and then met her gaze. "Thank you," he murmured.

Hastily Alexia dropped her hand and stepped back. "Let's go," she said.

Damon fell in beside her, and they set off for the temporary hilltop camp, moving in a random zigzag pattern to throw off potential pursuit and listening to every rustle of leaf and patter of tiny feet as birds and animals fled their approach. Naked as he was, Damon seemed little more than a ghost, sometimes ahead of her, sometimes behind, his skin absorbing what moonlight reached them as they kept to any cover they could find.

The deceptive quiet made what they found halfway back to the camp an ugly shock. Damon stopped abruptly, head lifted, and gestured to Alexia. Within seconds she smelled what he had, and the two of them crept under the trees to the source of the stench.

The first corpse was a Daysider, his head nearly severed from his body, a pool of black blood soaking the earth underneath. Alexia guessed he'd been dead for at least six hours, probably longer. Damon crouched beside the body and touched the Daysider's shoulder, his jaw clenched hard.

Alexia knew it was too risky to speak, so she let Damon examine the body and then went with him to find the second one. It lay a good dozen meters away—a female Nightsider, dressed in vampire daygear. Her helmet was missing, leaving her beautiful face exposed. A rash of burns pocked her skin, but they were not as severe as those of the double agent. She had been killed before the sun could complete its work, and the large, scorched hole in the chest of her suit made clear how she had died.

Damon studied her for a few moments, nodded to Alexia, and set off again. Neither of them spoke; there was far too much to say, and they were still in a very vulnerable position. By the time they reached camp—which was untouched, and still apparently safe—Alexia had managed to sort a dozen questions into some semblance of order.

She wiped her dry mouth with the back of her hand and paced in a circle around the hilltop, VS at the ready, trying to steady her emotions and buy a little more time while Damon dropped his pack and began unfolding his spare set of clothes. He seemed as reluctant to begin the conversation as she was.

"Who were they?" she asked at last.

"Council operatives," he said, laying a neatly folded shirt, pants and socks on the top of his pack. His voice held no emotion, but Alexia had begun to learn how to read in it what might not be evident to anyone else.

He was angry, perhaps even grieved that his fellow agents had been slaughtered. It didn't take much guesswork to figure out who was responsible.

"I'm sorry," she said softly. "Lysander?"

"He wasn't the only one."

That wasn't a very comforting answer, but it didn't surprise her, either. God knew how many of them were running around the area now, setting up their little scheme to wipe out the colony.

Busy killing any and all opposition they could find.

"Did you know them?" she asked.

He gave short nod.

"Were they the other agents you mentioned when we met?"

"Yes."

"Do you think they were looking for enemy operatives when they were killed?"

"It is possible."

Alexia knew he wasn't going to say anything more about it, at least for the time being. And they were still in grave danger.

Alexia's grim reflections were cut short by Damon's next words. "You should never have left camp alone," he said.

The tension, uncertainty and violence of the past few hours had left Alexia with only the merest thread of control to hang on to, and now it snapped.

"Did you expect me to ask for your permission?" she demanded.

He stood up abruptly, his clean pants hanging from his good hand. "If you had been hurt—"

"Who *was* Lysander?" Alexia interrupted, taking the offensive. "What was between you two that made you hate each other so much?"

Damon jerked on the pants one leg after the other, testing the tough fabric to its limits. "Lysander is—" he reached down for his shirt and shook it out "—was," he corrected himself, "a midrank Freeblood with ambition. And a traitor to the Council."

A Freeblood…one of the four basic ranks in Nightsider society, and the second lowest. Freebloods were no longer vassal to any Bloodmaster or Bloodlord, but they had yet to establish households with serfs of their own, and so competition among them was particularly fierce.

"You didn't know he was a traitor when you first found

us, did you?" she asked. "You obviously wanted to kill him the moment you laid eyes on him, and he felt the same, whatever he was trying to achieve by lying to us."

Damon crumpled the shirt in his good hand. "He would have behaved the same with any Darketan."

"Maybe. But before you showed up, Lysander tried to convince me that he killed the other Nightsider because *you* had a personal grudge against the Expansionists that would make you believe what his victim said about not trusting him. But Lysander must have known all along that you'd never believe anything *he* said." She lowered her voice. "He mentioned Eirene. What happened, Damon? How was he involved?"

Fabric hissed as it tore in Damon's fists. He stared down at the damage he had done to his spare shirt—and undoubtedly to his wrist, which he had pulled out of its sling—before letting the garment fall to the ground.

Alexia tried again.

"Lysander said you were more driven by 'irrational impulses' than others of your kind. That that was why you were sent to work with me. What made him say that, Damon? What does it have to do with what you and I discussed before, about Darketans and feelings?"

His flat expression told her he wasn't going to let her break him down. "We have far more important matters to discuss," he said, "if we want to stay alive."

He was right. She couldn't waste time and energy trying to drag the truth out of him now, especially since there was one particular thing she had needed to know ever since she'd left camp late that morning. A question only Damon could answer.

Which was why *she* was alive at all.

Chapter 12

"Very well," Alexia said, hardening her voice, "let's talk about what happened yesterday."

Damon pushed his good right arm through the sleeve of his shirt and took a deep breath. "It was necessary, Alexia," he said.

So he wasn't going to pretend he didn't understand her line of questioning. That was something, anyway.

"Necessary to use sex as a way to make me bite you?" she asked, carefully controlling her voice so as not to reveal how much even the thought of his lovemaking aroused her even now.

"It wasn't like that," he said, easing his other sleeve over his injured arm with exquisite care. "I didn't have it planned."

"Didn't you?" Alexia slung the strap of the VS back over her shoulder and turned her back on him, walking to the nearest tree. She rested both palms on the trunk, inhaling and exhaling slowly the way she had been taught in the earliest years of her training. "You said, before we…you said you wouldn't take my choice from me. You lied."

"And you broke *your* promise," he retorted with some heat. "You tried to back out of it by asking me to remember your exact words. I believe they were 'hang on as long as necessary.'"

At least he didn't seem to remember what she had told him when he had been under his "spell," demanding so ferociously that she stay alive. "That's right," she said. "As long as necessary. But once Michael was dead—"

"It was even *more* necessary," Damon said, "because you were the sole survivor of your team and the only one capable of completing your mission."

The anger went out of his voice. "I didn't even know it would work, Alexia. I could only hope."

"You've used that word before," she said. "I never thought you really believed what it meant."

"Have *you* abandoned it, Alexia?" he said, his voice thick with emotion that only confused her more. "Would you rather have died?"

As much as she wanted to say yes, she knew it wasn't true. Maybe seeing Damon fight Lysander to the death had made her cherish life more than the principles she had thought were unbreakable. Maybe she valued her own existence more because she valued Damon's.

No, she couldn't lie to him. But she couldn't dismiss her anger, her sense of betrayal, so easily.

"Do you expect me to thank you?" she asked.

"Do you think you had no part in it?" he asked, the edge returning to his voice. "Whether you admit it or not, even you are a creature of instinct, driven to survive."

He was right. He could not have forced her teeth into his flesh. But she *couldn't* admit it, because that meant she was no better than a Nightsider. No better than the monster Michael had become, or the thing inside Damon that would gladly have slaughtered Lysander with nothing more than his teeth.

Damon's footsteps, barely audible, whispered across the ground behind her. "You were born as you are, Alexia," he said. "It does no good to fight your nature."

Or his. Even if she could despise herself, her weakness, she couldn't despise him. The fact was that something had happened to her when she and Damon had made love—not just a matter of bodies coming together in sex, or even the ecstatic joy that had taken her at the end. Their lovemaking had hurled her into territories uncharted and far more dangerous than their tentative friendship.

Even the matter of taking his blood couldn't diminish what she had felt then, what she was feeling now. He was so close now, and she could draw every familiar line of his body in her mind: broad shoulders tapering to taut stomach and trim waist; long, muscular legs; and the part of him she so badly wanted to feel inside her again.

She closed her eyes and turned her face up to listen to the rustle of the leaves in the midnight breeze, forgetting everything but the vivid memory of Damon's passion.

Once that passion had been for Eirene. Perhaps he had been thinking of his former lover when he kissed Alexia, when he entered her and possessed her and accepted her bite.

She couldn't believe it. Even if he wasn't capable of regarding any other woman the way he had Eirene—even if what he and Alexia had shared was only a matter of the "attachment" Lysander had spoken of so mockingly—he cared. Genuinely and truly. And *she* could no longer put off acknowledging the overwhelming truth.

She laughed. No, she couldn't hate Damon. Or even herself. Not as long as she was with him.

"I am what I am," she said, turning to look at him. "I know I can't change that. But I can still live in service to something bigger than myself, and die honorably."

A sudden gust of wind lifted the unbuttoned placket of Damon's shirt, blowing the edges away from his chest. "Honor is a human concept," he said softly.

Alexia tried not to let herself become distracted by the sight of his partially naked body. "Is that why you have so much trouble keeping your promises?" she asked. As soon as the words were out of her mouth, she regretted them. "I—"

Damon looked away. "Why did you leave camp?" he asked again, as if their previous discussion had never happened.

"I went back to take care of Michael's body," she said, and then hesitated. Surely she could wait just a little longer to tell Damon about Michael, even though the mystery of his transformation, his behavior and his words remained unsolved. "It was gone when I got there."

"I'm sorry," Damon said. His voice turned gruff. "I should have seen to it earlier. It was still foolish for you to go out alone."

"I felt fine. And if I hadn't, I never would have had the chance to talk to the first Nightsider before Lysander killed him. I wouldn't have been so much on my guard when Lysander gave me the line about stopping a traitor from deceiving me and getting me on his side."

"And since Lysander was almost certainly lying or twisting the facts most of the time, everything the first Opir told you must have been the truth. What exactly did he say?"

She repeated what the man had told her. Damon hissed sharply through his teeth.

"Drugs," he said. "The patch. He knew about it."

"Yes," she said, "but I don't think *he* took it. I think he knew who did, and tried to tell me he knew where it was. He spoke of the colony in the same breath."

"Interesting," Damon murmured.

"Isn't it? Lysander heard the first Nightsider mention the drugs before he killed the poor bastard, but he himself never once referred to them. I think he was trying to avoid the subject, because *he* had something to do with stealing the patch. I know he thought I was too stupid to notice."

Damon smiled, displaying the tips of his incisors. "Arrogance. It's a common failing among the Opiri. I wonder if he knew the nature and effects of the drugs and expected you to be weak and helpless without them."

"Maybe," she said, "but Lysander made a couple of other mistakes. He said the Expansionists want to destroy the colony because they expected the colonists to support their policies, and that wasn't happening. But he also clearly implied that the Expansionists already had the plans in place, even though the man he killed hadn't yet reported back to his masters."

"Lysander already knew what they were going to do," Damon said, echoing Alexia's earlier conclusion. "In the past, he appeared to support the Sophist Faction, but his behavior was never in keeping with their desire for peace. He aspired to become a Bloodlord with his own harem, but he knew there are already too many in Erebus. He could never advance himself until Opir territory expands."

Alexia nodded. "And so it would make perfect sense that he'd support the faction that would risk war to grab more turf."

Damon crouched by the pack again and withdrew a pair of sturdy socks. "Maybe Lysander *was* originally sent out by the Council, but they don't know he's betrayed them."

"Whatever they know or don't know, I'm sure Lysander was involved with whoever was shooting at us before, even if he wasn't one of the snipers himself. His surprise was just too off to be believable. And then there was that bit about not seeing Michael. That might be possible, but I think it's far more likely that either he or the dead guy was the one Michael was following."

Damon's face settled into grim lines as he used his good

hand to pull on his socks. "Either he was unaware that your partner was dead, or he was lying about that, as well."

At least I know he couldn't have killed Michael, Alexia thought with a rush of sadness.

"We still don't know if all the shooters were the same," Damon said, "or if they had different motives. There are plenty of those to go around."

"Michael raised a good point about the colony probably not having the tech to do anything with the patch," she said. "Unless, as he also suggested, they were trying to buy freedom from Erebus by selling it to them."

Damon untied the laces of his boots. "You said the colony wanted equality for all Opiri, regardless of rank."

"That's what Lysander told me."

"Did he say who established the colony?"

"Someone named Theron, I think."

Either it was her imagination, or Damon suddenly went unnaturally still all at once, like a vid caught between one image and the next.

"You know the name?" she asked.

He continued with his boots as if nothing had happened. "It is familiar," he said. "But such a philosophy, if viable, would be anathema to all of Erebus, including the Council."

Alexia searched his face. Was he admitting that the Council would be just as hostile to the colony as the Expansionists? Maybe enough to want it destroyed, too?

"We still can't be sure how much of what Lysander said about the settlement or the Expansionists' plans were lies," she said.

Damon put on his boots, unfastened one of the outer pockets of his pack and withdrew a spare knife, smaller than the other but every bit as nasty-looking. "The first Opir's warnings seem to confirm at least some of it was the truth. There must be a great deal more Lysander didn't tell us."

"And none of this explains why none of the shooters killed us."

"Indeed."

Alexia went to join Damon, aware in every nerve of the heat of his body, the smell of his skin, the planes and angles of his face. As crazy as it was under these very dangerous circumstances, in spite of the matter of the blood, she wanted him again.

From the way Damon's muscled clenched up, Alexia had an idea he was thinking the same thing she was. She could almost feel his desire, like static electricity raising all the hair on the back of her arm. His nostrils flared and the corner of his mouth twitched.

But he resisted his body's demands. Even without moving, he seemed to lean away from her, putting more space between them.

It hurt. But Alexia was glad. Whatever Lysander had said, they could still both control their "irrational impulses."

"We know Lysander was lying about your new 'orders,'" she said, "unless you think the Council would really change your mission right after you left."

"Unlikely," he said, staring into the darkness clotted among the branches of the old oak.

"Then why would Lysander pretend that the Council wanted you to escort me back to the Border when he knew I'd report my suspicions to Aegis?"

Damon balanced the knife's blade on one extended finger. "The orders Lysander gave me are not what he told you," he said. "They instruct me to take you and Michael back to Erebus, where we would be met secretly by Council Security. They claim this is to protect you from the Expansionists, but I believe members of the Expansionists would be the ones to meet us, and probably before we ever reach the Citadel. They wouldn't risk taking us too close to Erebus."

"So they just want us to walk into a trap so they can kill

us? What would be the purpose, considering how many times they've had a chance to do it already?"

"I don't know." He stabbed the knife's tip into the dirt between his feet with enough force to bend the blade. "I think they'd keep you alive, if possible. You have too much potential value to them."

"Why? Why me in particular?"

He shoulders hunched as if to ward off her question. "It would be too much a risk to take you for such a reason."

"What *is* the reason, Damon?"

Damon turned the blade from side to side, catching the moonlight so that the metal seemed to burn with cold fire. "As you once noted, the offspring of Opir and human are forbidden in Erebus. There are no dhampires there. But sometime during the War, an Opir was said to have discovered that dhampir blood acts as a stimulant and aphrodisiac on the Opir system."

Alexia lost her balance, dropping from a crouch to her knees. "You mean like the drug that keeps my kind alive?"

"This one is purely recreational." His teeth flashed in a humorless smile, bright as the blade. "To many, it is only a myth. You probably know better than I how many dhampires have disappeared in the Zone since the Armistice. Some Bloodmasters may have obtained dhampir serfs born before the end of the War, but they would be rare. As you can imagine, the demand is quite high."

"And Aegis…" She felt bile climb into her throat. "They can't possibly know this."

"As I said, it may be only myth."

That was scant comfort, Alexia thought ruefully.

"Would it work the same on you?" she asked.

"No. I am not full Opir."

The statement was so final that Alexia decided he was telling the truth.

"And in spite of all this," she said, struggling to find a little humor, "you don't think the Expansionists would try to sell me for some fabulous sum?"

"They know Aegis would investigate your and Michael's complete disappearance."

"But the enemy would expect that no matter what happened," Alexia said, shivering in spite of herself. "They've got my patch. Maybe they can use me for some kind of experiment."

Damon frowned and looked into her eyes. "Such speculation is pointless. We still can't be sure who stole it, the colony or the Expansionists. Even if we knew the Expansionists had it, we're not going anywhere near Erebus. I won't risk it until we have more concrete information."

"Then I guess we'd better start looking for answers closer to home."

"Some answers aren't worth the price." He reached over and laid his hand on her arm, so lightly that she barely felt it. "Lysander did say one thing of value. You shouldn't be further involved, Alexia. Your partner is dead, and you've suffered a grievous injury. Aegis would not expect you to continue this mission under the circumstances, and—"

"You just said since I was the sole survivor of my team, I had to finish the mission myself."

She'd caught him, and he knew it. But that wasn't enough to make him give up. "I was wrong," he said.

"Forget it."

He tightened his grip. "Michael would have reported the theft of the patch, but now that task is yours. Our new information makes it even more essential that Aegis be informed of the Expansionists' plans so that there will be no misunderstanding if and when the colony is attacked. They *must* know that the Council is not involved."

"You said yourself that you aren't privy to the Council's deliberations. Given what you've said about how Erebus would feel about the colonists' philosophy, what if they aren't controlling the Expansionists because they want them to do the Council's dirty work?"

"They are not involved," he repeated.

"Isn't that just what you want to believe, Damon? Because if the Council is just as bad as the Expansionists, you have no reason to serve any of them?"

He got up and moved away from her, a few uneven strides in one direction and then back again. "You're wrong. We agree that any overt move on the colony could be interpreted to be an act of war. The Independents' entire purpose is to maintain the status quo."

"Do you really believe Aegis would send soldiers into the Zone because Erebus eliminated its own illegal colony?" she asked, rising to follow him. "That would make war a certainty."

"How can you agree that this is a highly volatile situation for both sides if you don't believe Aegis would take action in that case? Why would they have sent you to investigate at all?"

He was right, of course. It was all imprudent talk on her part, an effort to make herself feel less helpless.

"Then explain to me why you told Lysander that Aegis might be pleased if the colony were destroyed?" she asked. "Why would you even suggest that to him?"

"I *don't* believe it, Alexia. I was attempting to throw him off his stride in any way possible, and see what might result." He held her gaze intently. "We once discussed the fact that the Enclave is just as responsible for the serfs in Erebus as the Opiri. The reason I am convinced that your government *would* act in the case of violence against the colonists is for that very reason. The Treaty specifies that no humans may be killed in Citadel territory."

He was silent for some time before he spoke again. "There must be much hostility and resistance to the custom of sending condemned criminals to Erebus, and guilt is a very powerful human emotion," he said. "Would your government dare remain indifferent to a few dozen human deaths, even if the dead were merely cast-off criminals?"

Pulling back a clenched fist, Alexia swung at Damon's face. He caught her hand with his own good one and held her still, breathing as hard as if they had just finished a knock-down, drag-out fight.

"What is it?" he taunted, leaning toward her. "Is the hypocrisy of your own people too difficult to bear?"

Alexia squeezed her eyes shut. *Oh, Garret.* "You son of a bitch," she hissed, hating him even as the feel of his skin on hers sent a spike of desire through her body.

He tightened his fingers around her fist. "What were your orders coming into the Zone, Alexia? Were you only to observe? Or were you perhaps sent to find a way to get the humans out of the colony before Erebus's factions tore it apart?"

"Where in hell did you get that idea?" she spat, struggling to free herself.

"It would be a way for your government to avoid open warfare and still retain the goodwill of those citizens who reject their method of holding the Opiri at bay with condemned prisoners," he said, keeping his iron grip on her wrist. "If they made the case that the Council could not keep the Treaty by protecting its serfs from destruction, they could avoid hostilities completely."

"That's insane. You're assuming Aegis already knew what was going on here!"

"You never denied they might have sent another agent ahead of you and Michael."

"I never *said*—"

A muscle flexed in his cheek. "And the Council's first agent investigating the colony *was* killed by an Enclave weapon."

"I don't know anything about that!" Her chest grew tight as it occurred to her just how much she might not have known.

"I was never told about any previous mission to investigate the settlement."

"Then consider that Aegis might already have been well-informed about the situation in the Zone and has already planned its response. You would want Aegis to save the colony's serfs, would you not?"

"You don't know a damned thing about it!"

Abruptly he let her go. "I, too, have my secrets, Alexia." He sighed and backed away. "The current situation makes it impossible to keep them any longer."

Alexia rubbed at her cramped fingers, her stomach rolling over and over like a trained circus dog. "What?" she said.

"You should know the real reason why I was sent to meet you and your partner."

"You didn't come to help us observe the colony?" she asked, anger fading to a formless sense of dread.

"No. I was sent to prevent you from getting near it."

Chapter 13

All the nerves in Alexia's body seemed to jump at once, lifting her like an express elevator and then sending her plummeting all the way to the bottom of the shaft.

"Then I was right after all," she whispered. "The Council *is* involved in this, up to its eyeballs."

"No, Alexia. My orders were to keep you away until the Council could complete its own investigation of the colony, without Enclave involvement, so that they might resolve the situation internally. I knew no more until we met Lysander."

"You didn't know about any double agents running loose?"

"Until I spoke to Lysander, I wasn't aware that the Council had employed such an agent."

"But you weren't even aware there *were* enemies out here. You denied the possibility." She took several deep breaths to calm herself. "You suggested that Aegis might be working with the Council. Was that to trick me into admitting something you might find useful?"

"I said it was possible, not that I knew it to be a fact."

"What other little white lies have you been telling me, Damon?"

He hesitated, and then met her gaze. "Those other hypothetical Council operatives I told you about when we met," he said, "were sent to fire on us so that we would remain together."

Now that the first shock was past, Alexia found that she felt very little, not even anger.

"Those people out there?" she said numbly, the faces of the slain Council agents still vivid in her mind.

"I don't know. I was not told their names. But it seems…" He trailed off, bowing his head.

"Whoever did it," Alexia said, "it worked." Oh, how well it had worked. She swallowed, searching for words that could find their way through the vise clamping her throat. "I take it they weren't supposed to actually kill us?"

Damon crouched to pick up the knife, testing the fingers connected to his broken wrist. "I considered the possibility that the first shooter we encountered might be one of them. Then, when we were attacked again, I initially thought it could be the same agent or agents. Until they nearly killed us and removed your patch. That was not in the plan."

"I guess something went a little wrong."

He continued to gaze at the knife, carefully brushing dirt off the blade with the pad of his fingertip. "Yes," he said. "Very wrong."

She knew then that he had no idea his confession had revealed much more to her than the mere facts of his orders. Oh, it must have been inconvenient for Damon when Michael had "refused" to join him and Alexia on their trek to the colony.

Had Damon been amused when he'd "saved her life" from the first shooter, whom he'd presumed to be one of his own? And what about the second attack? If he'd thought, even for a moment, that the ones who had tried to kill him and Alexia might be on his side, why hadn't he warned her then?

"We are partners, Agent Fox," he had said. *"That makes us equals, does it not?"*

How could they be? He had kept too much from her, vital information that could have helped her make the right decisions, might even have saved Michael somehow. She had believed Damon when she should have been most suspicious.

"Either the Colonists or the Expansionists attacked us to get the patch," Damon continued, oblivious to her inner turmoil. "As you said, I made an unforgivable mistake in assuming that the Expansionists would not have their own covert agents and risk firefights between Opiri in the Zone. I fear they have already done incalculable damage."

He feared, did he? Were *any* of his emotions real? Had all the feelings Damon had expressed for her since the theft of her patch, the intensity and sincerity of his lovemaking, been lies, as well?

"Yet you still have such utter faith that the Council didn't decide it was more convenient to deter me and Michael by eliminating us outright…and blame it on somebody else?"

"You must trust me, Alexia—"

She laughed. *"Trust* you?"

"Why would they send me if their purpose was to kill you and Michael?"

"Why did the Council send only one agent to stay with us? How could they *not* know that Expansionists agents weren't loose in the Zone?" She shot him a withering look. "None of this says much for your Council's ability to gather intelligence and deal with unexpected contingencies. Or for yours."

He glanced up at her, all earnestness and remorse. "What do you want me to say that has not already been said?" he asked. "That we are dispensable pawns in a game we cannot understand?"

"Aren't we, Damon? Haven't we always known that, you and I?"

"Yes," he said heavily. "We are pawns, Alexia, one way

or another. But I still have my duty, as you do. I must do it as best I can."

"And so must I."

"You will not return to the Enclave?"

The very fact that he had to ask that question again was testament to how little he knew her.

"You'd like to get rid of me, wouldn't you? Maybe you didn't kill Michael, but you're glad he was cooperative enough to die."

He jumped to his feet, the knife clenched in his fist. "So my honesty has led you to decide that I really would have harmed you or your partner to keep you away from the colony?"

She glared at him. "Wouldn't you?"

"Have you forgotten that I know as well as the Expansionists do that Aegis would investigate your disappearance?"

"And that's always been your motive, hasn't it?"

"No," he said in a very low voice. "I once said I would never harm you, and I swear by the Blood of the Sires that is still true."

"Oaths. Promises." Alexia turned away, feeling as though her bones had melted and her body was filled with air, ready to collapse like a balloon pricked by a pin. "They mean nothing."

"You no longer believe...I care for you?"

"What do *you* think, Damon?"

For an endless span of time all she could hear was his breathing, harsh and heavy. "I'm sorry, Alexia."

Sorry. What idiot had thought up such an inadequate word? "Maybe it is time we parted ways. I'll continue with my mission, and you can do whatever it is you think you need to." She released a sharp, angry breath. "I guess that would be reporting what you've learned back to Erebus, since you won't have me to worry about. That is, of course, unless you intend to stop me. Just be aware that I'll try to kill you if you do."

"Alexia."

She wanted to hold her hands over her ears and babble like a child. "There's nothing more to say."

"There is. We have no idea how long the effects of my blood will continue to sustain your body. If you go it alone, you may find it suddenly betraying you."

Alexia swung around to face him, eyes wide. "Are you actually suggesting we should do it again?" She nearly choked when she realized what she had just said. "Take your blood, I mean?"

The ghost of a smile crossed his shadowed face. "Surely you had already considered that possibility, Agent Fox," he said.

Oh, yes. It had crossed her mind, and she'd quickly erased it again.

"Maybe the one time was enough," she said quickly. "Maybe I'll find the patch."

"Alone?"

He was right, of course. The odds were incalculably against it. She didn't know her way around this part of the Zone, and they were probably surrounded by enemy agents.

"There is no telling how long your current condition will last," Damon said, pushing his advantage. "Are you as prepared to die as you were before?"

He was taunting her now. Somehow he knew that her life had become important to her again, something to be guarded and cherished.

"I'm prepared to take my chances," she said, pulling her arms tight across her chest.

"Even though your mission may die along with you?"

As useless as it was, she longed to hit him again, smash his handsome nose and bloody his lip. But then she saw the healing gashes on his face, the wrist he still moved so gingerly, and was deeply ashamed.

"What do you want?" she asked, turning her back on him.

"I propose a truce."

"Like the one you offered when we met?"

He cleared his throat. "I will not lie to you again."

"Never?"

His silence told her all she needed to know. She went to gather her things.

"Never, Alexia," he said quietly.

She stopped. This was the moment of decision. She knew she should never trust him again, that just being with him would create an open wound that could never heal.

That was *her* problem. But what about his? What about his shadow-self? It was still a complete mystery to her. She had no idea how long it had been part of him, if his masters knew about it, when it would arise again. He didn't seem to remember his spells, but she had seen the pain and confusion in his eyes after they were over.

Could she find some way to help him if she stayed with him? Or would she only make it worse? How could she possibly know?

Only by refusing to leave him. Accepting that he lied to her over and over again.

Lowering her arms, she felt the bulge of something under her jacket and remembered what she had hidden there.

What about your *lies?* she asked herself. The communicator seemed to burn like a hot coal inside her jacket, though it gave off no warmth at all. She still didn't know why Michael hadn't told her about it before he'd left. Why had Aegis entrusted it to him, and not her?

Signal, he'd said. Was he saying he'd received a signal, or had sent one? Did he want her to complete some task his transformation had made impossible? Had *he* been part of a plan to remove all the humans in the colony? Was Damon's theory really so crazy after all?

If it was true, then she had been much more a pawn than she ever could have imagined. But she didn't dare take the

time to try to track Michael down and see if she could communicate with him again…if he was even willing to be found.

I'm sorry, Michael, she thought. *So very sorry.*

But she wasn't sorry about keeping this secret from Damon
until she felt she could trust him again. If that was even possible.

"What did you have in mind as the next move?" she asked.

If Damon was relieved by her reasonable tone, he didn't
let on. He bent to retrieve the sheath of his knife, flexing his
wrist in a way that suggested it had nearly healed, and slid
the blade in.

"The center of everything is the colony," he said, his voice
turning brisk and businesslike. "We could hunt for other Expansionist agents and attempt to learn more from them, but
there is no guarantee we would find them, or be able to defeat them if we did. We cannot go to Erebus. If we are to
obtain useful information, we must approach the settlement
directly."

"You're suggesting making a move without instructions
from your Council," she said. "Up until now, everything
you've done could conceivably be justified as being within
the parameters of your assignment, even telling me what you
were really sent to do. But what you're proposing isn't anywhere in those orders, is it?"

She meant the question to mock him, hurt him…if he
could be hurt by something as small as her words. But when
he spoke, his voice was unmistakably humble.

"No," he said. "It isn't. Nor, as you have said, is it in yours.
Perhaps it is time these pawns became knights."

Slowly she turned to face him, caught unaware by a foolish and very dangerous undercurrent of pride. And yearning.

More than mere yearning. It was the need to be with him
again, in every way. To feel him on her, inside her, just as if
nothing had changed.

But if she gave in again, if she let herself be driven by

passion, she would almost certainly pay a price she could never afford.

"There's still a good chance that at least one set of gunmen was from the colony," she said, her voice not quite steady. "Even if they didn't steal the patch, they may still be shooting at anything that moves."

"That is the risk, of course," Damon said, studying her intently as if he had heard her highly inappropriate thoughts. "But I believe there is a way to obtain entrance to the colony without dying to achieve it."

Alexia braced herself. "What is it?" she asked.

"I know the man who founded it."

Damon experienced Alexia's shock as if they were attached by thousands of tiny cables that conveyed every emotion directly into every nerve in his body. He had felt that shock time after time in the past few hours: Alexia's grief, her suspicion, her hurt and sense of betrayal. Each one had destroyed a piece of his heart…the treacherous heart that could reduce a rational being to extremes of violence and tenderness all in the course of a moment.

He gazed at Alexia's calm face, amazed all over again at her resilience. He had asked—demanded—so much of her, and not once had she broken. She was capable of setting aside her intense feelings when indulging them became an obstacle to her mission; she could speak with complete poise and rationality even after he had repeatedly provoked and betrayed her.

In many ways she was so much stronger than he was. She could leave him without a second glance if it was necessary. But he…

Damon remembered the horror that had curdled in his belly when he'd seen Alexia with Lysander and realized his old enemy was loose in the Zone, claiming to be working for the Council. He remembered realizing that Lysander was trying to deceive both him and Alexia, an attempt ruined by the Opir's mocking words about Eirene, and Alexia's worth as a dhampir in Erebus.

What he didn't remember was what had happened afterward. He had attacked Lysander, and they had tried to kill each other. But the details were like a hole in his mind filled only with blood, rage and pain.

He thought it had happened before. It seemed as if he'd woken from a bizarre nightmare—the kind only humans were supposed to have—and quickly found the details burning away in the light of the sun, as if his mind refused to accept that he had somehow lost his ability to control his every thought.

But until Alexia, with such worry in her eyes, had asked him what he remembered of the fight, he hadn't really understood that something dark inside him had claimed his mind, a darkness he couldn't see when he was normal. If he had ever been "normal" at all.

What the Lamia had done, interfering in the fight and killing Lysander, was far from normal. Nor was what Damon had sensed when the creature had looked into his eyes with an intelligence and purpose none of its kind had ever revealed before.

Protect, it had said in his mind. *Save.* And an image of Alexia had filled his head, shaded with emotion no Lamia should have been capable of feeling.

That was when he had known what the creature was. *Who* it was. And knew, too, that Alexia had recognized the truth before the creature had killed Lysander, and kept it from him.

He had told Alexia truths he had never meant to share, revealed his original mission, exposed inner thoughts and feelings he had once rejected with all his will. He had wounded her, turned her against him, flinched at the agony in her eyes.

Irrational impulses. Lysander had recognized that weakness in Damon far too well. But Damon hadn't known the

Council had chosen him to work with the Aegis operatives because of that weakness. Or how well it would blunt his intellect and competence. Lysander had taunted him about that, too.

Since Eirene died. But it wasn't just Eirene. It was Alexia. He would have given his life gladly to spare her one more moment of pain.

But he had no right to spare her any truth that might keep her alive. Thank the First Sires that his suspicions of Michael's involvement in the theft of the patch were no longer relevant to that purpose.

If only—

"Theron?" Alexia said, breaking his silence. "You *know* him?"

Damon shook himself out of his dark thoughts. "From Erebus," he said. "He was a Bloodmaster, and one of the few Opiri who treated Darketans as equals and believed they should have full representation in the government."

Alexia remained very still, barely breathing. "A Bloodmaster," she said. "Are you saying he was your *friend?*"

Damon remembered the long, philosophical discussions with Theron in his tower apartments, the only span of time in which Damon was free to speak, feel as he chose without consequences. It had all been so much illusion in the end.

"Friendship is not a concept easily understood in Erebus," he explained. "Darketans cannot advance in Opir society, and any relationships not based on alliances for power are considered deviant."

"Like your relationship with Eirene," she said.

There was no malice in her question, but Damon still felt the blow. "Yes," he said, "but Theron had sufficient influence to circumvent the restrictions placed on Darketans in Erebus. He had many unpopular ideas, including the concept of establishing what you would call more democratic methods of government. He did what he could to further the rights of Darketans and vassals, even though his stance put him in some danger from more conservative Opiri."

"The Expansionists," Alexia murmured. "Did Theron believe in human equality, too?"

Damon had known the question was coming. He had considered Theron far more than a friend; the Bloodmaster had been like a benevolent Sire as far back as Damon's memory reached, when he had discovered that Damon was one of the few Darketans unable to suppress his emotions with the rigid discipline imposed on all his kind.

But Theron had still been a Bloodmaster. He would never have considered that humans could be equal to Opiri of any rank. That would require setting them free, and losing access to the blood every citizen of Erebus must have to survive. Such a radical concept would shake the very foundations of Opir belief and society. It could destroy Erebus, and every Citadel like it.

"No," Damon said softly. "He did not."

Alexia was quiet for a while, but when she spoke again her voice held no trace of anger. "Is that why he decided to establish outside Erebus?" she asked. "To implement his philosophy?"

"So it appears. I was not privy to his plans to do so. The Council would have prevented it if they had known, so he must have worked subtly to evade their notice."

"So subtly you didn't know anything about what your 'friend' was doing?"

Damon smiled grimly. It was so much like Alexia to cut straight to the heart of the matter, like a surgeon with a scalpel.

"Theron disappeared from Erebus a year ago," he said. "I had no idea what had happened to him. Apparently neither did the Council."

"So you were led to believe."

He inclined his head to acknowledge her scathing comment. "Yes."

"But if the Expansionists knew about the colony early on and supported it, at least secretly, didn't they know that Theron's ideas went against everything they believed in?"

"Either they were unaware Theron himself was in charge," Damon said, "or they believed they could manipulate or force him into furthering their cause. Knowing what I do of him, I doubt Theron would have hesitated to deceive them as to his purpose if it would further *his* goals."

Alexia sighed sharply. "All right," she said. "But you're sure that your past connection will get us into the colony now, even though your 'friend' didn't bother to tell you what he was doing or invite you to join his experiment?"

"As sure as I can be."

She pushed her bangs away from her forehead as if she were brushing away her doubts. "Doesn't he know you're working for the Council?"

"He always knew."

"If he shot at us…"

He frowned. "I can't believe snipers from his colony would have known exactly who they were shooting at."

"They might not give you a chance to tell them who you are. You're taking a big chance, Damon."

"So are you," he said, hating the need for what he was about to say. "I told you about the potential worth dhampires have to Opiri. It will be impossible to disguise your eyes. The colonists will know what you are at once."

"And that means?"

"I will have to lay claim to you as my serf."

Chapter 14

Alexia pulled back, her eyes unreadable. "How is this going to work when they'll know Darketans don't have serfs of their own?"

"Ordinarily, they would not. But there is nothing ordinary about what Theron has apparently attempted to do. Assuming he has enough control over his people that there will be no open challenges—which would make his entire philosophy untenable—I may be able to keep you with me. But I don't know how he deals with serfs at all. He might—"

He stopped, wondering how he could make what he was about to say remotely palatable. "He might keep them in common for the use of all Opiri in the colony, as is the case in the Darketan dormitories."

"What would you do in that case?" she asked as if the answer were nothing more than a matter of idle curiosity.

"I would fight for you."

Her eyes widened. "That would be a very bad idea."

Remembering how it had been with Lysander, Damon

couldn't have agreed more. "Normally, a Darketan is no match for an Opir in a head-to-head fight," he said. "And there is also the complication of your nature as a dhampir. That may create conflict where there might have been none."

"Sounds reasonable."

He stared at her. "I don't think you understand me."

"Oh, I understand just fine. We go in, I'm your slave, someone decides they want me and challenges you, a fight ensues…what then?"

"If I win, I keep you. If I lose…"

"But this whole challenge thing might not happen at all."

"There is no way of knowing. It is possible that, in recognizing you as a dhampir, they will realize you are an Enclave agent and will leave you alone, or even let you go."

"Maybe they would answer our questions without all this playacting."

"I would not risk a direct approach with so little information to go on. But your danger would be great, either way. That is why I must ask again that you return to the Enclave— or, failing that, remain under cover until I return from the colony."

For the first time since this painful conversation had begun, there was a real light in her eyes, a vivid reflection of the life and spirit that had drawn him to her from the very beginning like a bee to a blossom.

"Do you think I'll let you have all the fun?" she asked with an impish grin.

"Alexia—"

"When do you want to leave?"

It was quite hopeless. He *knew* that, and though part of him wanted to rage at her and threaten her into submission, he knew she would never be cowed by him again.

"We will leave tomorrow afternoon," he said, "after I have fully explained the situation to you and you understand what you must do."

She adjusted the strap of her VS130 on her shoulder, her smile fading. "Do you want to do anything with those bodies back there?"

"They died in the course of their duties," Damon said. "They may yet serve to make the enemy believe any direct threat posed by Council agents has been eliminated."

"They're almost right," Alexia said. She moved briskly to kneel beside her pack. "But we're going to show them almost isn't enough."

Damon was too humbled by her indomitable courage to answer. He watched her as he pretended to check his own weapons and equipment, wondering how it was possible that he had never recognized the value and worth of her kind. Not just the Opir half, but the human, as well.

"You were human once," Alexia had said. And though he didn't remember, now he had cause to be proud of that blood.

As he prepared to fieldstrip his rifle, an explosion of pain burst inside his stomach, sending a volcanic rush of acid into his throat. He dropped the weapon and doubled over, turning away so that Alexia couldn't see.

The Hunger. But that wasn't possible. It was too soon. Much too soon. When Lysander had taunted him about needing blood, he had discounted it as sheer maliciousness, an attempt to frighten Alexia and arouse her suspicion.

But he remembered his powerful reaction when he had tasted Alexia's blood, however briefly, and how he had stared at her lip when she had bitten through the skin.

Now he wondered what Lysander had seen in him that he hadn't seen himself. And why it should be coming on him *now*.

"Damon?"

He straightened and turned, schooling his expression to neutral inquiry. "Yes?"

"Nothing." She frowned. "I thought… Never mind."

She returned to her work, but Damon remained very quiet,

listening intently to his body. The flare of pain was gone, but he could still feel its aftereffects. He stared at Alexia's back, imagining them entwined together, his mouth on her neck, taking her blood as he took her body.

No. He was imagining this need because he wanted her, that was all. He would simply have to be at his most disciplined the next time she needed *his* blood.

Hands trembling, he bent back to the rifle and went to work.

They encountered no interference as they descended out of the hills and entered the valley. The quiet was almost ominous, but Damon knew he and Alexia were as prepared as they could be. They had advanced within five hundred meters of the colony walls, crossing open fields and cleared pastures, before the first bullets bit the dirt on each side of their feet.

Damon put his arm out to hold Alexia back. "Say nothing," he reminded her. "No matter what happens, hold your peace."

"Like a good serf should," she murmured.

Even as he winced at her wry comment, he recognized the courage it had taken for her to accept his plan. Asking her to lie down and die would have been easier.

Much easier. But she had decided to live, even at the price of relying on his blood and his word. He wouldn't let her down again. He would give his last breath to save her.

If his judgment was wrong, that last breath might be coming at any moment.

He and Alexia remained silent and motionless, waiting for more direct acknowledgment of their presence as their shadows stretched before them across the rough native grasses. Damon heard the distant sound of cattle lowing from the direction of the colony, undoubtedly kept behind the high walls for protection after all the hostile activity going on around them. After nearly half an hour Damon heard footsteps approaching from behind them. Alexia stiffened. He raised his hands above his head.

Damon felt the muzzle of an automatic weapon dig into the back of his skull. Alexia's hands curled into fists, but she stayed absolutely still.

"Who are you?" the man demanded, his voice muffled behind his visor.

Opir, Damon thought. The rustle and creak of his bulky protective suit gave him away.

"I've come to speak to Theron," Damon said.

The Opir laughed. "Everyone wants to see Theron," he said, "especially to kill him."

Did that mean they'd already been attacked? Damon wondered. "Tell Theron that Damon of the Darketans has come under Blood-truce," he said. "If I make any hostile move, you can always kill me."

"Gallows humor, I believe the humans call it," the Opir said. The rifle's muzzle pushed into the back of Damon's neck with bruising force. "Who sent you?"

"I come on my own."

"A Darketan?" the Opir asked, incredulity in his voice.

"I was originally assigned by the Council to observe your colony," Damon said.

"Spy, you mean."

"I was one among many, as you are undoubtedly aware," Damon said, disregarding the Opir's remark, "but my fellow agents were killed by Expansionist operatives. I learned that Theron was the leader of this settlement, and as I have been left without orders…"

"You thought you would join us?"

"Theron was my mentor, and—"

"You're lying," the Opir interrupted. "No Darketan abandons his duty to Erebus."

"Not all Darketans are alike," Damon said. "I value my

life as something more than a tool of the Council. I know you seek independence from Erebus. So do I."

"And you claim to *know* Theron?"

"I was his student. If you are familiar with his philosophy, you must realize that he regarded my people as equals to Opiri. He treated me as such when I knew him in Erebus."

He could hear the stark skepticism in the Opir's silence. "I have no reason to accept your claims," he said. "We know the Expansionists have their own agents watching us constantly. Why should I believe you?"

"The Expansionists would never use Darketans to do their work," Damon said. "I encountered a few of their operatives, and now they are dead. I have important information for Theron that cannot wait."

The Opir grabbed Damon's shoulder, his fingers pressing so hard they numbed Damon's arm all the way down to his healing wrist, and spun him around to face Alexia. "Who is *she?*" he asked.

"My serf," Damon said.

"A dhampir?" The Opir leaned toward her, his eyes barely visible through the tinted visor, and inspected her badly torn and stained clothing, her dirty face and tangled hair, all arranged specifically for this moment.

"She was in the company of one of the Expansionist operatives," he said. "I found her as you see her now."

"And the operative?"

"Dead, like the others."

The Opir's expression was invisible, but his scorn was evident in his posture. "Why do you bring her here?" he said, giving Damon a hard shake. "Darketans keep no serfs."

Damon refused to react to the provocation. "As I said, I am not like other Darketans. I have no weapons, and any Opir has strength superior to mine. You have nothing to lose by taking me to him."

For a few moments Damon was certain he had miscalculated in his confident approach. He caught Alexia's eye, and she nodded slightly. They were together in this, even if they could never be together in any other way.

If he was never to touch her naked body again, move deep inside her, feel her mouth pressed to his neck while she drank his blood, he would cling to those memories in the last instant of his life.

But it seemed that moment was not to come just yet. Abruptly the Opir dropped his hand from Damon's shoulder. Without lowering his weapon, he faced the settlement and raised one hand in a gesture obviously meant as a signal. Two colonists, both in the same bulky clothing he wore, emerged from the gate set in the settlement's high wooden wall. One figure was smaller than the other—female, Damon guessed—but just as heavily armed as the taller one.

The Opir continued to hold them until the other two had come half the distance across the open field. As soon as they had trained their own weapons on Damon and Alexia, he turned back toward the hills.

Damon made no attempt to talk to the two new guards, nor did he try to communicate with Alexia in any way, though he was constantly aware of the humiliation she must be enduring every moment this masquerade continued. The larger of the two new colonists moved in to pat Damon down while the other continued to stand guard, and then the smaller did the same with Alexia. After a seemingly endless wait the first Opir returned, carrying the weapons Damon had left behind as a sign of good faith.

The shorter of the two guards gestured with her rifle, making clear that Damon and Alexia were to precede her while the other two fell in behind their prisoners. The five of them covered the distance quickly. Though the area was quiet and Damon had never sensed the presence of other Opiri or Darketans in the area since he and Alexia had left their camp, the behavior of the colonists made clear how threatened they felt.

The gates swung open soundlessly as they came within a dozen meters of the wall. More well-armed colonists in protective suits met them just inside. As the gates closed, Damon made a quick assessment of the area immediately inside. It was bare dirt, clear of anything that might impede movement or catch fire. The colony proper—several clusters of buildings of various sizes, a half dozen well-tended gardens, a barn for livestock and other facilities appropriate to a small, self-supporting community—lay scattered around a commons, stretching some one hundred and fifty meters to the far wall built up against the eastern hills at the foot of the Sonoma Mountains.

The Opir who had first confronted Damon strode past him and gave Damon's various weapons to the men who came up to take them: two male humans, one dark and short, one tall and fair, both dressed in typical serf's tunics and pants. The immediate difference Damon noticed was that neither man wore the usual mark of ownership. One had a leather cord strung around his neck, what looked like a melted piece of metal hanging from it, and the other wore a colorful armband of cord and beads. At second glance, Damon saw that even their tunics were different in design and detail, as if the humans had been personally responsible for the decorations.

The two men glanced at Damon with open curiosity, looked with more intense interest at Alexia behind him, and carried the weapons toward one of the nearby buildings. Damon heard a whistle from overhead and saw that one of the several guards pacing the battlements at the top of the wall was waving to Damon's original captor. He, too, was human.

"Fresh blood, Sergius?" he called down, startling Damon with his familiar manner of address.

"We shall see," the Opir said. He bent to speak to the shorter of the two Opiri watching over Damon. She gave a quick nod and set off toward a low building with rows of windows that Damon guessed was a serf's dormitory.

"Where is Theron?" Damon asked.

Sergius's visor swung toward him. "Be silent," he commanded. "You have no status here, Darketan."

"I am not seeking status," Damon said, making his scorn clear in his voice. "I said I have urgent—"

He broke off as a crowd of humans, most dressed in the same cut of shirts and trousers, a few of the females in well-cut shifts embellished with ribbon, leather and colored thread, gathered in a loose crowd to stare at Damon. If they had come from Erebus—which was Damon's understanding—they might have seen a Darketan in passing, but it would be a rare occurrence.

What seemed odd was that none of the Opiri appeared to notice or disapprove of their gathering. Serfs in Erebus were not permitted to congregate in numbers above a handful unless they were all the property of one Opir. And in a colony like this one, each of these humans would have a well-defined task to keep the settlement running.

But no one interfered with the humans at all, and after a short time another Opir joined them, speaking casually to the human nearest him. There was nothing in the posture of either one to suggest mastery or servitude. The human neither bowed his head nor flinched away.

Despite his earlier resolution, Damon glanced again at Alexia. She, too, was staring at the crowd, a faint frown on her face. She looked at Damon and cast him a puzzled glance.

Neither one of them had much time to consider the implications of the Opiri's strange behavior, for the female Opir whom Sergius had sent away was returning, without her helmet and suit. Her pale hair was loose around her shoulders, and her honey-colored skin glowed with health and well-being.

She was not Opir, but human. She walked past Damon without a glance and stopped before Alexia.

"My name is Emma," she said, offering her hand. "You're welcome here."

Alexia stared at Emma's hand and then looked toward Damon in confusion.

"Don't look at him," Emma told her. "You are no longer his property." She took Alexia's arm in a firm but gentle hold. "What is your name?"

"Alexia." She hesitated. "Alexia Fox."

"You are safe here, Alexia Fox." Emma tugged on Alexia's arm. "Come, now. Everything will be all right."

"Let her go," Damon said, starting toward them. Sergius grabbed his shoulder and yanked him back.

"Don't even think of trying to keep her," the Opir warned. "She doesn't belong to you."

Damon wrenched free of Sergius's hold and spun to face him. "I claimed her fairly, in challenge. You have no right."

"No right? Where is your sigil of ownership?" He spoke again before Damon could find an answer. "You do not have one, because you are Darketan, and your claim would never be sanctioned."

Damon knew there had always been a chance that his and Alexia's plan would involve separation, but he hadn't expected the challenge to come so soon. He backed out of Sergius's reach, swept his gaze over the other Opir guards and then met Alexia's eyes. Her expression was strained as she tried to determine what her next move should be.

Damon had no intention of leaving her alone with Opiri who would be eager to claim such a prize, even if they would be breaking the Treaty by doing so.

Since they had already broken the Treaty merely by existing, that would seem a very small infraction.

"I said I had information to give you," Damon said, "information that may save your settlement. But my price is the girl."

"You cannot have her," Emma said, stepping between him

and Alexia. "You may have forced her to submit to you, but that's over now."

The confidence of her words left Damon at a loss. She spoke as if she had power in the colony, and she had gone out with the other Opir guards, disguised as one of them, to confront him and Alexia. But while it was clear human serfs were much more leniently treated here than most in Erebus, Emma's assertiveness went far beyond the privilege permitted a well-favored servant.

"I will Challenge anyone who attempts to take her," Damon said in his coldest voice.

"Even if you did," Sergius said behind him, "no one here would accept. And you will not get the chance to make such a Challenge."

Damon worked his hands into fists, carefully noting the positions of the Opiri around him. The humans would be no trouble, but the Opiri would likely shoot him before he got anywhere near Alexia. They wouldn't even bother to pit their superior strength against his.

He had made a terrible mistake in bringing Alexia here, a miscalculation for which he could not forgive himself.

"If you move against any of us," Sergius said, "you will die. But the dhampir will live no matter what happens to you. Make your choice."

"Don't hurt him," Alexia cried, breaking away from Emma. "Please."

As much as she tried to sound frightened and uncertain, Alexia was incapable of behaving like a serf or a beaten prisoner. Her voice was too strong, her manner too bold. Everyone looked at her, some with surprise, others with calculation. Emma regarded her face with extreme interest.

"He said he found you with an Opir. Is that true?" she asked Alexia. "Did he challenge for you and win?" She leaned close, her voice soft with concern. "What did he do to you?"

"He saved my life," Alexia said, meeting Damon's eyes.

They gazed at each other, and Damon felt as if they stood alone again in their hilltop camp, speaking as equals, bickering and threatening and making love.

Making love. A human phrase that had no equivalent in the ancient Opir tongue.

"You owe him nothing," Emma said. "Whatever you need you will find here." She tried to take Alexia's arm again, but Alexia backed away.

"Why should I trust you?" she asked. "You're from Erebus. I was taken…" Her lower lip trembled. "All of you are alike!"

"You're wrong." Emma held out her hands, palms up. "We want to help you."

"Then let me go!"

"That would be too dangerous for you, Ms. Fox," Emma said. "But you will not be treated as a prisoner here."

"Do you speak for the rest of them?" Alexia demanded, gesturing toward the Opiri who had gathered around them. "For *them?*"

"I swear you will be left alone."

"I'll go with you," Alexia said, "if you *swear* you won't harm Damon."

Frowning, Emma looked at Sergius, who inclined his head.

"He won't be harmed," Emma said. "Come, now."

With a last, hooded glance at Damon, Alexia went with the other woman, her feet dragging with reluctance. Damon knew she was afraid for him. She understood that both their positions were precarious, and the colonists were making no secret of their hostility toward him. But she knew that she would better be able to gain intelligence if she pretended to cooperate.

Damon couldn't blame her. But their separation was doing something to his heart, threatening to pull it through his ribs and out of his chest.

"Where are you taking her?" he asked Sergius.

"That is no longer your concern," the Opir snapped,

abruptly switching to the ancient Opir tongue. "Emma may have promised that you would not be harmed, but 'harm' is a matter of interpretation."

"I don't expect you to abide by the word of a serf," Damon said with unfeigned scorn.

"I see you will have to be taught to speak with respect."

"To you?" Damon asked with a curl of his lip. "An Opir who will not accept the challenge of a Darketan?"

Sergius seized Damon's arm in a punishing grip, jarring Damon's nearly healed wrist. "You aren't worth it," he said. He removed a short, dark rod from his belt: a prod, used on uncooperative or rebellious serfs. "Move ahead of me."

Damon knew that resisting would be worse than foolish, yet a familiar anger was festering inside him, the anger he had felt when they had taken Eirene away, when he had believed Alexia might die, and again when he had found her with Lysander. It made his fists clench and his muscles harden, his vision grow sharper and his sense of smell become so acute every scent was like an assault.

"Get going," Sergius said, poking at Damon's spine with the prod.

Damon moved, looking for Alexia. The women had crossed the perimeter and were walking toward one of the dormitories. Sergius steered Damon toward a small wooden building that stood apart from the rest.

"Where are you taking me?" Damon asked.

"To a holding cell."

Digging his boot heels into the dirt, Damon came to a halt. "Tell Theron I am here. He will see me."

Sergius pushed his visored face close to Damon's. "You have a choice, Darketan. You're less than nothing in Eleutheria, and my authority overrides Emma's. Do as you are told."

Damon hardly heard him. Eleutheria, he called this place. It meant "freedom."

Freedom from Erebus. But not for him, or Alexia.

"You have one more chance," Sergius said. "If you—"

Before he had finished speaking, Damon was spinning, striking out at the least protected part of Sergius's body. The side of his hand slashed into Sergius's neck in a disabling blow. The Opir staggered back, choking and coughing as he reached up to protect himself. Damon ripped the prod out of Sergius's hand.

He had no chance to use it. There was a flash of movement behind him, and he felt a stunning blow to the back of the head.

After that there was nothing but darkness.

Chapter 15

Damon woke up with a head as heavy as the great statues of the Sires in the Grand Concourse and a clot of intense pain at the base of his skull.

"Get up," a masculine voice ordered.

Faint light seeped through Damon's half-closed lids. The floor on which he lay was hard, and the room was dark, but that dim glow gave him a sense of the details before his eyes came into focus.

The holding cell was perhaps two by two meters, bare except for a wooden chair in one corner and a heavy door, currently blocked by the Opir—Sergius—standing over Damon. The sliver of light came from outside, where the door must open onto the commons. The smells were those of night, and Sergius wore not the protective daygear of before but a long, loosely belted tunic and close-fitting pants tucked into high boots.

Damon struggled to his knees, gasped as a white lance of pain plunged into his skull, and planted his hand on the wall for support as he stood. His formerly broken wrist protested the incautious movement with a deep throb of discomfort.

"I see you have survived," Sergius said in a dry voice. His eyes reflected red in the darkness, and though Damon's vision was slow in returning, he knew that the Opir was smiling. More or less.

"How long?" Damon asked, resisting the urge to rub the back of his skull.

"Six hours," Sergius said.

Blinking several times, Damon struggled to make out the Opir's face. Though the details remained blurred, Damon recognized the long elliptical shape and finely sculpted features typical of high-rank Opiri. Sergius wore his hair cut level with his shoulders and swept back from his forehead, held in place with a small silver circlet that might have represented a dragon. Everything about him exuded elegant disdain.

It was difficult to believe he was the same man who had behaved so roughly before. Sergius's stare suggested that his opinion of his prisoner had not improved over the intervening hours. Damon was keenly aware of the fact that his vision had not yet recovered, but he had no intention of letting Sergius know he was vulnerable.

"Where is Alexia?" he asked.

Sergius sighed. "We're back to that again? Nothing has changed."

"Are you taking me to Theron?"

"Not like *that*." Sergius moved away from the door. "You will clean yourself first. You stank even before you came through the gates."

Damon bowed mockingly. "I will endeavor to correct my condition."

Without comment, Sergius indicated that Damon should precede him out the door. If he was armed, he made no attempt to advertise it, and he offered no threats. He followed Damon out onto the commons, lit with lanterns hung on sturdy poles spaced just closely enough for night-blind humans to find their way from one area of the settlement to the other. The windows of the several dormitories were mostly dark, and only a few Opiri were abroad. Vague shapes—sentries—moved along the battlements.

At the end of one of the dormitories was a lavatory, where Damon and Sergius met a human coming out. The human, a young male, raised his hand to Sergius, glanced at Damon and continued on his way without any further sign of respect, let alone the wariness or outright fear most serfs displayed in the presence of strange Opiri.

Sergius waved Damon through the door and pointed out the clean towels hanging on racks along the wall. Damon did the best he could to scrape off the dirt and blood he hadn't been able to wash off after the fight with Lysander. As he worked, he listened for voices within the building.

There were none, nor could he identify any trace of Alexia's scent. He assumed she was in another building and reminded himself that he would learn nothing unless he controlled his emotions.

When he was finished, Sergius nodded grudgingly and took Damon back across the commons, this time toward a small wooden house which, like the holding cell, was set apart from the others. Damon lengthened his stride.

"Stay behind me," Sergius said. "Theron—"

Damon ignored him and went on to the door. He hesitated only a moment and walked in, Sergius at his heels.

Theron sat behind a neatly made but very plain desk, a stack of papers on one side and a statue of a graceful woman on the other. There was no sign of a computer or any other technology more advanced than the humming generator that stood against the wall and the portable intercom on a table beside it. The generator provided the only light, which outlined the shape of a narrow cot against the back wall.

As soon as Damon had crossed the threshold Theron was

on his feet, his mouth stretched in the grin that had always set him apart from any Opir Damon had ever met.

"Theron," Sergius said, anger in his voice, "this Darketan—"

"Damon!" Theron exclaimed, coming around from behind the desk with arms outstretched. "My dear boy." He embraced Damon briefly, nodded to Sergius and stepped back.

"Forgive me," Theron said, his smile fading. "This is quite unexpected. When Sergius said a Darketan by your name had come to Eleutheria claiming to know me—and with a dhampir prisoner, no less—I didn't believe it at first."

Damon examined the Bloodmaster's face. Though his vision was beginning to clear, he found it difficult to accept that Theron could have aged so much in the two years since they had last spoken. Yet the fresh lines were there, lines that would ordinarily indicate extreme old age in an Opir.

Theron was old, but he was not one of the Elders, who were rare and usually lived alone in their towers. His face was still handsome, more rugged than that of most Opiri, his hair still thick and his gaze direct. He was only worn down, bent under the care of bringing together Opiri who would normally resist living in such close quarters.

"You didn't see us before we entered the valley?" Damon asked. "You didn't shoot at us?"

"We don't have the resources to send our people out to shoot at passers-by," Theron said. "This is all quite a shock to me. Only when the young lady—" He broke off, looking Damon up and down. "You have not been treated well, and for that I apologize." He indicated the chair facing the desk. "Sit. Sergius, would you find us some refreshment?"

Damon could hear the Opir's sharp intake of breath, as if he were about to argue. But after a moment Sergius opened the door and walked out, leaving Damon alone with his old mentor. Theron went back to his seat, but Damon remained standing.

"I am at a loss," Theron said, the words steeped with weariness. "I have been told that you have come to bring some warning to us, but I have difficulty understanding under what circumstances you would arrive without orders from Erebus. You have been observing us on their behalf, have you not?"

"It is true," Damon said, holding Theron's gaze. "I was sent to observe your settlement, but I am not here under orders from Erebus. The instructions under which I was operating no longer apply, and I have had no direct contact with other Council agents for days." He leaned over the desk. "There is war going on outside your walls, Theron, and it is about to sweep you up."

"Do you think I am not aware of this?" the Bloodmaster asked. He leaned back in his chair, gazing up at the ceiling. "I am not totally cut off from Erebus, Damon. I know how fortunate we are to have been left alone as long as we have."

"Left alone?" Damon asked. "Or is it that you have deceived those who supported you, and they are no longer accepting your claims of cooperation?"

"They," Theron said. He looked at Damon again. "You mean the Expansionists, of course. Naturally the Council believes we are in league with them."

"I was not told what they believe. But the origins of this settlement are an open question, and since by its very existence it is attempting to expand Opir territory, it seems logical to assume a connection with the Expansionists."

Theron's gaze hardened. "Look at me, Damon. You know what *I* believe. When have I ever agreed with the Expansionists or supported their positions? You have seen how we have created our little town as a place where Opiri live in peace as equals, without challenge or vassalage. Can you tell me to my face that I have conspired with the enemy?"

"I can tell you that they plan to attack you, wipe you out if possible, no matter the consequences to the Armistice or the political balance in Erebus."

"Is it possible you haven't noticed our defenses?"

"The wall? Do you think that will keep out Opiri bent on killing?"

Theron waved his hand in dismissal. "What of you, Damon? Have you come out of your personal loyalty to me?"

Damon took his seat. "I won't lie to you, Theron. Once I learned you were here, my primary purpose was to discover why the Expansionists are so eager to destroy you, and why an Opir working as a double agent for the Council would say that the colony was not what they believed."

"Out of curiosity? Or to gain status in Erebus by dealing in useful information?"

Damon countered with a question of his own. "Did you intend your idea of a free society to include Darketans?"

Theron sighed. "When I began this experiment," he said, "I knew it was little more than a dream. I knew it would provoke strong, even dangerous reactions from all factions in Erebus and from the Enclave, as well. I understood the risks. But I had hoped Eleutheria might somehow set an example...." He shook his head. "Yes, that was my intention, Damon. I had many of what humans call 'good intentions.'"

"You no longer stand by them?"

Theron's hand twitched to the stack of papers. "Where do we begin, my boy? You have questions, and so do I. It seems—"

"I have only one question now. The dhampir I brought with me, Alexia Fox—"

"Ah, yes." Theron smiled again, but sadly, and spread his palm flat over the papers as if he feared they might blow away. "The young agent. You said you had taken her by challenge from another Opir, and that you claimed her as your property."

The words sounded almost obscene as Theron spoke them, and they felt that way to Damon. "Yes," he said. "But your people took her, and I want—"

"You *want*," Theron repeated, his eyes gone cold. "I would not have believed that you, of all Darketans, would be so foolish and greedy as to claim an Enclave agent as a serf." His chair scraped back, and he rose to walk to the single window. "Is it because you have freed yourself of the Council that you make so bold a move?"

Damon rose, as well. "I have determined to make my own choices, Theron."

"You will find your choices here are limited." The Bloodmaster turned to face him, no trace of warmth left in his face. "Whatever you had intended for the young lady, you will find you have no power over her in Eleutheria. You see—"

The door burst open behind Damon, and Alexia's fresh scent filled the room. She was almost on top of Damon when he turned around. He had a few seconds to note that she was wearing a tunic and pants in place of her badly torn uniform, and that she was smiling.

Sergius strode in after her with a lantern in his hand, a barely concealed scowl on his face. "I found her on her way here as I was returning," he said. "Shall I—"

"It's all right, Sergius," Theron said just as Damon put himself between Alexia and the younger Opir. Theron nodded gravely to Alexia, who took Damon's arm and turned him around to face her again.

"Didn't he tell you?" she asked, her eyes very bright in the lantern light.

"Are you all right?" he asked. "Have they hurt you?"

She laughed with an ease Damon had never seen before. He tried to make sense of the joy in her eyes and failed.

"What is this?" he asked Theron, who returned his stare without softening.

"She is not yours," he said. "She is not anyone's now. There is a reason we call this place Eleutheria, and it is not only because here we regard all Opiri as equals."

And then Damon understood. The humans he had seen

gathering when he and Alexia had arrived hadn't been afraid of chastisement from their owners, because they were not possessions to be berated and punished for the smallest disobedience. The young man outside the lavatory had seen no need to genuflect because he had nothing to fear from Sergius or any other Opiri in the settlement.

Eleutheria. Freedom.

Damon's head and wrist began to throb again. "It seems we didn't have to be quite so cautious," he said to Alexia.

"I can hardly believe it myself," she said. "Emma told me what had happened to you. I asked her to get you out of the holding cell, but she wanted to give the colony leaders time to discuss it." She grinned wickedly. "Serves you right for playing your part a little too well."

Theron cleared his throat. "Apparently I was mistaken in my suspicions, Damon," he said. "I had to be sure that Ms. Fox was not under duress when she told us of your purpose here."

"I did not enjoy the deception," Damon said stiffly, "but we couldn't be sure of the reception we would receive, and we had no reason to believe Agent Fox would be treated as a free woman. She is an extraordinary person, and I had no pleasure in treating her—" He broke off before his emotions could become too apparent. "We had no way of knowing you had taken your philosophy to such extremes."

"Now you see why the Expansionists want to see us destroyed," Sergius said.

Damon glanced at Sergius and then did a double take. Now that his vision had returned to normal, he saw the Opir's features clearly for the first time.

"Nikanor!" he said.

"I no longer go by that name," Sergius said, meeting Damon's gaze with a little more friendliness than he'd shown earlier.

"Many of us have changed our names since we took up

our new life here," Theron said. "We wish to forget the way of life we once took for granted. No one has been more devoted to our goals than Sergius."

Nikanor inclined his head in acknowledgment of Theron's praise. "I was not the first to see the wisdom in Theron's philosophy, but when I did I knew it must be put into practice as thoroughly as possible."

"He has been invaluable to the colony," Theron said, fondness in his voice. "He has risked much."

Damon wasn't surprised that Nikanor was involved with Theron's experiment. He had been one of the Bloodmaster's most devoted disciples. Once Theron had freed him from vassalage, he could have struck out on his own and worked to move up the ranks, but instead he had chosen to remain with Theron and reap the benefits of the Bloodmaster's considerable wisdom. For a time, he and Damon had shared Theron's tutelage, and Nikanor had treated Damon as a fellow student rather than an inferior.

"You knew I wasn't able to see the details of your face," Damon said, meeting Sergius's gaze. "Why didn't you tell me who you were? Why didn't you acknowledge me earlier?"

Sergius's expression was grave. "None of us could be sure of your motives when you first arrived," he said, "especially given your treatment of Ms. Fox. We wished to keep you uncomfortable until we could learn more about your purpose in coming."

Damon touched the back of his head. "You did that very well," he said drily.

A slight smile touched the corner of Sergius's mouth. "I only just learned what Ms. Fox had told Emma when Theron sent for you."

"He hurt you?" Alexia asked, stretching to peer at the back of Damon's head. She glared at Sergius. "I was told he would not be harmed."

A weight in Damon's heart lightened at the anger and concern in her voice. "I believe I will survive," he said, briefly meeting her troubled gaze. He turned to Sergius again. "I thank you for seeing to Agent Fox's welfare."

"It was my pleasure, though Emma deserves the credit," Sergius said with an approving glance at Alexia.

Too approving, Damon thought. He rested his hand on Alexia's shoulder.

"You house the humans in the dormitories, I take it?" he asked. "Where will Ms. Fox—"

"For pity's sake," Alexia cut in. "There's no need for such formality. All the rules seem to have been broken here already." She smiled up at Damon, and he felt as if that smile alone could send him crashing to the floor again.

"Alexia," he breathed, wondering if she recognized what he meant to express in that single word. She held his gaze a moment longer and then looked away.

"We shouldn't waste any more time," she said, sobering. "I told Emma about the Expansionists' plan to move on them soon, but I'm sure Theron and his Council will want the details of what we managed to find out from Lysander and the other Nightsider."

Damon hoped she hadn't told Emma more than they'd agreed to reveal. "It would be wise to put more sentries on your walls immediately," he said to Theron. "The Expansionists may take action at any time."

"Perhaps you have forgotten that Theron was sired before humans built their first city," Sergius said. "He needs none of your advice."

Just as he finished speaking, a young human woman entered the room with a tray bearing a decanter, five wineglasses—two filled with clear water—and a plate of biscuits. She set the tray on the small table next to the generator, smiled at Theron and went back out the door.

"Ah," Theron said. "Let us have a little refreshment before

we continue. It does no good to talk of such serious matters on an empty stomach."

He moved to the table and picked up the tinted glass decanter. "Damon," he said, "you will not be surprised, I think, to learn that we do not force any human citizen of Eleutheria to provide blood. They do so because it is their desire to contribute to our community and build new bonds of trust between our peoples."

Carefully he poured the rich red liquid into one of the glasses. The blood was fresh and pungent, and the smell alone seemed to choke off Damon's breath.

He had tried to disregard his growing hunger, refusing to acknowledge the warning signs since Lysander had mocked him about taking Alexia's blood. Now he was in a place where he could find nourishment, and yet he didn't reach for the glass Theron offered. He looked down at Alexia's face for the expression of revulsion he expected to find.

Instead, he saw neither approval nor disgust, only a faint frown accompanied by an unreadable glance at Damon's face. He raised his hand to refuse the glass. The door opened again, and Emma came into the room with another plate of fresh bread and a wedge of cheese. Her gaze lingered on Sergius, and then she joined Theron at the table.

"You must be hungry," she said, smiling at Alexia. "Since you wouldn't eat earlier, I thought—"

Damon didn't hear the rest of her words, for he was staggering, falling, his stomach turning inside out as he caught himself against the desk and cracked his head on the edge. Alexia cried out, her small, strong hands clamping around his arm. His vision dimmed again.

"What's wrong?" she demanded, her voice thin and far away. "Help him!"

"He needs blood," a male voice said.

Someone lifted Damon's head from the floor and pushed a glass to his lips. He nearly gagged before the blood flowed over his tongue, and then there was a profound relief, as if his body had been numb for years and had suddenly come back to life.

"He never said anything," Alexia said. "I should have recognized—"

"He needs rest," Theron said. There was a sound of feet moving on the floor, and then the cup was taken away.

"This will serve only temporarily," Theron said. "He is clearly starving. He must have fresh blood from a vein if he is to take full benefit."

"That can be arranged," Sergius said. "If you are certain you are up to speaking with us while he recovers, Ms. Fox—"

Damon growled and reached out blindly, struggling to find Alexia through a vast inner blindness. Sergius had no right to speak to her so intimately. He didn't know her.

And she was *his*.

"It will be all right, Damon," Alexia said. He felt the slightly calloused pads of her fingertips brush his cheek and the corner of his mouth. "You can join us again when you recover."

Driven by fury that seemed to consume every last drop of blood he had taken, Damon ordered his muscles to lift him from the floor. His will overcame their feebleness, and he was on his feet again, swaying, his hand gripping the edge of the desk. His vision cleared enough for him to see Alexia's beautiful, anxious face, and then he pushed past her, heading straight for Sergius.

Theron caught him from behind and held him, speaking low in his ear.

"This is the Hunger talking," he whispered. "I will take you to your room myself."

"Go with him, Damon," Alexia said. "I'll tell you what we've discussed after you've done what you need to do."

Done what he needed to do. The very thing she most despised. As he despised this helplessness and what it made of him.

That was the last rational thought he had. He made for the door, finding his way more by memory than sight. Sergius moved quickly out of his way and held the door open. Damon blundered out, all raw instinct now, all need. His legs tensed to carry him in a sprint toward whatever prey he could find.

The woman who had brought in the tray was crossing the commons in the direction of one of the dormitories. Damon smelled the scent of the blood pulsing beneath her skin and started toward her. Voices called behind him, but he was already running. As he reached her, the woman turned to face him.

Her expression showed no fear, only calm acceptance. Damon skidded to a halt, his boot heels digging furrows in the dirt.

The woman held out her hand. "I can give you what you need," she said. "You don't have to take it."

Damon closed his eyes, feeling a strange sense of weightlessness as his mind began to hold thoughts again. *He didn't have to take it.* Not like all the hundreds of times before, when humans serving the Darketan dormitories were sent to him and the others, nameless men and women who were nothing more than cattle. Even to him.

Back then, before he had met Alexia, he had never considered any other way. And now this woman, who had full freedom to choose, was willing to ease his hunger. To trust him, as Alexia did.

"You don't have to give him anything," Alexia told the woman, coming up behind Damon. "I'll take care of him."

Damon turned his head halfway, afraid to move lest his body overwhelm his mind. "No," he said hoarsely.

"You gave me your blood," she reminded him. "Now I give you mine, freely and gladly."

Theron, Sergius and Emma arrived a moment later, forming a tense tableau behind Damon, Alexia and the human woman. Alexia pressed her soft, supple body to Damon's back, her arms wrapping around his waist.

"Come with me now," she said. "You want me, Damon. And I want you. In every way."

Chapter 16

At first Alexia wasn't sure she'd reached him. He didn't move; every muscle was rigid in a battle for control, and if he could see her he showed no sign.

But he heard her. Slowly he turned, forgetting the petite, dark-haired woman who had been so willing to share the very essence of life with a man she didn't know.

But *she* had no right. Damon had hidden the extent of his need from Alexia, and in spite of—no, *because* of—Lysander's remark about Damon's hunger, Alexia had pretended she didn't recognize the signs.

Now they were unmistakable. *She* was responsible for his condition, because she had been afraid. Afraid of her own need for him, both physical and emotional. Afraid of letting herself become a mere source of nourishment, no different from the human convicts in Erebus. Afraid of forging the final link in the chain that bound her and Damon together.

She had hated what Damon had done to her when they'd arrived at the colony, even though she had agreed to the necessity of becoming his serf. He had almost managed to convince her that it was not merely a ruse, that all her doubts since their last conversation in camp were justified and that somehow she had missed a crucial element of Damon's character. For a few terrifying minutes, she had believed the life she had always known was over.

But even if the colony had been what she and Damon had both believed, a place where Opiri might be free but humans were still cattle, she would not have denied him now.

"He must have fresh blood from a vein if he is to take full benefit," Theron had said. Even if the blood in the glass had given him the energy to move again, it could not sustain him long.

"Come," she said again, offering her hand.

When he finally reacted, it was not to take her hand but to sweep her up in his arms and carry her off to the nearest building, one much like Theron's and no more than a dozen meters away. She wrapped her arms around his neck and pressed her face into the hollow of his shoulder, where she could hear and feel his blood moving sluggishly through his veins.

I'm not afraid, she told herself with wonder. *I'm not afraid.*

Without pausing to see if anyone was in the house, Damon kicked the door open and strode inside. Sergius had brought a lantern into Theron's house to provide light for human eyes, but this single room was dark. It smelled of Sergius.

If Damon was aware of the scent, he ignored it. A low cot similar to Theron's stood against the wall in the far corner of the room. Damon carried Alexia to it and laid her down with a gentleness she hadn't expected. He gazed into her eyes, and once again she saw a war within him: savage instinct against concern and something akin to shame.

She reached up to touch his face. "It's all right, Damon," she whispered. "This is what I want."

Her words seemed to release the terrible tension in Da-

mon's body. He put one knee on the edge of the cot and his
arms to each side of her head, opened his mouth and bit her.

The instructors at Aegis had tried to explain what being
bitten would feel like, intending to prepare operatives for the
experience and help them avoid the natural panic they would
feel if they ever faced such a situation. But classroom theory
had never been put into practice, for no Opiri were allowed
in the Enclave, and dhampires were taught to loathe the idea
of taking blood.

Now Alexia knew how inadequate that theory had been.
She gasped and closed her eyes, her senses exploding with
pleasure that radiated out from the point where Damon's teeth
pierced her skin. In a distant part of her mind she asked herself if this was what all humans experienced, but she already
knew the answer. For if they did…oh, if they did…

Her thoughts disintegrated as Damon's tongue stroked
the curve of her neck, his warm mouth moving over her
skin in a way every bit as erotic as his lips on her nipples
or between her thighs. She arched against him, urging him
to drink deeper still. He moaned inside his throat, and she
could feel the pressure of his erection against her thigh as he
straddled her. He slid his hand down along her belly to the
drawstring waistband of her pants and beneath, reaching the
nest of curls. Alexia gasped as he found her clitoris with his
thumb and began to stroke it in time to the rhythmic motions
of his lips and tongue.

Reckless with excitement, Alexia pushed her arm between her chest and his, feeling for the fly of his pants. But
he trapped her hand with his free one and, withdrawing his
other hand from within her pants, lifted himself on his arms
and moved his mouth from her neck.

She groaned in protest, but he silenced her with his lips on
hers. They still tasted of her blood. He kissed her, touching
her tongue with his, as if he would devour her completely.
He pushed her arms above her head and began to lift the hem

of her shirt. Alexia helped him, seething with impatience to feel his mouth on her breasts and something more substantial than his fingers between her thighs.

The shirt came off, and Damon tossed it aside. A second later he was at her throat again, this time biting the other side of her neck, carrying her to that indescribable, euphoric state she hadn't believed could possibly exist.

It didn't last. It couldn't. But when Damon licked the blood from her skin, sealing the wound and trailing his mouth down to her breasts, she remembered that there were a thousand other ways of pleasure she could give and receive without any blood at all.

As Damon's lips closed on her taut nipple, Alexia laced her fingers in his hair and whispered encouragement he obviously didn't need. He suckled her breast with the same hunger with which he had taken her blood. He reached down again, finding his way to her waistband, and dragged the pants down to her hips. She wriggled under him, freeing herself to the knees, gasping as he moved to her other breast.

Somehow, between them, they managed to get her pants off. Damon sent them to the floor with a nudge of his knee and rolled his tongue in tight circles around her nipples, first one and then the other. His palm curled under her waist, lifting, positioning her so that her thighs spread wide without any help from her.

Once again he found the almost painful ache beneath her damp curls, but this time he slid his finger past her clitoris and between the hot, wet lips. He stroked his finger slowly from front to back, dipped it inside her and slowly pushed until his finger was all the way in. Alexia strained against him. He began to move his finger in and out as his thumb found her clitoris again. Just when she was certain she was going to come, he withdrew his finger and began kissing his way down from her breasts to her belly.

Even though she knew what was coming, she wasn't prepared when his lips and tongue replaced his finger. He licked along the same path his finger had taken, sliding between her swollen lips, teasing her clitoris and finally reaching the molten center of her need. He stiffened his tongue and pushed it inside. Alexia thrashed on the cot, lifting her legs higher, knowing she couldn't stand much more. She had to have him inside her, all of him. Now.

He didn't make her wait much longer. Suddenly his shirt and pants were gone, too, and his hot, naked flesh was pressed to her body. She reveled in the feel of firm muscle flexing as he positioned himself between her legs.

Before, when he'd entered her, he had moved with urgency and impatience. Now he took his time, teasing her lips with the head of his cock, stroking her the same way he had with his fingers and tongue. He managed to keep it up for a good five minutes before he drove himself to the point where he couldn't stand it any more than she could.

Still he didn't enter her. Instead, he lifted her with one arm—obviously no longer troubled by the damage to his wrist—and turned her over onto her hands and knees. Her excitement intensified as he knelt behind her, grasping her hips with his hands. Suddenly he thrust into her, driving deeper than ever before, and she gasped again as she felt his big cock fill her more completely than she had ever been filled before.

As he moved inside her, he leaned over her bottom and bit the back of her neck, his incisors piercing the skin just beneath her ear. He hardly had time to enjoy the sensation before her body released in a flood of hot wetness and throbbing pleasure.

She felt Damon begin to move away and made a sharp sound of protest. He stopped, and she rolled over to face him, holding out her arms. He fell into them, and once again she guided him inside her. Then she bit his neck just to the side of his Adam's apple, sucking the blood that trickled over her tongue.

He reached his own completion not long after, pumping so fast and furiously that she came again. He rolled over and pulled her close to his side, murmuring senseless words of endearment into her hair.

Sometime later, as she lay there in blissful contentment, Damon gave way to exhausted sleep. Alexia draped her arm across his chest and listened to the night sounds outside the cabin. She couldn't hear anyone moving about, not even the nearly silent Nightsiders, and she was pretty sure every last human had long since gone to bed.

That didn't mean they were necessarily asleep.

She sighed and nestled her face into the hollow of Damon's shoulder. She had thought she'd known what sex was like before she'd first made love with Damon, that day when she had thought her time on earth was almost over. But she'd had barely a taste then, and now she knew what it really meant to give herself to another person in every way, and take everything she was offered. Not as an operative doing a job, or a serf, or one dependent on another for survival. Not even for friendship, or "caring." This was what she had fought against every moment since she recognized the depth of her attraction to her enemy.

It wasn't just sex. It wasn't need or hunger or even comfort.

It was love.

Her throat suddenly tight, Alexia disentangled herself from Damon's body, rolled off the cot and picked up the tunic that lay on the floor beside the bed. She brushed it off and pulled it over her head, smoothing the soft fabric over her body from chest to upper thighs. Every nerve felt raw, exposed, vulnerable to the slightest sensation from the brush of the almost imperceptible draft coming from under the door to the feel of wood on the soles of her feet.

"Alexia?"

She turned to find Damon propped up on one elbow, the sheets draped over his hips in a way that made her wonder if he was actually trying to be modest. He smiled, his sapphire gaze wandering over her body with undisguised admiration.

Alexia blushed and mocked herself for her self-consciousness. There wasn't any part of her Damon hadn't seen, and that included a good chunk of her heart and soul.

"Good morning, I think," she said, returning his smile.

He tilted his head. "Two a.m.," he said huskily, "if I'm not mistaken." He stretched, long muscles shifting under night-pale skin, and lifted the blanket. "Come back to bed."

There was no doubt that he was ready to resume their sexual gymnastics, but Alexia couldn't stop her mind from working over everything that had occurred in the past few days and what was likely to happen in the very near future.

First there was the question of the patch, which she and Damon had speculated might be in the settlement. She hadn't been foolish enough to ask about it outright; if the colonists *did* have it, they would have responded quite differently when they had first seen her. It would be pretty difficult for all the people she'd met to hide the reaction she would expect.

Assuming her judgment was correct, she and Damon still had to share what they'd learned with Theron and find out what he planned to do. And now that Damon had no orders or direct line of communication to his own masters, he still had a few very important decisions to make.

Alexia didn't know how much he and Theron had discussed before she had arrived at the Bloodmaster's cabin, but Emma had told her that the colony had accepted some clandestine support from the Expansionists at the very beginning. Theron had never been under any illusion as to how the Expansionists would react once he broke off their "alliance." What Alexia had seen since her arrival made clear why the Expansionists would want to eradicate the settlement.

Not what we believed, the Independent double agent had told her. If that information had reached the Council, there was no telling what *they* would do about it.

And Aegis? Wouldn't this colony's mere existence force them to change their assumptions about Opiri and their approach to Erebus? If there was even a chance the settlement could be a basis for a new kind of civilization…

For the first time since she'd arrived, Alexia was struck by the full recognition of what Eleutheria could become. A symbol, not only of equality and friendship, but of the hope of peace founded not on mere truce but true understanding. Understanding that could end the deportation of convicts from the Enclave. That could bring people—*people, not Nightsiders and humans*—together as she and Damon had come together.

"Are you all right?" Damon asked with a worried frown.

Belatedly Alexia realized that they hadn't talked since he had taken her blood. She could imagine the thoughts racing through his mind: he had taken advantage of her, he had behaved like a savage, he had hurt her. She could feel those fears as if they were her own.

She went back to the cot and perched on the edge, hands braced on the frame and gaze fixed on the floor. "I've been thinking," she said slowly.

"About what?" Damon asked, hesitantly reaching out to tuck a strand of her hair behind her ear. "Did I do something wrong? Did I…" His fingers stopped, and she heard his teeth clench. "Did I hurt you?"

She turned to catch his hand and pressed his palm to her mouth. "No, Damon. If you had, I wouldn't be sitting here, wishing we could start all over again."

His expression relaxed all at once. He took her hand between his and brought it to his chest. His heart was beating strongly, and his dark eyes were warm with relief.

"I didn't know what I was doing last night," he said.

"Oh, yes, you did." She spread her fingers across his chest. "You knew exactly what you were doing, and you were extremely good at it."

He ran his thumb gently across the places where he had bitten her. "No discomfort?" he asked.

"No. Should there be?" She smiled. "There was never any pain, Damon. Only the most indescribable—"

She broke off, knowing she could never explain. Knowing if she did, she'd only want it again and again, like an addict who had no idea when to quit.

Damon's lips brushed her neck. "It was indescribable for me, as well," he murmured.

His voice had a little growl in it, provocation and promise, but Alexia didn't fall into his trap. "Does it always happen that way?" she asked, leaning back. "Between Nightsiders and their vassals and humans?"

He sat up cross-legged on the cot, the blanket still draped across his lap. "I know only what I have been told," he said, his voice roughening. "With vassals, it is said to be mutually pleasurable, but there is always an imbalance of power. With serfs…" He worked his fists into the sheets. "Whether or not they receive pleasure is of no interest to the Opir who owns them."

"Except in this place," she said. "If it was unpleasant, I can't imagine the humans in Eleutheria would be so ready to provide blood at the drop of a hat. Like that woman last night."

Damon shifted. "I apologize," he said, a little stiffly. "When I find the woman, I will ask her forgiveness."

"Oh, I don't think you need to look for her yourself," Alexia said hastily, wishing she hadn't raised the subject. "Emma planned to introduce me to some of the other colonists once we finished our business with Theron. I'm sure I can pass on your apology."

Damon looked up. "You have no reason to be jealous, Alexia."

"Jealous? Because you were going to take her blood without asking me if I was willing?"

"I was incapable of discussing it at the time."

"You could damned well have told me what was happening before it got so bad," she shot back. "If you were so out of control, you could have hurt that woman. I know you would never have hurt *me,* no matter how far gone you were."

"She knew how to react without fear or provocation," Damon said, utterly serious. "I don't know what I would have done if—"

"Nothing happened, Damon," she said, resting her hand on his knee. "Everything is all right now."

"Is it?" Damon stared blankly into the darkness. "Opiri can lose control like that if they're starving, literally on the edge of death. But I wasn't dying, Alexia. I was insane."

Chapter 17

Alexia went very still. She had known the time would come when the subject of his "spells" would arise, even if she had to introduce it herself. But now that it was here, she wanted to tuck the entire matter away into some forgotten corner where it could never disturb either of them again.

"You fell, Damon," she said. "You were sick. Even Theron recognized your condition."

"No," he said, setting his jaw. "You asked why I didn't tell you what was happening before. That was because I couldn't acknowledge it. The Hunger should not have come so soon. Something caused this to happen, something unnatural for my kind."

Oh, God, Alexia thought. She reached out to take the hand he had clenched in the sheets and opened his fingers, lacing hers through them. "Tell me," she said.

"I have felt this before," he said. "Not this level of Hunger, not so quickly. No. But the savagery…the rage…" He met her gaze. "What did I look like when I left Theron's house, Alexia? A monster?"

"Is that what you felt like?" she whispered, beginning to shiver.

"I don't know." He disengaged his fingers from hers. "Answer me, Alexia."

"You never looked different," she said, careful not to glance away.

"But I *was* different," he said. "Wasn't I?"

She couldn't answer the pain in his eyes. They went distant with some ugly memory.

"Until I nearly killed Lysander," he said, "I didn't realize that there was a pattern. But the first time I felt it was in Erebus. The *first* time I fought him."

"The first—" Alexia couldn't forget a single brutal moment of the battle in which he and Lysander had almost killed each other. She had known then that there had been something very bitter between them. Lysander had compared her to Eirene. "Spirited," he'd said. As if he had known the Darketan woman. Very well.

"You fought over Eirene," she said, trying to keep her feelings from her voice. "You both wanted her."

She expected Damon to bolt from the cot and begin striding around the small room, agitation translating into frantic motion. But he remained where he was, blank-faced and emotionless.

"After the Master of Agents discovered my relationship with Eirene and separated us," he said, "Lysander tried to claim her. No Opir had ever attempted to claim a Darketan before, but he convinced the Master to give her to him rather than sending her away. She was forced to go with him."

Alexia imagined the scene, the depravity of it, the pain and fear. Darketans had a kind of freedom—freedom from service to anyone but the Council and the Citadel. Eirene had had that taken from her after being forcibly parted from the man she had—

Loved. As Damon had loved her.

"I was kept confined for a week," Damon continued. "When I was released, I obtained permission to enter the Citadel proper. I was planning to break in on Lysander in his quarters, but I found him on the Grand Concourse instead, parading Eirene around and showing her off to the other Opiri as if she were a valuable serf."

"But she was, wasn't she?" Alexia said, longing to reach out to him. "And you couldn't bear it."

"No. I attacked him on the Concourse. I remembered almost nothing except sinking my teeth into his neck. And rage. Boundless rage."

The kind, Alexia thought, that would make him equal in strength to a full-blooded Nightsider.

"When I woke, I was in a cell," Damon said. "I was told Eirene was being sent on a solo mission, and that it would be highly dangerous. I was also told that in spite of my actions, I was too valuable to Erebus to be expelled from the Citadel."

"Expelled?" Alexia said, momentarily distracted from the tragedy of his story.

"Criminal acts by those of rank, Bloodmasters and the most powerful Bloodlords, are seldom punished by execution. Doing so would instigate more problems than the criminals themselves. That is why most who break the law are sent outside the walls."

"To die in the sun, or of starvation?" she asked.

"Yes. Or to be changed."

She didn't know what he was talking about. "Changed?"

"As those humans selected to become vassals are changed. Only our criminals are not as fortunate as humans. They become something both our peoples fear and despise."

All at once Alexia understood. He was talking about Orloks. Aegis had speculated that the creatures were in some way like Nightsiders, capable of converting humans into blood-drinkers like themselves.

But now Damon was saying they *were* Nightsiders. And Michael had become one of them.

"But how?" she asked, tears thickening her voice. "We never saw these creatures before the Armistice. How did the first ones come to be?"

"Mutations," Damon said. "Grotesque reflections of Opiri. Like Darketans."

"Not like Darketans. You can't possibly think you're anything like an Orlok."

But he had asked her what he'd looked like when he had left Theron's house. As if he'd almost expected...

She couldn't complete the thought. "You aren't a monster," she said.

"They are mindless creatures who attack both humans and Opiri indiscriminately," Damon said, as if he hadn't heard her. "But recently it had been reported that most Lamiae had left the region. That was why when the thing attacked Michael and me, I——" He drew in a deep breath and released it slowly. "I wasn't prepared."

And Michael had never guessed what might happen to him. But he'd spoken to her, after. Warned her. He hadn't been mindless at all.

"If you had been expelled," she asked dully, "would the change have happened to you?"

"I don't know," he said. "No Darketan has ever faced that particular punishment. But I asked for it, after Eirene left Erebus. I begged them to throw me into a pack of Lamiae. Either the creatures would kill me, or I wouldn't care any longer."

Care. The one thing Darketans were not supposed to do. Damon's punishment had been worse than any death or transformation.

He hadn't been sent out to become an Orlok, but the savagery he claimed they possessed was part of him, too. If she hadn't seen that shadow inside him before he and Michael had been attacked, she might have had reason to believe that he had also been affected by his contact with the Orlok.

But he had said he'd felt it in Erebus. It had already been there when she and Michael had met him.

She became aware that he was staring at her, his gaze fixed on her face with a kind of obsessive dread.

"You *have* seen it before, haven't you?" he asked. "This is not the first time." He edged farther away, ready to swing his legs over the side of the bed. "Was it when I fought Lysander?"

Lying, even evading his questions, was no longer possible. "Yes," she said, holding his gaze. "It happened then, and once before."

"When?"

"When you first swore you wouldn't let me die. When you made *me* swear to stay alive."

He closed his eyes. "Did I threaten you?"

"No! No. Nothing like that. Damon—" She reached across the cot for his hand. He jerked away, but she managed to grab hold again. His muscles twitched under her fingers. "Damon, whatever this is, you're not alone. If we can be rational about this—"

"I knew where you were concerned I wasn't rational," Damon said. "I wanted you from the start, and I knew…if I gave in to those impulses, I would be no different than an Opir with his serfs."

"You're not a Nightsider, and I'm not a serf. I was never helpless, Damon. And I wanted you from the beginning, too. I just refused to let myself believe it."

"*Your* feelings have nothing to do with it," he said harshly. He opened his eyes, and she saw despair so great she couldn't begin to touch it. "It is *my* feelings."

Fast as a striking cobra, Damon seized her shoulders in his hands and dragged her toward him, lifting her until her face was level with his. "Emotions," he said. "The trainers have always forbidden them, from the earliest part of our lives. We are little more than children when we come to the Master of Agents."

"Children?" Alexia repeated in astonishment. "But you said you're mutations! Nightsiders don't convert children!"

"So they say. None of us remembers what came before, except one thing. We are not to shame ourselves with emotion."

Tears spilled from Alexia's eyes. "Because Nightsiders don't understand it. They *have* no real feelings."

"And whatever mutates Darketans, makes us what we are, gives us too many. Every day of our lives we are reminded that we are like humans, inferior, driven by primitive sentiments that have no value in the Opir world. They must be beaten out of us before we are worthy to serve." His gaze revealed his inner torment. "They should have been beaten out of me, as they are out of most Darketans. But Eirene—"

He broke off, and Alexia was grateful. Because she was remembering how difficult it had been for Damon to admit he "cared" for her, how much he had fought against it. Not only because of what had happened with Eirene, but because he had been raised from childhood to despise emotion as weakness. He had been abused, both emotionally and physically. He had been made to believe what his masters wanted was the only thing that gave him worth.

Irrational impulses. Lysander had taunted him about them, said that he had been sent to join the Enclave agents because of them. And she still didn't know why.

Anger pushed aside Alexia's anguish for Damon. "They didn't beat it out of you," she said. "You beat *them*. You were never just a pawn, Damon."

His mouth contorted in a bitter smile. "Humans believe in souls, do they not? I would have sold mine to destroy that part of myself that was never anything but a slave to these *feelings*."

"No." She took his face in her hands and forced him to look at her. "Do you believe humans are inferior, Damon? That we are weak for daring to feel for each other, for caring about justice and equality and freedom?"

"No," he said, his breath hitching as he let it out. "I no longer believe that. If I hated the Enclave—" He covered her hands with his own. "In this place I've seen another way. A good way."

"If you've recognized that after only a few hours, some part of you must always have believed the Nightsiders were wrong about humans all along. And that meant they were wrong about *you*."

His hands slid down her arms and dropped to the cot. "They weren't wrong, Alexia. I know now that every time I *care,* I change. I cared too much for Eirene, so I attacked Lysander. I care for you—" He stared into some hell of his own creation. "These emotions are the triggers that turn me into a monster."

"Because your mind was twisted," Alexia said. "You were abused as a child and an adult. It probably isn't any coincidence that you don't remember the time before you went into training." She squeezed her hands together in her lap to keep from touching him again. "I'm no shrink, but even I can see that the psychological trauma you suffered in denying your feelings could push you to extremes your conscious mind would never permit."

"Others endured the same," he said, "and did not change."

"How do you know? Have you spoken to every other Darketan in Erebus?" She leaned toward him, praying he was listening. "You can be helped, Damon. Not in Erebus. Not by Nightsiders, but by people who understand—"

"When it happens," Damon said, looking through her, "I can't control it. What if I had killed your partner, Alexia? I wanted to do it more than once. You make excuses for me, but it doesn't change what I could do if it happens again."

Even as he spoke, Alexia knew she was losing him. Losing him to despair, to resignation, to death. *Because* he cared, he would do anything to keep her, or any other innocent, from suffering what his rage might unleash.

"I know what you'd like to do," she said with quiet intensity. "You'd like to hole up somewhere out there where you'll either let yourself starve or become an Orlok. Well, forget it. I won't let you."

He focused on her again and brushed a tear from her cheek with his thumb. "If emotion is what awakens this thing inside me, then I must be away from anything that provokes it." He lifted his thumb to his mouth and tasted her tear. "From any*one*. You must see that, Alexia."

"I see that you're giving up without any real understanding of what this thing is and how to fight it." She heard her voice begin to rise in desperation. "You said Theron was a Bloodmaster. Maybe he's heard of this condition, or even seen it. You don't know it can't be cured. How can you make any decision without more information?"

For one precious moment there was a flash of uncertainty in his eyes. The shadow of hope.

"Perhaps," he murmured.

"I won't lose you, Damon. I lost Michael to something I didn't understand, and I won't let it happen again."

"Michael—" Damon began.

"Michael wasn't…killed," she said slowly. "He was changed. Into an Orlok."

She expected to see shock on Damon's face, but he hardly reacted at all. "I know," he said. "And I know you were keeping this from me, and that I should wait until you felt safe enough to tell me."

More deception all around, Alexia thought grimly. "He was trying to protect us," she said. "And he…he communicated with me, Damon." She touched her temple. "Here. In my mind."

Like a child playing Simon Says, Damon touched his own forehead. "Yes," he said. "I heard him, as well. 'Protect,' he said. 'Save.'"

"Then he didn't become a monster when he changed. He retained at least some of his intelligence, his loyalty. He tried to warn me. He said that someone was coming, and right after that the double agent showed up. He said something about an attack, and war. Somehow he must have known what the Expansionists had planned for the colony."

"How?" Damon asked, riveted by her words.

"I don't know. Between the time you last saw his body and he came to me as an Orlok, anything could have happened. If Lysander was the Opir he followed, he could have overheard Lysander conspiring to attack the colony."

Damon looked away. "Alexia," he said heavily, "I didn't plan to burden you with this, since he can no longer do any harm. But I believe Michael had some part in stealing your patch."

Alexia stood up so suddenly that she shoved the cot, Damon still on it, seven or eight centimeters across the floor. "What did you say?" she asked, her heart freezing in her chest.

"I didn't want to share my suspicions," he said, "because I had no proof. But now it seems evident to me that Theron does not have the patch. He would have no use for it here. It appears more and more likely that Expansionist operatives took it."

"What the hell does that have to do with Michael?"

"Someone from Aegis must have told the operatives what to look for. There were many aspects of your partner's behavior when he learned your patch was gone that seemed strange to me, and—"

"Strange?" she echoed. "To *you,* who have admitted that you can't control or understand your own emotions?" She heard the cruelty of her words but was too furious to stop.

"I know you never liked him, but to accuse him *now,* when he has no way to defend himself…"

The cot creaked as Damon got up. "I should not have told you."

"Setting aside the fact that he would have no motive, how do you think he managed to do it?"

"I have no theory as to his motive," Damon said softly, moving to the small window.

"Oh, that's just wonderful." She glared at him, wondering how any person could go from love to hate, from sympathy to antagonism so quickly. "Do you have any idea what he sacrificed to be an agent? How loyal he was…how dedicated to his work?"

"I know he was your friend, Alexia."

"And you expect me to think you're—" She stopped, arrested by a thought that no longer seemed so ridiculous. "Are you jealous, Damon? Jealous of how I felt about Michael and he felt about me?"

He turned to look at her. "I have no reason to be jealous of a man who—" He broke off and looked away again. "You said you were not lovers."

"No. But if you think that gives you the right to dishonor his memory…"

He's not dead, she reminded herself. "You're calling him a traitor, not only to Aegis, but to me. No dhampir would ever go over to the enemy. It's never been done in the whole history of the Enclaves." She strode across the room to confront him. "How can you possibly justify such a bizarre claim? A *feeling?*"

He didn't answer, and Alexia was left to pace from one wall to the other and back again, too enraged to think.

Except to remember, again, what Michael had said after he'd changed.

Coming. Signal. Attack. Warn. War.

Automatically Alexia reached for the communicator, but

she had left it in the room Emma had assigned her in the east dormitory. Suddenly it seemed necessary—no, imperative—that she look at it again, study it carefully as she should have done when Michael had given it to her.

Without a word to Damon, she grabbed her pants, pulled them on and rushed out the door. The colony was still quiet, but dawn was breaking and all the lanterns, widely scattered across the commons, had been put out. She found the device where she had left it on the neatly made-up cot, along with her belt and her cleaned boots. Nothing else of her clothing had been worth saving. She snatched up the communicator and held it in her trembling hand.

As before, it appeared featureless with its beetle-black shell. But after a minute of careful examination, she found the nearly invisible recessed button at one end. She pressed on it, and a touch screen lit up, marked with only two symbols. One was the emblem for Aegis: the famous da Vinci Vitruvian Man with arms outstretched within a circle and square superimposed over the figure's legs. The other was a red square.

It was flashing.

Alexia's fingers almost lost their grip on the device before she could touch the square. Immediately the flashing stopped, and a blue screen took the place of the two symbols, a field covered with small print spelling out terse sentences Alexia took in at a glance.

Message received re: colony. Strike force deployed. Maintain position. Report only in emergency. Do not intervene.

As soon as she had finished reading, the screen went blank. Even the symbols disappeared.

Alexia dropped the communicator on the cot. Strike force. From Aegis. They were deployed only in the rare case of a situation where more than the usual agent pairs were required for an assignment, where stealth and speed and force were all equally vital. Its operatives were heavily armed and trained to go in quickly, complete their missions and get out without regard to the Armistice or the rules of the Zone. In case of casualties, no bodies would be left behind, nor any other evidence that they had ever been in the Zone at all.

Using them meant that Aegis was willing to risk a complete breaking of the Armistice.

Coming. Signal. Attack. Warn. War.

Someone had sent a message calling in the strike force. Had it been Michael? Was that the signal he was talking about? What had he told them that would cause Aegis to act so precipitously? Even if he had learned the Expansionists' plans for the colony, how could that be a good enough reason for Aegis to bypass all diplomatic channels?

And why hadn't Michael told her?

He did, she thought. *Just not soon enough.*

Frantically she grabbed for the communicator again and punched on the button. Nothing happened. As far as she could tell, the device was dead. "Alexia?"

Damon stood in the doorway, dressed in the same tunic and pants she wore but cut in a masculine style. She saw her terror reflected in his eyes.

"You were right, Damon," she said, her voice shaking. "Michael was keeping secrets. I don't know why he didn't tell me, but he sent a signal to Aegis requesting a strike force, and they're on their way. Do you know what that means?"

He knew. His concern hardened to a mask of grim resolve.

"War," he said.

Chapter 18

"Why?" Theron asked, leaning on the table with his hair loose and undressed around his shoulders. "Why should your people attack us? We have heard nothing from the Council at all, nothing from the Expansionists in weeks that would suggest a motive. What could have happened to provoke this?" He fixed his intimidating stare on Alexia. "What did your partner tell them?"

"I don't know," Alexia said, meeting his gaze steadily. "I'm by no means certain the strike force actually plans to move on the colony at all. I have simply told you what the message said, and what happened from the time Damon met with us."

She hadn't wavered under the fury of the Bloodmaster's attention, but Damon moved closer to her nevertheless, interposing himself slightly between her and the table at which she sat. The other members of Theron's local council—Sergius, Emma and six other Opiri and humans—looked on with faces drawn with worry, every one of them knowing their time was running out.

"He disappeared for a day between the time he left us and the time he returned," Damon said. "There is much he could have accomplished in those hours."

"He never came within sight of the colony," Sergius said. "How could he know enough about us to report anything to Aegis?"

Alexia bit hard on her lip. Damon rested his hand on her shoulder, knowing how much she was blaming herself for Michael's involvement in this volatile situation.

On their way to speak to Theron, they had discussed the possibility that it was Michael's discovery of the theft of Alexia's patch that had motivated him to call in the strike force. But that assumed he hadn't been involved in stealing it himself. Now it was looking increasingly likely that Damon's "feeling" that the dhampir had taken the patch was correct.

There was much he and Alexia had told Theron, and much they had not. They hadn't yet mentioned the patch and Alexia's dependence on Damon's blood to counteract her condition. Nor had they raised the subject of Damon's "spells."

"The only thing I am certain of," Theron said, breaking into Damon's thoughts, "is that neither the Council nor the Expansionists have done anything but observed from a distance."

"They were busy killing each other," Damon said, "and making plans to move on you."

"Which they have not done." Theron resumed his seat and swept his hair back with his hand. "The very existence of such strike forces is in violation of the Treaty. We know of nothing in Eleutheria that would arouse such a reaction."

"Not directly," Sergius said, "but we would not necessarily know of every political intrigue going on in Erebus. Perhaps the Council deliberately chose to provoke Aegis into breaking the Armistice, using the colony as a pretext."

"Ridiculous," Theron said. "The Expansionists might be stupid enough to try it, but not the Council. They could not conceal the kind of preparations they would need to make in order to fight another full-scale war, even if they desired it." He hesitated. "I know several of them personally. I know the way they think. No, this did not come from the Council."

Damon glanced at Sergius, noting the rebellion in the set of his face. The younger Opir was not pleased at having his idea so casually dismissed. But he would defer to Theron because he knew as well as Damon did that the Bloodmaster understood the politics of Erebus better than any living Opir.

"Hatred, greed and ambition are powerful motivators," Damon said. They *want* to see Eleutheria destroyed. Sending the right message to Aegis would serve them by causing the Enclave to break the Treaty and spare them the effort of getting rid of you."

"Obviously," Sergius said. "And since the dhampir Carter sent the communication, he must have been working with the Expansionists."

Alexia made a small sound of protest but didn't speak. Damon squeezed her shoulder.

"It is difficult to fathom his motives, given the dhampires' hatred for Opiri," he said. "But I agree with Sergius. It only remains to determine what his reasons might have been."

"If Alexia can't figure it out," Emma said, "how are *we* supposed to do it?"

"I missed something," Alexia murmured, clenching her fists on the table. "Something important. My partner was angry when Damon came. More angry than he should have been, but I didn't pay enough attention."

"What of the attacks on you and Damon?" Sergius asked.

"Now that you have confirmed that your people were not in the area firing at intruders," Damon said, "we cannot be sure of the identities of any of the shooters. The first may or may not have been the Council agents assigned to keep me and Agent Fox together, the ones I found dead later."

Theron smiled tightly. "Peculiar, is it not, that the Council sent you to keep the dhampires away from the colony, but you brought one of them directly to us instead."

Since the answer to that unspoken question involved far too much private emotion, Damon spoke with care. "Priorities can rapidly change in the field," he said, "and it became apparent to me that Council orders were not as important as dealing with what came to light as a result of Lysander's revelations."

"You made the correct choice," Theron said. He looked at Alexia. "Both of you."

"No," Alexia said. "I failed. Michael tried to warn me, and I didn't see…"

"The fact remains that he *did* try to warn you," Damon said, speaking softly as if for her ears alone.

Alexia lifted her hand and touched his fingers. "I know," she whispered. "But that doesn't help us now."

"And neither does wasting time trying to dissect the thinking of a dhampir traitor," Theron said. "We must focus all our efforts on defense. Once the Council becomes aware of the intrusion, they must act, if the Expansionists don't do so first. We will be caught in the crossfire."

"We don't even know what they're coming to do," Emma said. "Invade us? Take us prisoner? Wipe out any Expansionist operatives they can find?"

"They wouldn't come for a purpose that minor," Alexia said. "It has to be something much bigger. So big even the prospect of a new war doesn't seem as bad." She raked her slender fingers through her hair. "But on those rare occasions when they've been sent into the Zone, they carry through their objective regardless of loss of life on either side."

The people at the table looked around at each other in silence.

"I have already told you I will start for the Border immediately," Alexia said, beginning to rise, "and do what I can to intercept and explain that whatever Michael told them has to be a mistake. If they listened to him, they'll listen to me."

"No," Damon said, pushing her back down. "You said yourself they will not allow themselves to be seen, let alone delayed, even by another Aegis operative. I will not allow you to put yourself at risk for no reason."

"But I—" she began.

"Damon is right," Theron said. "You must be here if and when an attack comes. Perhaps then your words will be of use."

"In the meantime," Sergius said, "we must decide how we can best defend ourselves. Most of the Opiri here know how to shoot and can hold off any attack for a time."

"They could move today," Alexia said. "Do you have enough daygear for all the Opiri willing to fight?" She glanced around at the others. "If they're intent on getting inside these walls, you'll have to kill all of them to stop them. And you have to *find* them first."

"We will send our own scouts to meet them before they get close," said one of the other Opiri, a female with short-cropped hair and unusually light eyes. She glanced from Damon to Alexia. "We have enough daygear for that, and we're still stronger and faster than either dhampires or Darketans."

"Some of us humans are very good at fighting, too," Emma said with a pointed smile. "And sneaking around, for that matter. We were all convicts, remember?"

"And some of you were no more than petty thieves," Sergius said, "or less."

Alexia stiffened. "Sergius is right," she said in a strained voice. "They aren't trained for this."

"That is why we must evacuate them," Sergius said. "Send them to the caves until this is over."

Emma shook her head vehemently. "We ex-serfs have something here we never dreamed could exist outside the

Enclaves," she said. "Do you doubt we would defend it with our lives?"

"From your own kind?" Sergius asked mockingly. "Could you kill them, if you had to?"

"The ones who sent us to Erebus in the first place?" said the dark-haired human male named Cullen. "We aren't Enclave citizens anymore. Whatever they want here, I doubt they'll be too concerned with our welfare."

"If that is true, why would there be a law against killing humans in Erebus?" Sergius asked.

"That law is a joke," Cullen interrupted with open dislike. "Both sides know it. The strike force might not try to hurt us, but if we're collateral damage..." He glanced at Alexia, who seemed to have some difficulty meeting his eyes.

"I can't tell you anything," Alexia said in a low voice. "I wish I could. The strike force isn't made up of agents like me and Michael. They're specially trained. As far as Eleutheria is concerned, I think we're all in agreement. The fate of the colony is *our* fate."

"I don't think—" Sergius began.

"We could simply surrender," Theron said.

Everyone fell silent. Then they all began to talk at once.

"Out of the question—"

"They'll only—"

"What makes you think—"

"Silence!" Theron said, his voice booming across the table. He swept his gaze over each of the council members in turn. "We built this colony on the precepts of peace, cooperation and freedom. We knew that this great idea might not survive the first time it was put into practice. I appreciate your willingness to die for it, but martyrdom will serve nothing. We must be alive to serve as living proof that this philosophy is viable."

"You can't surrender to a strike force," Alexia said urgently. "It's not an army. Since we have no idea what their orders are, there is no guarantee a mass surrender will make any difference."

"Regardless of their reason for entering the Zone in force," Theron said, "they surely have no intention of killing indiscriminately. If we fight, we cannot negotiate. If we put up no resistance, however, bloodshed, if there is to be any, will be minimized."

"There *will* be bloodshed," Sergius said in a tone just short of contempt. "If any Expansionists or Council agents are in the area, *they* will fight. Projectiles and bullets are no respecters of persons. If the Aegis operatives don't attempt to kill us, someone else will." He stood to face Theron. "As you so wisely said, when we began this colony, we knew the obstacles we would face and that a time would come when we would be compelled to make a difficult decision. Now that time has come."

Damon watched Sergius out of the corner of his eyes. Nikanor, as he had been in Erebus, had never been particularly passionate about anything except long philosophical discussions, all on a theoretical plane. Like most Opiri, his emotional range had always been limited, particularly compared with Theron.

But he was passionate about this, and Damon found it more than merely strange. Though it was hardly rational, given the little information Sergius had possessed at the time of Damon and Alexia's arrival at the colony, Damon hadn't forgotten the way Sergius/Nikanor had treated him. The fact was, he didn't trust Sergius, rational or not.

"I propose that we evacuate the humans to the caves, as I suggested before," Sergius continued. "Those Opiri who wish to leave with them may do so. The rest of us will stay and defend the settlement against any who would destroy it."

Cullen and Emma immediately protested. The short-haired Opir woman nodded firmly. The remaining Opiri exchanged

glances and then sat without speaking, their faces expressionless as they weighed the options.

"Sergius," Theron said heavily, "I cannot prevent you or
the others from fighting. I am a leader, not a tyrant. But I beg
you again to think what you are doing."

"I *have* thought about it," Sergius said, holding the old
Opir's gaze like the young wolf who planned to be the next
leader of the pack. "You should go with the humans, Theron.
You'll be needed later."

Theron shook his head. "I still hope to speak with the Enclave forces. I assure you, I have no personal wish for martyrdom, either, but it is my choice." He looked around the
table again. "Emma, I believe you, Cullen, Beth and Jonathan should help lead the others to the caves. If you will not
think of yourselves, think of those who lack both the skill
and the will to fight such a battle."

Dropping her gaze, Emma stared at her folded hands. "Let
some of us stay, so we can—"

"*All* of you," Theron said gently. "Please, go into hiding
just until this is resolved."

After a long hesitation, Emma nodded. Cullen and the
other two humans pushed back their chairs and rose.

"We will gather the others," Cullen said, "but we aren't
going to be ready to move until near nightfall." He looked
across the table at Alexia, inclined his head and left the room.
Emma, Beth and Jonathan followed.

"One of us must accompany the humans," Theron said to
Damon, Alexia and the remaining Opiri.

"I will do it," Sergius said. "As soon as they are safe, I will
return to help defend the colony."

"*If* the strike force and any other combatants are not already in the way," Theron said. "Agent Fox, earlier you were
willing to remain with the colony at this time of crisis, even
though by doing so you may be considered a traitor to your
own people. You have no connection to us except through

our human citizens. Again, I ask—is this what you want? Do you truly accept that you may face extreme sanctions from the Enclave if you do?"

Damon waited tensely, hoping she would change her mind. He hadn't even suggested that she leave Eleutheria before the strike force arrived, because he had known what she would say.

Just as he knew what she would say now.

"I know that is possible," Alexia said. "But it's because I work for Aegis that I believe I am in a unique position to help There is something here that doesn't exist anywhere else." She rose to face Damon. "It's the only place where Damon and I can be together, as equals, without fear of reprisal. *I* have to believe Eleutheria will survive this crisis and become stronger because of it. I want to be a part of the change it has begun, and the hope it represents."

Her words stunned Damon, not because they were out of character, but because they were so much more than he had ever expected. Their relationship had always stood on shaky ground, and they had never questioned their divided loyalties.

Those loyalties, and the hatred their peoples had for one another, would ordinarily have made any thought beyond the present impossible. Until he had seen how Opiri and humans interacted in Eleutheria, he wouldn't have believed there was any path around those seemingly immutable obstacles. Yet now Alexia spoke as if there might be a future, fragile as it was, and her eyes were asking him if he felt the same.

How could he accept what she offered? She was throwing aside her past, all her connections to her city, all the human parts of her life she had never shared with him. She was willing to accept the necessity that she might always need his blood to survive, and that he would continue to drink hers. And she knew she would be taking a Darketan who could become a savage every bit as subject to his emotions as a serf was to his Bloodlord.

But she wasn't deceiving herself. Her gaze was clear and direct and unafraid. It was *he* who was afraid: that he'd hurt her during one of his rages, that he'd fail to protect her—not only from every outside danger, but from her own stubborn, fierce will.

He didn't insult her by asking her again if she was sure. He took her offered hand and raised it to his lips. A moment later he remembered where they were, and so did Alexia. Her cheeks flushed. She ducked her head and sat down.

Damon took up his position behind her again. Theron looked him in the eye, his brows arched and a slight smile touching the corners of his lips.

"I will not ask if *you* recognize the consequences to yourself if the Council ends up in control of the colony," he said. "It may be worse than the other alternatives. But if you have made up your mind…"

Damon nodded. Sergius made a sound that eloquently combined impatience with mild disgust. "May we continue?" he said acidly.

Ignoring him, Theron turned to Alexia. "Since you wish to help, I think you and Damon should accompany our human citizens to the caves. You both have the skills necessary to defend them, and I know Emma trusts you, Alexia."

"No," Alexia said. "You can't keep me safe by sending me to hide. And I may still be able to speak to someone from the strike force before this gets bad."

"It will be no less dangerous guiding the others and protecting them," Theron said, "especially since we have no idea where the Aegis forces or their enemies may appear. Perhaps Hera—" he glanced at the short-haired Opir woman "—will accompany you, and Alexia can return when the others are safe."

Damon thought of Sergius's sudden change of plans from wanting to remain at the colony to accompanying the humans to the caves. And he'd been the one to suggest the caves in the first place. Damon trusted him even less than before. He had to be watched.

"We'll go," he said.

Alexia shot him a troubled look, but she must have known as much as he did that the old Bloodmaster was deliberately trying to get him and Alexia out of the way. He must truly believe the colony would fall to one force or another, and for some reason he wanted to be sure Damon and Alexia survived.

The hard fact was, no matter where Damon went, any violence aimed at Alexia—and likely any other innocent from the colony— could provoke one of his spells. His shadow-self could be a potent weapon turned against an enemy, but there was always the risk that it would endanger friends, as well.

That was why he would see that Alexia and the humans were safe, make sure that Sergius was no threat to them, and then go looking for the strike force himself. Maybe he could stop or delay them as no one else could.

"I agree," Alexia murmured, reaching behind her for Damon's hand. He took it, enfolding her fingers in his. Immediately Theron turned to Sergius.

"I have an even more difficult job for you," he said. "I want you to go into the mountains and look for movement from Erebus. If you discover any sign of Opir troops in this area, return to report immediately."

"You can send someone else for that, Theron," Sergius protested. "Since you refuse to leave, I should stay here to protect you."

Damon watched Sergius out of the corner of his eye. Yet another about-face on the Opir's part. There was something very wrong here.

"I would not ask this of you if it were not necessary, my friend," Theron said.

The flicker of a scowl crossed Sergius's face and then quickly disappeared. "As you wish, Theron."

"Then it only remains to discuss what we who remain in Eleutheria will do to prepare." Theron cleared his throat. "Agent Fox, Sergius, Damon and Hera, when you leave, go by the postern gate. My thanks to you all."

Hera and Sergius stood, covering their heads and faces with the cowl and goggles of their light daysuits. Alexia rose as well, and all four of them headed for the door. Sergius and Damon reached it at the same time. Sergius shouldered past Damon without a glance and strode across the commons.

Damon considered telling Alexia—or Theron—of his unease about Sergius, but sharing his vague suspicions might result in Sergius becoming aware that such suspicions existed. Damon wanted the Opir off his guard, confident that his scheme—if, indeed, he had one—would succeed.

And Alexia would only be in worse danger if she got in Sergius's way.

One very tense and busy hour later, Damon's pack, along with his weapons and those of Alexia's he had been able to fit in it, lay beside Alexia's cot in the dormitory. Damon still had his uniform, but he chose to continue to wear the simple clothing he and Alexia had been given earlier. Both of them had laid out and carefully inspected their combat knives, pistols and rifles. Alexia pushed the strange communicator into her belt; she had told Damon that even though she couldn't find a way to send an outgoing message, there was still the chance Aegis or the strike force might try to contact Michael again, unaware of his fate.

When she and Damon had completed their preparations and had nothing more to do but wait until twilight, a charged silence fell between them. Damon studied her face, memorizing its familiar, beloved lines: the fringe of red hair across her forehead, her tilted cat's eyes, her full lips curved in a brave smile.

"Well," she said. "It seems we're to have another adventure together."

All Damon wanted then was to take her into his arms and kiss her, absorb her into himself and never let her go. He saw the same yearning in her eyes. But he had to make her understand what had to be done, and nothing else could get in the way.

"When we go," he said, "I'll bring up the rear. It would be better for me to stay away from the others so that I can move freely in response to any attack."

Alexia didn't misunderstand his meaning. "If you think I'm going to leave you alone, think again."

"It is necessary, Alexia," he said. He put his hands on her arms. "If you are attacked, I might lose any ability to control my actions."

"That's why I'm not running away from you." She laced her fingers behind his neck and brought his head down to hers. "We never had a chance to talk about what to do about your spells. We think we know what causes them, but there must be a way to control them. I have a theory—"

"This is not the time for theories, Alexia," he said, stroking her cheek with the pad of his thumb. "If I become a beast, I would rather turn it against my enemies."

"Listen to me, Damon. If certain kinds of strong emotion make this happen to you, maybe others can save you." She swallowed, her eyes flickering away. "Like love."

The words came haltingly, and Damon knew how difficult it had been for her to speak them aloud. He knew she didn't expect him to reciprocate. He couldn't, though he understood the miracle they represented.

He had once told her that love was a word Darketans had no use for. She had acknowledged that there was a Zone of difference between caring and love.

Both statements were true. But he no longer knew where to draw the line.

"I think I can help you," Alexia continued through his silence. "I think that by staying with you when it happens, I can find a way to help you use it instead of letting it use you."

Damon shook his head. "Alexia—"

She pressed her finger against his lips. He knew defeat when he met it. He grabbed her wrist and kissed her, pulling her body hard against his. She melted into him as if she, too, were trying to merge with him so completely that they could never be parted again.

But they both knew this was a moment out of time, whatever Alexia had implied about a future together. The one thing she refused to give up was hope, and he would never deny her that comfort.

Closing his eyes, Damon smelled the scents of approaching twilight. "They will be waiting for us," he said, letting her go.

She wiped her tears away with the heel of her palm and nodded.

Together they found their way to the eastern wall, butted up against the hills. Sharpened spikes rose from the tops of the battlements to discourage potential enemies from approaching from that direction, and there was a very small postern gate set where the wall turned away from the hill.

Two dozen humans, alerted by their representatives on Theron's council, had gathered there, a few with rifles and others with packs, moving restlessly as Hera spoke to Emma and Cullen. Sergius was there as well, still wearing a cowl and gloves but dressed in clothing more practical for travel in the bush. He avoided Damon's gaze and passed through the gate first.

Damon hesitated, torn between the desire to follow the Opir and his implied promise to remain with Alexia and the humans. If he left, he'd have to tell Alexia of his concerns, and that would help nothing. All he could do was wait. And watch.

Hera, dressed much like Sergius, nodded to Damon and

Alexia and followed him, taking point. Half the humans followed her, Alexia went next, and the second half trooped behind her with Damon taking up the rear.

The caves in question were less than a kilometer away, but no one in the group let his or her guard down for an instant. Damon walked in a zigzag pattern to cover the most ground as he kept watch. Once Hera called a halt to listen to the rustle of something large moving in the bushes, but it turned out to be a brown bear, which reared up on its hind legs to watch them pass. The sun sank below the horizon, and a jay scolded in the pine branches as they walked beneath.

"Nothing," Alexia whispered, falling back to join Damon. "Either the strike force hasn't arrived yet, or they're watching before they make their move."

And even if they were not yet in the vicinity, Damon thought grimly, Expansionist or perhaps even Council agents might be. If his instincts about Sergius proved wrong, the Opir would eventually return with a report on any movement to the east toward Erebus.

"You go ahead now," Damon told Alexia. "Keep the others safe."

"You come with *me*," she said. "I know I can—"

"Damon!" Hera cried from somewhere ahead of them.

All the humans fell flat as they had been instructed, except for Emma and Cullen, who had their own rifles and immediately took up defensive positions. Damon and Alexia joined them, standing back-to-back with their rifles ready.

They knew in a very short time that they were surrounded.

Chapter 19

Hera was first to appear, hands raised, with an Opir in day-gear driving her at gunpoint ahead of him. The fact that he wore the suit told Damon that he had anticipated being out in daylight, though dawn was very far away. And by the number of weapons he carried, he expected to fight.

"It seems we were a little too late," Alexia whispered as a half dozen other suited Opiri approached from every direction.

She felt behind her for Damon's hand, and he squeezed her fingers. They both realized what was likely to happen to them, no matter how hard they fought, but Damon knew that Alexia was thinking of the humans. At best, they would be taken back to Erebus to resume their former lives as serfs. Damon guessed that some, like Emma, would rather be dead.

They still might be.

When Sergius strolled out to meet them, his helmet tucked in the crook of his arm, Damon knew how thoroughly he'd failed. He should have acted the moment he had felt those "vague" suspicions about Theron's former disciple. He should have fully recognized the rebellion in Sergius's eyes. Resentment, not only against Theron, but against his place in the world.

He should have killed Sergius at the very beginning.

"Damon," the Opir said. "Agent Fox."

"Sergius," Damon said, his voice eerily calm. "How long have you had this planned?"

"Not long." Sergius smiled, though without the mockery Damon would have expected. "It just happens that the opportunity has come to act, and delaying would be foolish and unnecessary." He signaled to his agents, who closed their circle around the humans. Hera's captor shoved her close to Damon and Alexia.

"Put down your weapons and no one need be hurt," Sergius said. He dropped his helmet into the grass at his feet and casually brought his rifle to bear on Alexia. "Do as I tell you, Damon, or I will kill your little friend."

"I'm getting a little tired of being called 'little' by upstart Freebloods," Alexia said as she tossed her rifle down and removed her other weapons. "Am I too far off in guessing you knew Lysander?"

"Not at all, Agent Fox. We were working together, but unfortunately he never made our last rendezvous." He met Damon's gaze. "He knew his work was dangerous. Damon, I will not ask you again. Throw down your weapons."

He removed his rifle, pistol and knife and tossed them out of reach. Sergius was in a talkative mood in spite of the precarious situation, and Damon intended to take advantage of his bad judgment.

"We know Lysander was working for the Expansionist Faction," he said. "Are you?"

"Not originally. I was recruited to become the party's agent in the colony after I discovered what Theron's once-noble philosophy had become."

"A double agent, you mean," Alexia spat.

"Lysander was my contact. We both, however, determined the Expansionists' goals were not necessarily our own."

"And these others?" she asked.

"Fellow Freebloods who agree that our kind should no longer rely on any faction in Erebus to grant us what we have earned." He shrugged. "A pity Lysander didn't survive. He said he had an opportunity to obtain something that would be highly valuable to us in furthering our plans."

His eyes narrowing, Sergius stared pointedly at Alexia. "I was under the impression that this thing Lysander sought had something to do with you, Agent Fox. I know the Expansionists had assigned him to kill you and Damon. Perhaps you know what he was after?"

Damon felt Alexia stiffen. "I have no idea," she said.

"Why am I under the impression you are lying?" He clucked his tongue reprovingly. "No matter. We will have plenty of time to talk it over."

"Where?" Alexia asked. "In the middle of the firefight that's probably about to happen any moment?"

"Oh, we intend to stay out of the way," Sergius said. "We have no stake in Eleutheria or what Aegis and the Council do to each other because of it. Our only goal now is to wait them out and then move our resources—" he nodded to the humans "—to our new home."

"Your own colony," Damon said, noting the positions of each of Sergius's followers without turning his head.

"I must credit Theron with giving me the idea," Sergius said. "When we smuggled the serfs out of Erebus, he led me to believe that his colony would be one where Freebloods seeking to found their own households would be able to claim a certain number of humans in exchange for helping establish the settlement." He laughed derisively. "But, you see, once Theron had begun, he became obsessed with a new way. Freedom. Equality."

He glanced again at the humans, whose expressions ranged from defiant to dull acceptance, with Emma and Cullen among those who looked ready to fling themselves at the Opiri and die happily. "Theron's dream has no hope of surviving, but we intend to learn from his mistakes. When we found our own settlement, it will be truly Opir."

"A society based on brutality and involuntary servitude," Damon said, the rage beginning to smolder in his chest.

"Outrage, Damon? From you, when you so perfectly illustrate both these qualities?"

Damon felt Alexia push her body close to his, trying to get his attention. He glanced at her, but already he was having difficulty interpreting what he saw in her eyes. Just as he couldn't make sense of Sergius's comment.

"No matter," Sergius said. "We have what we wanted from Eleutheria. Theron may be sure we will put these serfs to good use." He signaled to one of his men, who slung his rifle over his shoulder, set down his pack and removed a coil of heavy rope.

Sergius addressed the humans. "I will kill two of you for every one who fights or struggles," he said. "Emma, that means you."

The young woman glared at him with hatred hot enough to set the air between them on fire. "Do you think the Council will let you get away with this?" she asked. "If the colony falls and the Enclave doesn't take us, they'll want us back in Erebus, not in the hands of rebellious Freebloods."

"That is a chance we are willing to take," Sergius said. "And from now on, Emma, you will learn to treat your betters with respect."

Emma spat. Sergius casually trained his rifle on Cullen and shot him. Emma screamed, dropped to her knees and took the dying man in her arms.

Damon lunged toward Sergius. Alexia grabbed his arm and held him back through sheer force of will.

"I won't let you kill yourself," she hissed. "We'll find a way, Damon."

He heard her, though his mind was beginning to fill with crimson haze and adrenaline raced through his body like a fast-acting poison. As he balanced on the thin wall between sanity and mindless violence, Sergius's henchman began to tie the hands of the nearest humans, leaving a length of rope between each captive.

"You aren't moving fast enough, Sergius," Alexia taunted, slowly working her way into a position between Damon and the Opir. "The strike force could be here any moment. If they catch you, I don't think they're going to let you walk off scot-free, humans or no humans."

"But I have a hostage, do I not?" Sergius said. "Your people will surely hesitate to attack when one of their dhampir agents may be killed."

"Don't bet on it," Alexia said. "Like Theron said, they aren't likely to be happy that I've countermanded my orders and haven't only approached the colony but am fighting for them."

"But you aren't with the colony now, are you?" He beckoned one of his other men, who approached one of the female humans, pushed her down and tore off a wide strip of her long tunic. He brought the scrap to Sergius.

"Come to me, Agent Fox," Sergius said. "And quickly, if you value the lives of these serfs."

Alexia glanced at Damon, a plea in her eyes, and started toward Sergius. From deep within the morass of dark emotion that was slowly swallowing his reason, Damon felt pride and humility at her courage. He had failed again and again to protect her, but she had never wanted him to steal her choices from her. And, knowing he might lose her, he had chosen not to take them.

Sergius was oblivious to what was happening inside Damon. He took Alexia's arm in a cruel grip. "Stand still," he commanded, and wedged the scrap of cloth into her mouth. Damon swallowed a howl as Sergius tied the gag.

"I see what you would like to do to me, Damon," the Opir said, glancing casually in his direction. "Your affection for this dhampir is clearly out of all reason. But then you were never quite right in the head, as the humans say."

"I will kill you," Damon rasped.

"I don't think so. Not as long as Agent Fox is in my custody." He looked away, dismissing Damon as if he were an annoying insect he intended to crush when he had a moment free. "You," he said to one of the humans sitting next to a weeping Emma, "help bind the others. You, as well."

The two of them, aware they would only bring on more death if they disobeyed, helped the Freeblood tie up their fellow humans and then stood quietly while the Opir finished with them.

"To the caves," Sergius ordered, gesturing with his rifle. "Move ahead of me, Agent Fox. We must be sure that none of our new acquisitions lose their way in the dark."

Alexia looked at Damon again. She knew he was on the edge, that any moment his fragile control would snap and he would strike at Sergius, no matter what the consequences. She hesitated, and Sergius struck the back of her head.

Damon sprang toward him, his muscles bunching and releasing as if they were made of steel cables, carrying him instantly across the distance between them as if it were no wider than a centimeter. Several bullets caught him full in the chest, and he dropped to his knees. Several more slammed into his shoulder and his left leg.

Somewhere, someone screamed. The voice was almost familiar, but Damon's ears were filled with a high-pitched buzz, and his nose was clogged with the smell of his own blood. He fell to his side, consumed by pain.

And something else far more powerful.

He spread his hands on the ground, splaying his fingers

to support his weight, and pushed up. His injured leg gave out beneath him, but he shifted to his other leg and heaved himself to his feet, his pulse blotting out every other sound.

He never heard the bark of the gun, only felt the bullet as it drove into his skull. He collapsed again, and darkness swallowed him.

When he woke, it took him some time to remember who and where he was. It was still well before midnight, and he lay in a pool of his own blood. As the recent past came back to him, he realized how close he had come to dying. The bullet had cracked his skull, but it had not struck his brain.

The shooter thought he'd killed Damon, or he would never have left his enemy here untended. But Sergius and his followers had done damage enough by keeping Damon from the others, and as he began to rise Damon had to fight for his balance and to hold the blackness at bay.

By the time he was certain he could move without falling, Sergius, Alexia and the others were long gone, and Damon knew he had a disadvantage in the dark. He began to track the others, loping awkwardly, his injured body fueled by ruthless need.

The Opir in the rear of the loose column heard him coming, but he never had time to raise his rifle. Damon hit him at a run and sank his teeth into the Opir's neck. He jerked his head sideways, ripping through the Opir's throat in a spray of blood, and left the man lying there as he raced for the next.

The second Freeblood pumped off nearly an entire round, but Damon dodged easily and wrenched the rifle from his enemy's hands. He reversed it, swung the stock at the Opir's head, and then shot the man as soon as he was down.

By then the commotion had been noticed, and for Damon the next sequence of events, passing in a matter of seconds, seemed to move as slowly as an Opir left to die in the sun.

Hera was the first to act, breaking the ropes that bound her hands and turning on the Opir who guarded her. She was not quite fast enough; the Opir jabbed the muzzle of his rifle into her chest and shot her point-blank. But her sacrifice created just enough distraction for Alexia to move on Sergius. As she slammed into him from the side, Damon broke into a dead run straight for his enemy.

He saw nothing of what happened then, for he was on Sergius the next moment, tearing the Opir's rifle from his hands and throwing him to the ground. Gunfire rattled and boomed, someone screamed, struggling bodies rushed by in a blur of motion as Damon went straight for Sergius's throat.

But Sergius was still Opir. He flung his arm in front of his neck and rolled to the side, sinking his own teeth into Damon's shoulder. Damon hardly felt it, as he scarcely felt the injuries that had barely begun to heal. He slammed his knee into Sergius's groin, flung him aside and forced him down again.

He might have made an end to it then if he hadn't smelled a scent he had never quite forgotten, heard a voice he had once cherished call his name. He froze, and Sergius surged upward, throwing Damon off balance and regaining the upper hand. Damon's vision pulsed red and black as Sergius bit the base of his neck, puncturing deep and filling Damon's throat with blood.

But he refused to die. He found the strength to fight again, his muscles swelling with fresh strength, his brain firing off signals his body obeyed before he was aware of them.

When once again he came back to himself, Sergius was limp under his hands, panting and bloody, mauled within an inch of his life. Damon looked up from the Opir's slack face. Alexia, gag gone, was standing with Emma and a human male, rifles trained on four Opiri sprawled in a heap at their feet. The humans crowded around them, looking very much as if they would appreciate being given the chance to tear the Opiri limb from limb.

Alexia, Damon thought. *Alexia is safe.*

He met her gaze, and she smiled. But as he rose, she looked past him at someone approaching from the south. Damon stiffened and turned.

An Opir, one of those Damon had taken down earlier, was stumbling toward him, hands raised, prodded along from behind by a rifle in the hands of a slim, light-haired Darketan woman, her skin pale in the darkness.

Damon knew her, just as he had known her scent, and her voice.

Eirene.

Three breaths was all the time it took for Alexia to recognize the woman who had come out of nowhere to help her take down Sergius's henchmen.

The "nice lady." The Darketan woman who had saved Alexia's life twenty years ago by sharing her blood.

Alexia's fingers went numb on the rifle, and she had to concentrate to make them work again. The woman was pushing one of Sergius's men, liberally splashed with his own blood, toward the other captured Opiri, and as she came she was looking at the Daysider who stood over Sergius's limp body.

Damon didn't move. He, too, had been badly injured, and it seemed a miracle to Alexia that he was still alive. But he seemed unaware of any pain as he stared at the woman, and Alexia could feel something almost tangible pass between them, more than recognition, more than wonder, more than joy.

"Who is she?" Emma asked.

"A friend, it seems," Alexia said. She swallowed and stared down at the Opiri, who were wounded badly enough not to cause any more trouble, at least for the time being. "We still have to get to the caves as quickly as possible."

Emma glanced at Hera's body. "She died for us," she said,

her voice thick with sorrow. "I wish we could take care of her."

"Maybe we can come back for her," Alexia said, silently offering thanks to the fallen Opir woman. "Right now I think she'd want us to make her sacrifice worthwhile."

"What about *them?*" Emma asked, gesturing at the Opiri with hatred in her eyes.

Alexia barely heard her question. She was watching the Darketan woman walk past Damon and Damon turning to stare after her as she urged her Opir prisoner to join the others on the ground. As the Freeblood sank to his knees, the Darketan stepped back and smiled at Alexia, her lovely face warm with approval.

"You must be Alexia," she said. "You're even more beautiful than you were as a child."

"Do you know her, Alexia?" Emma asked, staring at the stranger.

"Yes." Alexia shouldered her rifle and offered her hand. "I remember you," she said. "You haven't changed."

"Oh, but I have," the woman said. "In more ways than you can imagine. And so much of that is because of you." She turned to look at Damon, who was still standing over Sergius. "I think Damon is in need of help right now."

Shaking off her paralysis, Alexia told Emma to shoot the Opiri if they moved and ran to Damon's side. His knees began to buckle as she reached him, and she eased him down, her heart in her throat.

The Darketan woman came up behind her. "He's injured, but not dying," she said, kneeling beside Damon. His eyes were dazed and unfocused, but he glanced at her and then at Alexia with a deep bewilderment even his pain couldn't hide.

Alexia joined the other woman on the ground. "Damon, can you hear me?" she asked.

His mouth opened, but no sound emerged. Alexia had

the terrible feeling that he was keeping himself conscious by sheer instinct alone.

"I've never seen him this badly hurt," the Darketan woman said, the anxiety in her voice perfectly expressing Alexia's own unspoken emotions.

"How did you… Do you know him?" Alexia asked.

"It was a very long time ago," the Darketan woman said.

There was no time for Alexia to ask all the questions that crowded her mind, acknowledge the suspicions that were quickly becoming certainties. "I've seen him this bad," she said. "He recovered. But we need to get him to the caves, along with the others." She met the Darketan woman's eyes. "I don't how much you know about the situation here, but we're still in danger. A war is likely to start any minute."

"I know," the woman said. "I'll help you get to these caves." She looped her arm under Damon's shoulder and pulled him to his feet. Alexia let the woman handle him, knowing she had her own responsibilities that couldn't be pushed aside because of her personal concerns. She returned to the others, unslung her rifle and punched Sergius in the chest with the muzzle.

"I know you're not fatally injured," she said. "Get up, or I'll make sure you are."

Sergius rolled onto his knees with a grunt of pain. "This is only a temporary victory, dhampir," he muttered.

"It's good enough for me," Alexia said. "Move."

None too gently urging Sergius ahead of her, Alexia returned to Emma and the humans. "We can't take the Opiri with us," she said. "We'll have to—"

"Let us kill them," Emma said. The other humans murmured agreement.

"No time to make sure they're dead," Alexia said. "But we *can* make sure they can't get up for a while."

Without waiting for further instructions, Emma trained her rifle on the nearest Opir and systematically shot him in both knees and both arms. Alexia didn't stop her until she had done the same with all the groaning Opir, leaving Sergius for last.

"Where are my betters *now,* Sergius?" she asked, lifting the rifle again.

Sergius laughed and turned his head to watch Damon and the Darketan woman approach, Damon leaning heavily on her arm but still on his feet. "You were lucky," he said, "that you found an unexpected ally."

"Luck had nothing to do with it," Alexia said, following his gaze. "You were too arrogant, Sergius. And you underestimated Damon."

"Underestimated him?" Sergius coughed and wiped his mouth with the back of his hand. "I know him far better than you do, little dhampir. I know what he is, and why he has been allowed to live in spite of his unstable nature."

A fist of dread knotted inside Alexia's stomach. "I'm not interested in what you think you know," she snapped. "Emma, I'll take care of this one myself."

"Ask yourself why a Darketan is more powerful than a full-blood Opir," Sergius said with a twist of his lips. "Ask yourself who, and what, released that power." He seemed to run out of breath and waved his hand. "Finish your business, dhampir. I grow weary of this conversation."

Driven by fury that went beyond her hatred of Sergius and those like him, Alexia prepared to fire. Then she lowered her weapon again.

"I think we'll take you with us, Sergius," she said. "Who knows, you may be useful." She shot him in the shoulder and watched him writhe. "Would you mind tying him up, Emma?"

As the human woman went to work, grinning with savage pleasure, Alexia returned to Damon.

"Is he holding up okay?" she asked the Darketan woman.

"Yes," she said, meeting Alexia's gaze with her own dark

turquoise eyes. "But it may be too late to get away. I hear them coming."

Alexia listened. Others *were* coming, though she wasn't sure at first who they were.

"Aegis," the woman said. "I got here ahead of them, but just barely."

The fist in Alexia's stomach tightened its grip. "Where did you come from?" she whispered.

"San Francisco." She glanced over her shoulder. "And now it's time to run."

With a final glance at Damon's pale face, Alexia turned and hurried back to Emma and the humans.

"You take the others to the cave as fast as you can," she told Emma. "I'm sending the Darketans and Sergius with you, but I'm staying behind to hold off anyone who comes after you."

"You can't do it alone," Emma protested.

"I'll do what I have to." She waited for the Darketan woman and Damon to join them. "I don't care what's between you and Damon. Take care of him. He's going to need your strength."

"It is not what you seem to think, Alexia," the Darketan woman said. "But I promise I'll take good care of him. For you. Good luck."

As she and the others set off at a jogging run, Sergius limping ahead of Emma's rifle, Alexia quickly replaced the magazine in her rifle and arranged both her and Damon's weapons within easy reach. She was straining to listen for nearby movement when something vibrated on her hip.

The communicator. She reached for it, her gaze still sweeping the surrounding landscape. The touch screen had come on, flashing red. Alexia pushed the recessed button on the side.

There were new words on the screen, but they were not from Aegis. As she read, she began to understand the full scope of what was happening, and how one man's hatred might destroy them all.

Oh, Michael, she thought.

"Put the weapon down."

Alexia emerged from her trance and looked up at the soldier in Aegis camouflage gear crouched a dozen meters away. Slowly she put the rifle down and locked her hands behind her head.

The soldier ran to her, keeping low to the ground, and patted her down. He removed the communicator, glanced at the blank screen and attached it to his belt.

"My name is Fox," Alexia said. "Agent Alexia Fox. I need to speak to your commander immediately."

The soldier looked at her through his tinted visor. "I think that can be arranged," he replied.

Chapter 20

Damon opened his eyes. A face filled his cloudy vision, familiar even before he smelled her and heard her voice again.

"Damon," Eirene murmured, resting her hand on his cheek.

He closed his eyes again. This couldn't be real. Eirene was dead.

"I know it's a shock to you, Damon," she said softly. "They must have told you I was dead. I wish I could have gotten word to you, but until this happened I thought my remaining in San Francisco was more important than anything else, even though I knew you would suffer. I'm so sorry."

Half of what she said made no sense to Damon, and the pain coursing through his body made it difficult to concentrate. "You were...in San Francisco?" he asked hoarsely.

"The Council sent me there. Not to die, Damon, but as part of an agreement with the Enclave government. It was supposed to be a gesture of goodwill. Allow Aegis to study a Darketan for a time, within strict limitations." She stroked

Damon's damp forehead. "But the Council had another motive. I was supposed to spy on Aegis at the same time, collect
information and escape. But I chose to stay. I've learned so
much, Damon. About the dhampires, and—"

The moment she spoke the word *dhampires,* Damon was
pushing himself up from the hard ground, the by-now familiar shadow-strength surging in nerve and muscle and bone.
The bandages someone had wrapped around various parts
of his body began to come loose.

"You must rest," Eirene said, pushing him down again. "I
promised to take care of you, and I won't let you leave. You'll
have to walk through me to do it."

Damon fell back. "Alexia," he whispered.

"When I left her, she was fine."

"Does she…know who you are?"

"Not my name. Did you speak of me to her?"

"Yes, but—"

"It was her choice to stay behind, Damon. To make sure
all the humans would be safe. And because she loves you."

"Let me go, Eirene."

"I can't."

"The Expansionists… Sergius—"

"Disabled, and not likely to cause trouble for a while. Sergius is here in the caves, and so are the humans. I made sure
no one would find us."

Damon struggled to find the right words. "Aegis. The
strike force…"

"They are in the area. I discovered what they planned just
before they left the Enclave, and escaped in the hope that I
could warn you and Alexia in time."

"Warn…us?"

"I made myself so much a part of Aegis over the years that
they became less careful about what they let me hear and observe. I knew about the colony, and that Alexia and Agent
Carter were sent to observe it. But I also knew you had been

told to meet them, and that both of you would be in the area when the strike force arrived." She took his hand. "I know what they were sent to do, how Agent Carter lied to them so he could get them to help start a new war."

Agent Carter. Michael.

"What lies?" Damon asked, fighting against the drowning weight of exhaustion threatening to plunge him back into darkness.

"He sent a message to Aegis claiming that the colony was being used as a laboratory to experiment on humans, alter their minds to make them completely obedient to Opiri. I knew that many in Aegis didn't believe that could go on without their knowing about it, but there are certain parties in the Enclave government who want war as much as the Expansionists. They pressured the government to send the strike force to attack the colony and free the humans."

Suddenly, out of the tangle of bizarre events over the past few days, the pieces of the puzzle began to fit together. "The colony…" he said. "Theron wants peace. Equality for humans."

"Then it's worse than I thought," Eirene murmured. "And they're planning…" She broke off. "There's nothing we can do now, Damon. You're too weak. You could die if you try to move too soon." She squeezed his hand tight. "Alexia is a brave woman. But she always was, even when I gave her my blood."

"You…gave—"

"I have so much to tell you, but not until you and Alexia are together again. You are both unwittingly involved in an experiment approved by factions in San Francisco and Erebus. The truth has to come out, and I'm going to help make sure it does."

Now nothing she said made sense. But one thing did, and it was all that mattered now. Alexia was in danger, and he had to save her.

Levering himself up on his elbows, Damon pushed Eirene aside. She tried to hold him back, but the shadow-thing inside him was taking over again—not mindless, not savage, but driven by a purpose that would not be denied. His wounds were far from completely healed, but he hardly felt the pain, and they couldn't keep him from his objective, even though part of him knew that Eirene had reason to fear for his condition. He clambered to his feet, strode past the humans whose ghostly faces looked after him in astonishment, and found his way to the entrance of the caves.

"Damon!" Eirene called after him.

He forgot she had spoken the moment he stepped out into the night.

"It's a lie," Alexia said, crouching opposite the strike force commander under the cover of a dense stand of madrones. "The colony isn't conducting any experiments. They want peace, and freedom for humans."

The commander, his gray eyes unyielding, showed no sign of softening. "Where is Agent Carter?" he asked.

"I've already told you. He's dead, killed by an Orlok. You have his communicator. He left me a message, and—"

"We can find no message," the commander interrupted. "The communication Aegis received from Agent Carter claimed that your drugs had been taken by the Opiri, and you admit your patch has been removed."

"Michael also told you I was left for dead by the same Opiri, Commander, and as you can see I'm very much alive."

"Who were you waiting for when we found you, Agent Fox? Who are you protecting?"

"As I *also* told you, I'd already encountered hostile Nightsiders, presumably Expansionists operatives. I expected them to attack again, and—"

"Who took the patch, Agent Fox?"

"Michael did," Alexia said, holding on to her anger by her

trembling fingertips. "He admitted it in the message he left me, and sooner or later you're going to figure out how to access it. Michael had his own reasons for wanting you here to destroy what Theron worked for and to provoke the Council into stopping you."

"Because he wanted to take some personal revenge by fomenting open war between Erebus and the Enclave? You expect me to believe this of a seasoned, loyal operative, Agent Fox?"

"I couldn't believe it myself, but—"

"You have no proof for your claims, Agent Fox. Since you've confessed to having disobeyed your own orders and contacted the colony, your loyalty to the Enclave is in question."

"Do you think *I* went over to Erebus?" she asked, letting her scorn color her voice. "A vampire raped my mother. I have no love for them, and never will."

"Then tell me where to find the Daysider who was sent to work with you."

"I told you, he didn't know anything more about the colony than I did." Alexia chose her next words carefully, knowing she was withholding the truth of Damon's original mission. "The Council was still investigating the settlement when he was given his assignment."

"Your partner claimed that this Damon deliberately diverted you from your assignment, tried to kill him several times, stole your patch and left you—"

"—to die. I know. But we're back to the fact that I'm alive, and telling you Damon didn't do any of those things. If your mission was to 'rescue' the humans in the colony, you're wasting time with this line of questioning." She gave him a pointed look. "Do you think your presence here is going to go unnoticed much longer? Odds are that Erebus is already sending troops to meet you."

"Because the colony has contacted the Citadel?"

"That's not what I said. The colony has broken off from Erebus. Theron has founded a new philosophy that allows humans and Nightsiders to live as equals. If you go in there, guns blazing, you'll destroy it, and probably end the Armistice, as well."

The commander searched her eyes, his own flat and cold. "I was instructed to carry out a mission," he said. "I am not here to negotiate. If experimentation on human beings is occurring in the target location, Erebus will have already broken the Armistice. We will do whatever is necessary to free the convicts and remove them from the area."

"And if you're wrong? Do you think the Council will just accept an apology for your 'mistake'?"

"That is a matter for Aegis and the Mayor's Office," the commander said. "We have our orders, Agent Fox."

Orders. Orders of the kind Alexia would once have followed without question.

"Let me go to Theron," she pleaded. "Let me talk to him. I know he wants to talk to you, but the others won't let him out if there's a chance he'll be slaughtered the second he steps outside the walls. Give me your word you'll hold fire until I've brought him to you."

"How do I know you won't join him, Agent Fox?"

The man was clearly immune to reason, and Alexia knew she had no more time to argue with him. She hadn't wanted to tell him that the humans were already outside the settlement, since there was a chance he might decide to attack the colony and kill everyone left inside the walls. Now she knew she had no choice.

"Listen to me," she said. "The humans are no longer in the colony. They were evacuated hours ago. I can take you to them."

"And lead us into an ambush?"

"I am on *your side,* Commander!"

For a few tense moments the commander was silent, and

then he gave a hand signal to someone concealed in the brush. A soldier, his rifle trained on Alexia, emerged from cover.

"You will take Operator Willis to the human evacuees," he said. "He has orders to shoot if he suspects deceit, or if you try to escape. Is that understood, Agent Fox?"

"It's understood, as long as you give your word you won't move on the colony before you receive confirmation that the humans are safe."

"I am not authorized to give you my word, Agent Fox. I will act as I deem necessary. If you are still one of us, your only concern will be for the safety of our people."

Alexia hadn't expected him to say anything else, and she had never intended to take Operator Willis to the caves where they would find Damon and Eirene. The only thing she could do now was get Theron out of Eleutheria before the situation exploded.

"All right," she said. She got to her feet under Operator Willis's watchful eye, nodded to the commander, and then started off in the general direction of the caves. Willis, like most of the Special Forces, was human; if the strike force had dhampires with them, they would be acting as scouts on the lookout for Nightsider operatives or troops.

But that didn't mean Willis would go down easy. He wore the standard infrared visor, and he'd be watching for the smallest false move on her part. She didn't want to hurt him any more than was strictly necessary. It was going to take split-second timing.

"This way," she said, gesturing for the man to follow her. He did, keeping his distance, and she could feel the eye of his rifle fixed relentlessly on the center of her back.

The instant before she turned to attack, she smelled the Opiri.

"They're here!" she hissed. "Nightsiders! Get down!"

The soldier didn't move, but he wasn't stupid. Even without looking at him she knew he was listening, aware that she might be telling the truth.

The rattle of rapid gunfire came from the direction of the colony. Alexia spun and lunged for Willis's rifle. He got off half a round before she shoved the weapon aside, but it was enough to tear off a good chunk of flesh from her upper right arm.

That wasn't about to stop her. But Willis was good at his job. As she grappled with him, he pulled his combat knife and was about to plunge it into her side when some force of nature ripped Alexia away and held her suspended about a meter above the ground.

Damon, bare-chested and trailing bloodstained bandages like party streamers.

Alexia didn't ask him why he was there, why he'd left the sanctuary of the caves and ignored the fact that he wasn't in any shape to be rescuing anyone. She didn't have the chance. He set her down on her feet and went straight for the soldier.

The man would be dead inside of five seconds if she didn't do something.

Without another moment's hesitation she leaped onto Damon's back and wrapped her arms around his neck. His muscles, swollen with rage, tensed to fling her off.

"Damon!" she shouted in his ear. "He's not the enemy!"

He froze, his hand around the soldier's neck, teeth bared to bite and tear.

"We have to get Theron," she said, pressing her face into his shoulder. "If there's any chance of stopping what's about to happen, we're going to need him."

He released his breath, his body loosening just enough for Alexia to know she'd reached him. He dropped the soldier and took a step back.

"Operator Willis," Alexia said, keeping her tight hold on Damon, "you'd better get back to your commander and tell him Nightsiders are coming. I don't know if they're Council or Expansionists, but at this point it doesn't really matter. If he has the sense to realize what a new war is going to do to all of us, he'd better sit tight and hold fire." She grabbed the rifle she had taken from the soldier's hand. "Move!"

A single glance at Damon's savage expression convinced the soldier to do as she ordered. Running low to the ground, he melted into the brush.

Alexia moved in front of Damon and met his eyes, which were still nearly black with the darkness seething inside him.

"Are the others all right?" she asked.

He nodded and touched her face. "Alexia," he rasped.

"I'm fine." She looked him up and down, fighting an almost physical sickness at the sight of his partially healed wounds. Someone had treated his injuries, but *he* hadn't been thinking clearly enough to care that he looked like a madman.

More than a madman, she thought. Given what was going on, she doubted he'd be back to "normal" anytime soon. It wouldn't do any good to send him back to the caves—she'd been foolish to think anyone could keep him there—and she was the only one who could hope to control his shadow-side.

"We've got to get through to Theron, Damon," she said. "Maybe it won't do any good, but he's the symbol of everything decent in Eleutheria, and maybe we can get somebody to listen."

"Yes," Damon said.

"Let's go."

Together they ran southwest toward the colony, Damon moving much more slowly than usual but never faltering. There was another burst of gunfire somewhere ahead, but they didn't slow down until they were just behind the last tree at the foot of the lowest hill descending into the valley.

They were too late. A dozen Nightsider Council troops, wearing black uniforms and armed to the teeth, had formed a barrier around the settlement's front wall, facing outward across the valley. Even as Alexia watched, someone fired on them from the cover of a broad-trunked valley oak about three hundred meters to the southwest. The Nightsiders returned fire, and then silence fell again, as peaceful as the aftermath of a level-seven earthquake.

Whatever motive the Nightsiders had for defending the colony—whether it was because they actively meant to protect it or simply wanted to keep the Aegis soldiers away—the upshot was the same. The strike force wasn't going to leave until they'd "rescued" the supposed human guinea pigs, and the Erebus troops would never let them get anywhere near the walls. Since the Council obviously knew something unusual was going on, it was only a matter of time before they sent a larger force to deal with the human incursion.

"We'll have to try to get in from the back," Alexia said in an undertone. "I'm sure they've got it guarded, too, but it's the only chance we have." She grabbed Damon's hand. "Whatever happens, remember that you are still Damon. Use your shadow to protect, not to kill."

His eyes were almost clear now, reflecting starlight like indigo pools too deep to fathom. "You go in," he said. "I'll cover you."

She closed her eyes, grateful that he was himself in what might be their final moments together. She wanted to tell him what she had never quite said, not the way she'd wanted to say it. But she remembered the Darketan woman's lovely face, the look on *Damon's* face when he'd seen the woman with her Nightsider prisoner. Alexia refused to burden him with emotions that would only make things more difficult for both of them if they survived.

"All right," she said, opening her eyes again. "Good luck, Damon."

He grabbed her shoulders. "Be careful."

"I will."

Pulling her into his arms, he kissed her roughly and just as abruptly let her go. Alexia turned and started back up the hill toward the rear wall of the colony, her lips throbbing and her heart throwing itself against her ribs like a fox in a cage. Damon followed so quietly that only the scent of dried blood and the tang of the local flora on his skin told her he was behind her.

The Nightsider guarding the back wall never stood a chance. Alexia made only a small, token effort to get past him, and as he was about to shoot her Damon took him down from behind. She didn't wait to see how Damon would deal with the man or the other Nightsiders she knew had to be nearby, but continued down the hill to the eastern battlements and the row of sharpened stakes that rose a good two meters above her head.

The Nightsider colonists hadn't left this wall unguarded, either. A dozen bullets from above whistled past Alexia's ear, and she dropped into a crouch at the foot of the wall.

"It's Alexia!" she cried. "I'm coming in!"

There was no response, but Alexia didn't wait. She half ran, half slid the rest of the way down the hill to the postern gate, where she heard heavy objects being dragged around inside the wall. The door opened the width of an Armistice dollar and the sliver of a Nightsider's face appeared behind the crack.

"Get Theron," Alexia commanded. "Damon and I are here to take him to safety."

"You can't," the Nightsider said. "He—"

"I know he doesn't want to come, but someone's going to kill him if he sets foot outside the front gate. If we can keep him alive, there's still a chance he can—"

"You can't help him," the Nightsider said in a harsh whisper. "He thinks he can reason with them. He's about to walk out."

Alexia's shock lasted exactly as long as it took for her to draw a single breath. She turned and sprinted back up the hill, using her hands to pull herself along.

Damon was waiting for her, standing guard over two Council troops with a nasty little Nightsider pistol in one hand and an Erebus model assault rifle in the other. Both Nightsiders were bloodied but alive, wearing daygear but still protected by the darkness. "Theron is already leaving," Alexia said to Damon. "I'm going to be there when he walks out that gate."

Damon nodded, the shadow crouching behind his eyes, waiting to be summoned again. Alexia knew he was deciding whether or not to kill the troops, but he knew as well as she did that any chance he might have to talk to the Council would end if he took their lives.

"Surrender," one of the Nightsiders told Damon, "and you may be permitted to live."

Damon didn't answer. He dropped the pistol, tossed the rifle to Alexia, picked the Nightsider up by the back of his protective suit and charged down the hill the way she had come. She heard a low grunt, a cry of alarm and the thump of something heavy hitting the ground some distance away. The second Nightsider began to rise, but Alexia was ready, and he was in no position to resist when Damon came back for him.

"What did you do?" she asked when Damon returned.

"Over the wall," he said, grinning in a way that would have made even a Nightsider's blood run cold. "The colonists can deal with them."

Alexia returned his grin. She didn't wait to see if he was planning to kiss her again, though she wanted to feel his arms around her one last time. Moving as fast as the slope permitted, she plunged down the hillside parallel to the settlement walls and didn't stop until she reached the valley floor.

Damon ran up behind her, his breath stirring her hair, his body a wall of heat against her back. A Nightsider in Council blacks stepped right in front of them. Alexia dove for his legs while Damon went for his rifle and knocked him unconscious with a blow that might have felled one of the massive oaks in the woods above them.

An instant later they were running again, still alongside the wall and headed for the corner where it turned to face the open field. Someone shot at them as they raced toward the gate, but they didn't stop until they could clearly see what lay between them and Theron.

He stood just outside the closed gates, hands raised above his head. Behind him and to each side, Nightsider troops held him pinned under their weapons like a beetle on a display board. Half a kilometer across the valley, Alexia could make out the moonlit glint of more weapons and the motionless figures of Enclave soldiers, lying prone in the long grass and waiting for the signal to attack.

Humans and Nightsiders were so intent on each other that none of them noticed Damon and Alexia until they'd walked right into the open. Damon managed to keep himself between Alexia and the nearest threat, but he must have known neither of them could do anything but bluff their way into making someone—*any*one—listen to reason.

"My name is Agent Fox," Alexia said in a carrying voice, showing her hands. "This is Damon of the Darketans. We were both sent into the Zone to investigate this colony, and we speak for its members, human and Opiri alike. We speak for Theron, who lives his belief in the equality of all the people who share this Earth.

"We speak for peace."

Chapter 21

Damon listened for the first sound of a finger pressing a trigger, ready to throw himself on Alexia and take every bullet that came until there was nothing left of him to shelter her.

But no one fired. He saw Theron's face turn toward him and Alexia, his mouth opening as if to warn them away. Two of the Council troops broke from the others and edged in their direction, keeping close to the wall.

"Stop where you are!" a human voice shouted across the field.

The Opiri swung their rifles to face the new threat. In the brief silence that followed, all of Damon's senses began firing up at once, and he knew the chance of stopping this idiocy from spreading to engulf the entire West Coast was almost gone.

"More troops," he whispered to Alexia. "Coming west over the mountains."

Not just a handful this time, but hundreds, headed for the valley like army ants that would devour everything in their path. From the opposite direction came the thrum of helicopter engines. Enclave choppers.

Damon didn't have to ask Alexia what she wanted to do. As the Opir and Enclave soldiers became aware of the approaching forces, she ran straight for Theron, so recklessly that no one on either side was prepared to fire. Damon reached the Bloodmaster a second after she did, and together they dragged Theron to the ground. Sprays of bullets turned the wall behind them into confetti. The Opir troops lunged toward them.

Then there was a cry of horrified surprise, and another, and all shooting from the valley ceased. Damon, his arms spread wide to cover Alexia and Theron, barely had a chance to look up when a half dozen tall, pale figures appeared behind the Opiri and knocked them and their weapons to the ground.

The smell caught Damon just before he recognized what he was seeing. Lamiae, standing over the dazed Council soldiers, their attenuated bodies like ghosts stretched thin by the wind. One of them approached Damon and Alexia, bending low, its red eyes glowing with intelligence and purpose. Alexia raised her head to meet its gaze.

"Michael," she murmured. She pressed her palm to her temple. "He's talking to me," she said in wonder. "He says… he has all the troops on both sides under guard by…by Orloks, a whole army of them. My God."

Damon stared at Michael, barely able to wrap his thoughts around what was happening. Theron stirred, and Damon let him up.

"Lamiae," Theron breathed, the same wonder in his voice.

"They've stopped the fighting," Alexia said. "Michael says…we have to tell the troops to keep quiet, or they'll be killed."

She got to her feet, Damon helping her, and faced the valley. "Your voice carries better than mine, Damon," she said.

"Tell them not to struggle." She touched her temple again. "Michael says—"

She didn't finish, because the chopper was nearly overhead. A spotlight fell on the settlement walls and flowed down to catch Alexia, Theron and Damon in its bright circle.

"Agent Fox," an amplified voice boomed down from the chopper. "Are you all right?"

"McAllister!" Alexia called. She raised her hand and swept it back and forth, then held her hand palm out to the chopper. The craft rose abruptly and hovered about fifteen meters overhead, its light still focused on Alexia.

That was when the new contingent of Council troops appeared, announcing their arrival with a volley of heavy fire at the chopper. It stopped before the bullets could do any real damage, and Damon heard grunts of surprise and pain.

"How many Lamiae are there?" he asked Alexia.

"I don't know." She turned to face him. "You'd better make the announcement. There's going to be a truce as of right now, or no one's going to like what will happen."

It was almost too easy. One moment the tension and hatred was as thick as congealing blood, and the next contingents from both sides were approaching each other, weaponless and ready to communicate. The strike force commander was one of the humans; he eyed Alexia with enough hostility that Damon had to remind himself that *he* was part of the cease-fire, too. He remained close to her as Theron and the Opir commander, who had come forward with three of his men, spoke with the humans, including the man Alexia had called McAllister.

"Damon," Alexia said. "There's something I need to tell you."

The soft, sad tone of her voice cut through the drone of the negotiations like fangs through tender flesh. Damon took

Alexia's arm and led her away from the others, turning the corner to the north side of the wall where the voices faded to a murmur.

"Alexia—" he began.

"Damon—" She chuckled low in her throat, met his gaze and sobered again. "You had something to say?"

Something to say. Where could he even begin? He saw this woman before him, this remarkable, brave, intelligent woman, and found his tongue hopelessly inadequate to the task.

"You did this," he said at last. "It's because of you that Theron is still alive and these people are talking to each other."

"M-me?" she stammered, giving a quick shake of her head. "This is all because of Michael, because somehow he managed to get all these Orloks together and convinced them to intervene."

Damon had too many things on his mind to argue with her. "How is that possible?" he asked. "Lamiae are beasts, killers, incapable of reason."

"Are they, Damon?" She took his hand in hers and studied it as if she had never seen it before. "Michael isn't only capable of reason, he's capable of regret. Deep regret for what he did to try and start a war."

If he hadn't sensed a wrongness in Alexia's partner from the beginning, Damon might have been surprised. "Why?" he asked.

"He was so filled with hatred. Hatred for both sides, Nightsider and human." She dropped her gaze. "I never saw that side of him, Damon. I had no idea, until I read the message he left for me on the communicator. I didn't even know it was there until you and the others went to the caves."

"What did the message say?"

"It was because of his former partner, Jill. They loved each other, the way—" She broke off and continued in a near whisper. "About a year ago, they were sent into the Zone to meet a Daysider agent. Michael didn't go into details, but he said it was some kind of secret mission to determine if operatives from both sides could work together. They thought it might be some way to work toward peace on an individual level."

"They?" Damon asked. "The Council and Aegis?"

She nodded. "Michael, his partner and the Daysider did meet, and things seemed to be going well when Michael was called back to the Enclave. Jill remained behind. When he was finally able to return to the Zone, he found Jill dead, killed by the Darketan."

Damon felt a rising sense of dread. "I don't understand," he said.

"When Michael went to hunt down the Daysider, he met what he thought at the time was a Council agent, a Nightsider, who told him where he could find the Darketan. Michael killed the Daysider, and then the Opir agent helped him get out of the area before someone from Erebus found the body. Before they parted, the supposed Council agent told him that both Jill and the Daysider had been part of an experiment, and not what Aegis had told him."

She swallowed and looked up. "They starved the Darketan before they sent him out, Damon. He didn't know it, but they were injecting him with drugs that leached all the nutrients out of the blood he'd been drinking. Both sides wanted to see how long he could work with an Aegis agent, under orders not to hurt her, before he was forced to take her blood. They wanted to see if she'd cooperate, and if she didn't, if he would kill her."

"Sires," Damon swore. He cupped Alexia's hand between his. "That was why he hated his own people as well as mine."

"It gets worse." Alexia closed her eyes. "When Michael returned to the Enclave, he made it his business to find out if what the Nightsider said was true. He learned that Aegis had sent Jill out with a defective patch so that the Daysider couldn't find out about the drugs if he and Jill discovered a way to coexist without killing each other. She would have died even if the Darketan didn't kill her."

"That wasn't quite the way it happened," a familiar woman's voice said behind Damon.

Alexia's eyes widened, and Damon turned. Eirene stood a few meters away, Sergius nearly impaled on the muzzle of her rifle. The man Alexia had called McAllister stood a little distance from her, with Theron beside him. McAllister stared at the woman as if he were trying to silence her with his gaze alone.

"I learned almost by accident," Eirene said, as much to the human as to Damon and Alexia. "Alexia, I first met you after I was sent to San Francisco as an object of study for Aegis, a gesture of goodwill and a spy. I was trying to escape when I found you, and gave you my blood."

"I remember," Alexia said in a hushed voice.

"You inspired me in a way I didn't believe possible, Alexia," she said. "I decided to stay, to cooperate with Aegis and find a way to work for peace. Because my blood put your illness in remission, they found a way to derive drugs from it that could work to counteract the genetic condition that prevented almost half your kind from digesting human food."

Damon glanced at Alexia, wondering if she was as astonished as he felt. "You're Eirene, aren't you?" she asked, a catch in her voice.

"Damon didn't tell you?" She sighed. "How did you know?"

Tensing for Alexia's answer, Damon cursed himself for his blindness. Alexia had recognized Eirene as someone who had helped her long ago, but she must also have felt that there was something between him and the Darketan stranger. Somewhere along the way, she had put it all together. And he had done nothing to prepare her.

"I wasn't completely sure until now," Alexia said. "But Damon spoke of a woman he'd loved in Erebus, a woman who had been sent away on some kind of suicide mission. Other things you said, the way you acted…it all started to make sense."

"Yes," Eirene said softly, glancing at Damon. "As I told him, I made myself so much a part of the furniture at Aegis that I was able to learn things I never should have heard, about certain experiments they conducted with the Council's cooperation." She paused. "That first experiment with Jill and the Darketan… Her patch wasn't disabled because he might have discovered what it was. It was because they wanted to see if a starving Daysider and a dying dhampir could save each other."

"And not just *any* Darketan," Sergius said, his voice drawn in pain but still clear enough to express contempt. "One of that cursed mutant breed who never make the complete transition to Lamia, but carry the creatures' propensity for extreme emotion and violence."

He smiled at Damon. "Like you, Damon, he was driven by bestial urges but unable to understand why. The Council was also very interested in learning if he could control those urges in the presence of a food source. He and the female Jill would be entirely dependent on each other—she on his blood, he on hers. Just like you and Agent Fox."

Damon was too stunned to speak. He heard Alexia gasp, a sickened sound, and then Eirene spoke again.

"Yes," she said, "they chose a certain kind of Darketan, but not just to find out if he could control the Lamia side of himself. They also knew Damon was capable of the kind of emotion that would help him understand human, and dhampir, nature."

Eirene shook her head sadly. "That first time didn't work," she said. "The Darketan killed Jill, and Michael killed him before the Council could send agents to retrieve him. So they sent you two out for the same purpose, hoping for a different result."

"And they got it," Theron said. He moved to join Alexia and Damon, as if to lend his support in their time of trial. "You were able to build the bridge, and help each other survive."

"Because there was something special about Alexia, too," Eirene said. She hesitated, glanced away and looked back again with even greater sorrow than before. "When I gave Alexia my blood twenty years ago, I left a part of myself inside her, a trace of my signature that was never extinguished. Aegis chose Alexia for the experiment when they learned that I and Damon—" She swallowed. "When they, and the Council, realized that my previous connection to Damon might enable him to recognize that signature and be drawn to Alexia as he would be to no one else."

The shock was so thick in the air that Damon could hardly breathe. He felt blindly for Alexia, desperate to make sure she was still breathing herself.

As if to prove his fears were unfounded, Alexia spoke again, though she almost seemed not to have heard what Eirene had just told them.

"Michael found out about the first experiment," she said in a dazed voice. "Now it all makes sense. He managed to hide his knowledge so well that Aegis sent him in with me, even though his first partner had died under similar circumstances. He was supposed to leave me alone with Damon, but he had his own plans. He wanted to sabotage the second experiment, because he—" She nearly choked, and Damon reached out to steady her. His hand closed on empty air.

"He wasn't the only one who didn't want the experiment to succeed," Sergius said, filling the unbearable silence. "The Expansionists also learned of it and determined to stop it by killing you and Damon. After all, were you to build the bridge Theron mentioned—" he nodded toward his former mentor "—it would scarcely benefit those who wanted war."

"And Michael wanted war, as well," Alexia said, her voice

growing stronger, "no matter whom he destroyed in the process. He led the assassins to us. Lysander was one of them, and Michael made a deal that he'd deliver my patch to him as long as he and his men didn't kill me. It all went as Michael planned, and he took my patch. But other operatives, presumably from the Council, killed two of the assassins before they could finish Damon off, and Michael fled."

She met Damon's gaze with a steadiness that surprised and humbled him. "Later, Lysander killed the Council operatives—the ones we found—and Michael came back to us with the intention of murdering you. By then, he'd already sent the message to Aegis. He knew the colony was the other new hope for peace, and summoning the strike force would wipe that out, as well."

"How did he learn the true nature of the colony?" Damon asked, resisting his desire to sweep Alexia into his arms and carry her to that place out of time they had once—oh, so briefly—found together.

"I told Lysander, of course," Sergius said, "and he must have told Carter. How well it would have worked if he had not underestimated you, Agent Fox."

"And Damon," Alexia added, lifting her chin. "And Theron, and the colonists."

"And the Lamiae," Damon said. "Was that what made Michael decide to help us, Alexia? Changing into one of them?"

"He recorded his message to me before he became an Orlok," she said. "At the time, he was fully committed to his course and wanted me to understand why he'd done it. But yes, something happened to him when he changed. Something that made him realize what a terrible mistake he'd made and inspired him to fix it in any way he could."

"If he hadn't," Eirene said, "if Lamiae really were the monsters we always believed them to be, we wouldn't be standing here now." She met Alexia's gaze. "What became of your patch?"

"We don't know," Alexia said, glancing at Damon. "We thought it might have been brought here, to the colony. But we realized soon enough that it couldn't have been, and Sergius confirmed it. I'm sure Lysander thought they could gain some benefit out of the patch, maybe sell it to the Expansionists. But since it seems to have disappeared, we'll never know." She smiled. "And now that we're all such good friends, it doesn't really matter, does it?"

"You're going to need a new patch," Damon said.

"I should thing that the Enclave would be willing to provide you with one," Eirene said.

"Agent Fox—" McAllister began, clearing his throat.

"Director McAllister," she said, swinging around to face the older man. "What about you? What could have possessed you to send a strike force based on one agent's word?"

The man had the grace to look ashamed. "I was not told about this so-called experiment," he said, "and I was not informed about the deployment of the strike force until they had already left San Francisco. Certain members of the Enclave government acted without the approval of the Mayor or Congress. I was fortunate to learn what was happening before—"

He broke off, his Adam's apple bobbing. "The important thing is that a new war has been avoided, and we have begun talks to determine how this came about and what to do if something similar happens in the future."

"And will I and Damon be part of these talks?" Alexia asked bitterly. "We did what Aegis wanted, didn't we?"

"I know how much you sacrificed, Agent Fox, and if I had realized…" He folded his hands nervously across his groin. "It will not be forgotten, I assure you."

"Sacrifice?" Damon said, baring his teeth. "Your Enclave had no right." He walked away from Alexia and Theron, striding toward McAllister with fists clenched and head down.

"Damon!" Alexia cried, running to catch up with him. "Don't you see? No matter what we had to go through, we proved something important. Darketans and dhampires can work together. They can care for each other. And someone like you can become more than a Nightsider or a Lamia.

"You can see things from the middle no one on either side can imagine. What you have, the ability to truly *feel,* is a gift." She glanced at Theron. "The colonists have proved that humans and Nightsiders can live side by side in harmony. Isn't that worth any sacrifice?"

Damon stopped, intensely aware of Alexia behind him, of Eirene and Sergius, of the Opiri and humans and Lamiae on every side.

Alexia was right. She had always been able to see things more clearly than he could. And it wasn't only hope for a lasting peace she gave him now, but hope for himself. Hope that he could become what Alexia believed he could be. Hope that her faith in him would let him accept what he wanted so desperately to give her.

Abruptly he turned and took her arm. "If you will excuse us," he growled, "Alexia and I have something to discuss. Privately."

Striding past McAllister and the humans around him, he led Alexia back along the wall until he was certain not even the Opiri could hear them. Then he swung her to face him, trapping her face between his hands. "Alexia, I—"

She gazed up at him, lips parted, eyes shining with tears. He realized that it was fear he saw in them, felt in the trembling of her body.

Fear of *him.* All those brave words she had spoken. They had been said for the benefit of her audience, not for him.

He dropped his hands. "I'm sorry, Alexia," he said. "If I had known what they were trying to do, what they made me a part of—"

"I know," she said with such overwhelming sadness that Damon felt his own eyes grow moist. "I'm sorry, too, Damon. You suffered so much. And all this time Eirene was alive.

She was the one who saved me, who gave me the gift that helped us both survive."

Her blood signature. The most devastating revelation of all, that Damon had been drawn to Alexia—come to care for her—because he had sensed Eirene all along.

"I'm glad for you, Damon," Alexia said, her lips trembling in a smile. "For you and Eirene. After all this, I know they won't keep you apart again. You can be free. Really free."

Damon swallowed hard. "Is that what you want, Alexia?" he asked.

She took his hand. "I want you to be happy. You loved Eirene, even if you couldn't admit it at the time. And she loves you. It was always her. I should have known—"

Her voice broke, and her knees began to buckle. Damon bent to catch her and lifted her to face him again.

"Should have known what?" he asked. "That I couldn't care for you unless your blood carried Eirene's blood signature?"

"Not only that. They starved you, Damon. They took advantage of everything you are to make you turn to me. It was your own strength that kept you from hurting me, not anything I did or didn't do. It was only natural, when we took each other's blood—"

"Natural?" Damon's anger roughened his voice, but he couldn't hold it back. "Are you saying that what we feel for each other can't be real?"

"What *I* feel doesn't matter. Eirene—"

"Eirene was my salvation a long time ago. Yes, I loved her. But she knows that's over, Alexia." He cupped her cheek in his hand. "The first time we spoke in the caves, she knew I loved you."

Her gaze met his. "What?"

"I love *you*." He tried to smile. "You put me through Human Hell just to get me to say those words. And I won't forgive you for it. I mean to make you pay for the rest of your life."

"Damon—" She searched his eyes. "Do you mean—"

"I mean that I can't live without you. I mean that you're the most remarkable woman of either species I've ever met." He kissed her chin. "They said I can see from the middle. But I can't, Alexia. Not without you."

"You're wrong, Damon," Alexia said, still refusing to believe him. "You're more than just a symbol of peace. You can't just forget what you represent to all of us."

"A symbol doesn't feel what I feel for you," he said, kissing the side of her mouth. "It wasn't the blood signature, and it wasn't starvation that made me love you. That would never have been enough. It may have brought us together, but no one can force someone to love."

He kissed Alexia lightly on the lips, but he felt her holding back. She was afraid. Afraid that he was giving her what she wanted without regard for his own wishes.

"What can I do to prove myself to you?" he asked, stroking her cheeks with his fingertips. "I'd love you even if *you* became a Lamia, you little fool."

Suddenly she burst into laughter. "I…I know what they've done for us," she said, catching her breath, "but I'd rather stay just as I am, if you don't mind."

"Whatever you are, wherever you go, I'll be with you. No matter what happens from now on, whatever agreement the Enclave and Erebus reach with or without our help, we won't be parted again. We'll do whatever we can to convince them that the peace has to be maintained." He brushed her hair back from her face. "Maybe there'll be a lot more work to do. But we'll do it together."

"I don't know…Damon," she whispered. "I don't know what to believe anymore."

"Then believe this," he said. And he showed her with his mouth and his body and his heart until every last barrier fell and she was in his arms, loving him, his for all time. Together they watched the dawning of a new day.

And a love that could never die.

* * * * *

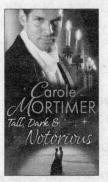

Join the Mills & Boon Book Club

Want to read more **Nocturne**™ books?
We're offering you **1** more absolutely **FREE**!

We'll also treat you to these fabulous extras:

- **Exclusive offers and much more!**
- **FREE home delivery**
- **FREE books and gifts with our special rewards scheme**

Get your free books now!

visit www.millsandboon.co.uk/bookclub
or call Customer Relations on 020 8288 2888

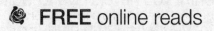